THE BOGANS

This is a work of fiction. Names, characters, places, and incidents are either the products of the author's imagination or used fictitiously. Any resemblance to actual persons, living or dead, events, or locales is purely coincidental.

Copyright © Channa Wickremesekera 2020

ISBN 978 - 0 - 6481349 - 1 - 6

All rights reserved

Cover and design by Brenda Van Niekerk

First published in 2020 by Wicks Publishing, Mt. Waverley, Victoria, Australia.

THE BOGANS

CHANNA WICKREMESEKERA

WICKS PUBLISHING

For Tessa

ACKNOWLEDGEMENTS

My thanks go to Sanjiva Weerasooriya for reading the very first draft of this novel, to Professor Yasmine Gooneratne for editing the first draft and to Elizabeth Cowell of Text Publishing for her valuable comments on an early draft of the novel. Brenda Niekerk's expertise in book designing was invaluable in preparing the book for print.

Bogan

bəʊg(e)n

noun Australian/NZ informal derogatory

plural noun: **bogans**

1. An uncouth or unsophisticated person regarded as being of low social status.

"Some bogans yelled at us from their cars"

ONE

"Come on, Vivienne, I think you are overreacting. Surely they have a right to raise their flag, in their own home and in their own country!"

Vivienne cocked her head and looked at Kumar as if to say that she had never doubted or questioned that, and that Kumar had got it completely wrong. Her small eyes opened wide to reveal the depth of her indignation. She opened her mouth, probably intending to express her feelings verbally, but Kumar's son, Rohan cut her off.

"This is not their country," he said, without looking up from his phone. "This is Aboriginal land."

Kumar looked at his boy with disappointment. Short, chubby and with a hairstyle that seemed to change with each haircut, he lounged in the recliner, eyes glued to his phone screen, utterly unconcerned about the effect his uninvited comment was having on the conversation between his father and their neighbour. No matter how many times Kumar had warned the boy, he never stopped butting into adults' conversations, often in the most casual fashion, while watching a video clip on the phone or texting someone, as he was doing now. He did this so consistently that Kumar was willing to believe that his son was just incorrigible until someone pointed out that maybe it was simply because Rohan faced no consequences that he continued doing it. Kumar had to admit that there was a lot of truth in that. He had only warned his son, but he had never really taken any action, nor had he indicated what consequences might follow if the warning was not heeded.

The only success he has ever had was with Rohan's swearing, and he was not certain whether that was entirely due to his stand on the issue. Some years ago, when he was navigating the challenging world of secondary school, Rohan had started swearing ever so often, even in front of Kumar and Indu. When confronted by his parents, the boy had defended his actions by saying that there was no harm in it. It was a very Australian thing, he had asserted, in fact, about the most Australian thing. If you live in this country, you have to swear. Kumar had to agree, ruefully. Almost everybody at work swore. Even David, his boss who was usually well-mannered and gentle, swore occasionally, whether he was expressing joy, dismay or anger. Swearing had appeared so normal that Kumar had himself tried to do it, in his early days at the job, in an attempt to fit in, but it had backfired badly. The attempt was so lame and was made with such little conviction that everybody had stared at him as if he had actually sworn rather than merely used the F-word as part of a conversation. It had convinced Kumar than swearing was not for everybody. Rohan had laughed when he heard about his dad's failure at swearing. It has to come from the heart, he had said. Not just from the mouth. Kumar had simply declared that he wanted no swearing in the house, whether from the heart or the mouth. To his great relief, the frequency of Rohan's swearing had diminished soon after his decree, but Kumar was not certain whether that was due to his request or whether the boy had come to realise that his own heart was not in it.

The butting-in however, showed no sign of abating. Rohan's heart seemed set on it, and now it was too late to do anything about it. The boy was pushing 18.

Vivienne seemed uncharacteristically offended by Rohan's observation. She usually didn't mind Rohan interrupting conversations, either because she really didn't mind people butting in or because she considered it the business of the parents to correct their own children. But now, she seemed to be taking issue with Rohan, her eyes lighting up with indignation.

"What Aboriginal land?" She asked in her distinctive Malaysian accent. If she didn't mind Rohan butting in, she was also more than happy to give him a piece of her mind when she thought it was necessary. "Everybody saying, Aboriginal land, Aboriginal land. When you see Aborigine last time? I am in this country fifteen year and never seeing Aborigine and everyone saying Aboriginal land, Aboriginal land!" She shook her head to emphasise her displeasure as she turned her eyes back to Kumar.

Rohan was trying to suppress a smile, and Kumar too felt the same. Vivienne did sound funny when she spoke, especially when she was agitated or excited.

"Maybe that is because most of them are dead. Killed."
Rohan said before his amusement got out of control. It only

increased Vivienne's agitation.

"Kill? Who kill? Me? You? Your father? Why we get blamed for killing hundred year ago?"

Kumar looked at Rohan with an expression of pure irritation. "Don't you have any school work to do?" He asked. Not that it really mattered whether Rohan had any schoolwork or not. The boy had little interest in studying. Long ago, when he was little and very ignorant of the ways of the world, Rohan had declared that he wanted to become an astronaut. However, as he grew up and realised how much studying such an occupation would require he had gradually lowered his expectations to engineer, builder and finally settling on becoming an electrician. He had declared to his parents that he was only doing VCE to make his parents happy and that after his exams he was starting an apprenticeship. This had worried Kumar and his wife Indu at first. They considered it a bad idea especially since all their relatives in Sri Lanka expected their son to become something more impressive than an electrician after going all the way to Australia, but Rohan had shown very little interest in the opinion of relatives. And caring more about Rohan's happiness than the approval of their relatives, Kumar and Indu had relented, though reluctantly. After all, they did not have any other children. And all their relatives lived in Sri Lanka.

Rohan looked up from his phone long enough to frown. It was the school holidays, he reminded his father before returning to his phone. Kumar's face assumed a worried expression at hearing this. Damn! He had forgotten all about the school holidays.

"When does school start?"

"Not until next week."

"Yes not till next week." Now Vivienne butted in. Perhaps one of the reasons why she didn't mind Rohan butting in, thought Kumar, was because she too did the same.

"Eric also start next week."

Eric was Vivienne's son, another only child. He was the same age as Rohan but went to a different school. Eric's was a private school where his parents paid a lot more money for their son to learn the same things that Rohan learnt at a state school, and where there was also much more homework. Kumar had heard Rohan teasing Eric about that.

Kumar sighed. One more week. He loved his son, but he had come to realise that, as Rohan grew older, he loved him more when he was at school. This was not because he had a bad relationship with his only offspring. Far from it. They got on very well, like mates. But Rohan, like most teenagers, was not very tidy, and when he was on his holidays the whole house began to look like his room. The loud music wasn't very helpful either. And there was always the butting in.

Realising Rohan was not interested in continuing the argument, Vivienne turned to Kumar again. She had lived in Australia for fifteen years, she said again. Fifteen years and she has had her fair share of encounters with racists, but she had never had the Australian flag shoved in her face like this.

"Well, they're not exactly shoving it in your face, are they?" Kumar asked, trying hard to sound reasonable while disagreeing with Vivienne.

But Vivienne refused to budge.

"Then what are they doing?" She demanded to know,

Rohan looked up from his phone again.

"Raising the Australian flag on their rooftop," he said and returned to his phone. Kumar winced as Vivienne's eyes widened in preparation for another sally against the boy, but she was interrupted by Indu who came out with a cup of coffee for Vivienne and a hot chocolate for Rohan.

"Who has raised what?" She asked, handing Vivienne her coffee. She placed Rohan's drink on the side table next to the recliner and perched herself on the arm of the seat.

Vivienne told her, her excitement hardly abated. The Bogans down the road and in the house opposite hers had raised the Australian flag. She considered it to be a direct challenge to her, and everybody else in the street.

"Why?" Indu asked, surprised. "I know they are terrible neighbours to have, but this is their country and it is their home. They can raise their flag."

"This is Aboriginal land," Rohan said again, without even looking up from the phone.

Vivienne started to respond but realising the futility of it, checked herself, instead simply raising her arms to the heavens in a gesture of resignation followed by a loud sigh. Indu grinned with frustration, and then ran her fingers through Rohan's hair.

"School holidays," she said, almost apologetically.

TWO

When the Bogans arrived in Kumar's street a few months earlier, they had created a big stir in that little neighbourhood.

Again, it was Vivienne who had brought the news. One Sunday morning, she came to Kumar's house, shaking, almost out of breath, and announced that something terrible had happened.

"What do you mean?" Kumar had asked, aware that in Vivienne's limited vocabulary, 'terrible' could easily stand for a wide range of problems, from a blocked sewer to a burst artery. But on that day, her tone, demeanour, and body language suggested that the situation was closer to a burst artery than a blocked sewer.

"What is so terrible?"

"I know not how to explain." Vivienne said, still shaking. "Come and look!"

Reluctantly, Kumar came out and followed Vivienne down the road. When Indu asked where he was going, he simply said that Vivienne wanted to show him something. Indu understood. This had become a common practice now, Vivienne calling and Kumar answering her summons. Vivienne always wanted to show something. Most times it was something trivial, but she always wanted to 'show.' And it was usually Kumar but sometimes Indu that she wanted to show things to. Ever since they moved in to the neighbourhood about five years ago, Vivienne had marked him and Indu as her confidantes, partly, no doubt, because they seemed tolerant of her ways and partly because, they, or rather Kumar, could be coaxed into coming and looking at anything.

Kumar and family lived in a court in south eastern Melbourne. It was called Park Court, not because it had any particular elegance to boast of, but because there was a little park at the bottom of it. The court spilled out of a long street called Jacob Street, spreading downhill until it reached the park. The park itself had no name, or if it had one, residents had long forgotten what it was. It was simply referred to as 'the park.' It was just a large oblong patch of grass with a couple of picnic tables, a swing, and a see-saw. On the far side, it was lined with a few trees and bushes, beyond which could be seen the walls and fences of houses from another street. It was used by only a few people, mostly Rohan and his friends in the neighbourhood who went there to kick the footy around or to sit around and chat. A few residents from other parts of the neighbourhood also visited the park, to walk, alone or with their dogs. Apart from that, it was left almost neglected. Even the council showed little interest in it other than to mow the grass now and then.

Vivienne lived in the last house on the left-hand side of Park Court, a brick veneer building with a short brick wall at the front and wooden fences that separated it from the house to the right and the park to the left. It was a fairly modest building that had been well maintained and had been renovated many times by its occupants. A pretty little front garden with a well-manicured lawn bordered by rose bushes gave its frontage the appearance of a scene from a picture book. Vivienne was very proud of her garden even though Eric often grumbled about having to mow the lawn ever so often, even in the winter.

When they arrived outside her house, Vivienne touched Kumar lightly on the shoulder and whispered in his ear, gesturing with her head towards the house across the road.

"Look!"

Kumar looked in the direction she indicated.

Across the road, on the edge of the park stood the house Mr. Andrews had occupied until about two weeks ago. Mr. Andrews, who was an Anglo-Indian, had moved out of Park Court to a bigger house a few kilometres away. His family, it seemed, was finally arriving from Calcutta and he needed a bigger house. A long-term resident of the street, he had cried almost uncontrollably the day he moved. Kumar and Indu thought that was because he could not bear to leave the place he had lived in for nearly ten years but Rohan, ever the cynic, had quipped that maybe it was because his family was finally arriving. There may have been more than a hint of truth to it as Mr. Andrews had lived the kind of carefree life that bachelors lived, entertaining friends often, staying out late at night, and flying to India once a year for a few weeks. He had lived there as if he was never going to leave the place, and when he finally left, he did so not with the joy of a man reuniting with a family from which he had been long separated, but like a convict being transported for life to some penal colony.

But now it seemed that the place was occupied again. The 'For Lease' sign on its lawn was gone and some of the windows in the house were open. Was Andrews back? Kumar wondered for a moment. Did he slip away from his family and return to his beloved home on Park Court? That was not altogether impossible. But then he saw the vehicle in the driveway. It was not Andrews' sleek red Honda but a hefty, old, station wagon that appeared to have been green once. It was parked facing the road, but you could see that the hatch was open. Someone had definitely arrived at the house, and it was not Andrews returning.

As Kumar stared wide-eyed at the decrepit car wondering who the newcomers were, Vivienne poked him sharply in the ribs.

"Come. We watch from inside." She said in a whisper.

Kumar followed her indoors, glancing back over his shoulder at the house and wondering what was going on. Obviously, Vivienne wanted to watch the house without being seen.

"What time did they come?" He asked Vivienne as they entered the house. Vivienne shook her head vigorously.

"Not sure. Last night not here. This morning, here."

From that vital piece of information, Kumar surmised that the newcomers had probably arrived in the middle of the night. But in the middle of the night? Who moves house *in the middle of the night?*

"Are you sure?" He asked. "Maybe you didn't see them arrive in the evening?"

Vivienne shook her head again like a woman who knew what she was shaking her head about. "Very sure," she said. "Last night, not here.

This morning, here."

Kumar scrunched his face with worry. This was disconcerting indeed. Not only did the car look like a travelling dump but the owners seem to have arrived at a ghostly hour. This didn't sound good at all.

"Have you seen any of them yet?"

"No." Vivienne shook her head again. "Not yet. As soon as I see car, I come and tell".

Kumar sighed. This was the problem with Vivienne. Getting over-excited with limited information.

Then, as they watched, the door of the house opened and someone stepped out into the garden. It was a man, White, tall, thin with long hair and a bushy black beard. He wore tight, black jeans and a dirty green jacket and also seemed to be wearing old, dirty sneakers on his feet. From that distance, his age could not be determined, but it appeared that he was not young. They also noticed that he was walking with a slight limp.

A loud gasp escaped Vivienne's mouth the moment she saw him. "Oh my God!" she whispered loudly. "It's one of them!" Her voice trembled with sheer terror.

"One of who?"

"Bogans!" She whispered, and Kumar saw her clasping her hands in front of her chest as if in prayer.

"How do you know?"

"I know!" Vivienne said with the air of one whose opinion should not be disputed. "One day Eric show me near shopping centre. Just like that man. He show and say, Mum, that is Bogan. Just like that man."

Yes, Kumar thought. Vivienne might be right. He had heard that word before but had never had Vivienne's opportunity of having one pointed out to him. But from the descriptions of Bogans he had heard, often from Rohan, Vivienne could be on the right track to correctly identifying one.

As Kumar and Vivienne watched in silence, the suspected Bogan approached the beat-up station wagon and opened its boot. He picked up what appeared to be a box and then turned towards the house and called someone.

A tall boy came out of the house followed by another, smaller boy. They both wore tight, dirty jeans and sweaters and had dishevelled brownish hair. When they came up to the car the older Bogan passed them boxes from the boot. It appeared that they were unloading their possessions.

"Don't tell me they bring everything in car!" Vivienne said. Kumar made no reply. He simply kept staring at the new arrivals unloading from the boot of their vehicle what appeared to be cardboard boxes full of clothes and other possessions.

After a few minutes, the two boys finished their work and went inside. The man too closed the boot and re-entered the house. Making use of the opportunity, Kumar quickly moved towards the door.

"I must get going," he said. "You are right. I think they are Bogans. But keep watching and find out what you can. I will call you later." Before Vivienne could say anything, he quickly got out of the house and hurried towards his own house.

This didn't look good, Kumar thought as he walked back home. It had been a peaceful neighbourhood until now. This could be the beginning of the end.

By noon that day everybody in the street had come to know that the last house in the street was occupied again. And that Andrews had been replaced by a Bogan family.

THREE

The Bogans were not the first White people to have lived in that court but they were certainly the first ones to live there for quite a while. And they were also one of the few White families Kumar and Indu had ever shared their neighbourhood with in Melbourne.

Before moving to their current house in Park Court Kumar and his family had lived in a small unit in south-eastern Melbourne. This was their first home in Australia, a rental property, which, though comfortable inside, looked from the outside like an ugly, brooding, block of bricks with windows. It was a multicultural area, mostly populated by Indians and Asians with a few other Sri Lankans. No White people lived there and had not lived there for a long time, according to some long-standing residents. According to Rohan, it was a similar story at school. The students were mostly Asians and Indians. There were some Sri Lankans too and even Africans but not many White students. "In fact," he said, "there were more Black and Brown kids than Whites."

It made Indu wonder where all the White people lived because they knew that there *were* White people in Melbourne. There were some at work and there were many in some of the shopping centres. "They live everywhere," Rohan had said. "But they are hiding from us." Indu chided him for being facetious and said it was a pity they could not see any White people because they always thought of Australia as a White country.

Kumar agreed. He was a firm believer in multiculturalism. He didn't mind seeing people of different cultures around him in Melbourne, even if he was often bewildered by the range of nationalities and cultures he encountered. All he asked for in Australia was a peaceful, quiet, affluent existence. He had achieved these simple ambitions to a great extent, and although he had not amassed the wealth of someone like Vivienne who could send her son to a private school, he was content. He was providing sufficiently for his family. He doubted if he could have done all that in the Sri Lanka he had left behind. Part of the deal of achieving this was sharing your workplace, suburb, your street, with all kinds of people. There were people from many different backgrounds working in the council offices. In fact, his section, the payroll department, consisted only of emigrants. Only his boss, David, was White. One of his co-workers, an Indian boy, named Dev, was even suspected of being gay. But no matter how multicultural it was, at the end of the day, he also believed that Australia was a country of White people. He and Indu had not come to Australia because there were Indians, Chinese, or Aborigines in this country. They had come because there were White people here and all the advantages they associated with Australia they associated with White people. That was why they had come to Australia and didn't go to China or India or Africa.

This is also why he believed it was silly to call Australia Aboriginal land, as Rohan was happy to chirp ever so often. Not because, as Vivienne seemed to imply, there weren't many Aborigines around, but because he felt there was nothing you could do about what occurred over 200 years ago. He found it very amusing that people acknowledged the traditional owners of the land at official ceremonies. Indu had told Kumar that they did that even at the start of their staff meetings at the bank where she worked as a teller and the manager of which was a very sensitive guy. At the local council where Kumar worked, it happened all the time. He still didn't know which tribe was being acknowledged even though he had heard it God knew how many times. In fact, he had seen people who did the acknowledging at ceremonies checking the name of the local tribe before the function just in case they acknowledged a tribe that had once hunted and camped in another area. And these were people who had done the acknowledging many times over. It all smacked of hypocrisy and stupidity, Kumar thought. Acknowledging indigenous people as custodians of this land was like someone who had stolen a car acknowledging the previous owner each time he drove it. Only White people could think up something as ludicrous as that. If Sri Lankans or Indians had come to Australia and found the Aborigines wandering around half naked and blowing into their didgeridoos, wouldn't they have done exactly what the British did? Kumar was not sure if they would even have kept any of the didgeridoos around to show later.

It was a pity then, he thought, that they saw so little of White people in their own country. It was as if Australia was neither White nor black but a mixture of everything and everybody in the world. It was interesting but also strange. As Indu put it, multiculturalism in Australia was not complete if there were no White people in it. "What nonsense!" She often huffed. "Indians and Chinese everywhere! Even Sri Lankans! What kind of diversity is this?"

When they moved to Park Court, having bought a bigger and better house with the money they had saved, Kumar and Indu hoped that the cultural mix there would be different. But they had no idea what kind of diversity to expect in their new neighbourhood. They hardly saw the other residents before they moved in. On the day they came for inspection, Indu said she caught a glimpse of an Asian-looking face in the house diagonally opposite the house being inspected and Rohan swore he saw a White man and woman in the two-storey house opposite to them, gazing at them from an up-stair window, which made Indu quite pleased. On the day they moved in, they saw nobody, it being around mid-day on a Friday when everybody was probably at work. They were so tired that after unpacking half their things, they went to bed early, leaving the rest for the following day.

The next day, which was Saturday, they had their first introduction to the neighbours, in dramatic fashion. Indu was a keen gardener, and in their previous home, she had maintained a sizeable vegetable plot which included some rare breeds of chilli. When shifting, she had uprooted these and brought them with her, planted in pots. That Saturday, she went out as soon as she had finished breakfast to re-plant the chillies. She had planted one and was half-way into digging a hole for another under the shade of the fence when she began to feel a presence above her. Part of the shadow of the fence, she noticed, was gradually and mysteriously, extending into an oblong shape. Startled, Indu stared at the strange shape for a few seconds with curiosity before she realised that it was, in fact, something behind her, over the fence. She turned around and was greeted by a face, dark, gaunt and wizened, topped by tufts of white hair, swaying above the fence as if moved by the gentle breeze.

Seeing that Indu's attention had been engaged, the face smiled, showing a full set of false teeth. Then, leaning forward slightly, it spoke with a glint in its eyes:

"Vanakkam!"

Indu stood frozen, gripping the digging fork. It did not take long for her to realise that the face with the flowing teeth and the flowing white hair belonged to none other than their next door neighbour. And he was Tamil! Indu's and Kumar's Tamil was close to non-existent but almost every Sinhalese in Sri Lanka knew the Tamil greeting.

The realisation placed Indu in a quandary. Kumar's and Indu's attitude to the Tamils was marked by caution. Even though they both believed that the war that had ravaged Sri Lanka for decades was largely the fault of Tamil terrorists, they did not think that the entire Tamil community was to blame. All Tamils are not bad, Kumar always believed, and Indu was often quick to point out that just as there were people among the Sinhalese who were against the war, there were probably Tamils who were against the Tamil Tigers also. "There are traitors in every community," she was fond of reminding friends and relatives who tarred all Tamils with the same brush. But the problem was figuring out who was a good Tamil and who was not, especially in a Western country like Australia, where the terrible Diaspora Tamils also lived and still campaigned for the division of Sri Lanka. You could never know for sure, and you could never say. Caution was the best policy.

But they had never bargained for having to exercise that caution with their next-door neighbour, of all people. Usually, it had not been hard to practice that caution in Melbourne. So far, their contact with Tamils had been almost non-existent. There was a distinctly Tamil looking woman working in the Planning Department in the council, but Kumar had no contact with her. There were no Tamils in Indu's bank branch. The only other contact they had had was seeing Tamil-looking people in the shopping centres. That was always fleeting. Occasionally, someone would nod at them, probably guessing they were Tamil - or Sri Lankan - and Kumar and Indu would nod back and smile faintly before moving off quickly lest they would want to dispel their doubts by starting a conversation, in Tamil. They would have probably evaded many Sinhalese also in this fashion, Indu often reminded Kumar as both groups looked alike. But it was better to be careful.

Now, confronted by a Tamil neighbour speaking to her over their fence, Indu could only stand and stare in bewilderment. Was this a good Tamil or a bad Tamil? She wondered as she surveyed the wrinkled visage above the fence. Or was it a Diaspora Tamil? He seemed friendly enough with that smile and cheerful demeanour. But then, that was probably because he thought she was Tamil too, she surmised. That is why he greeted her in Tamil.

Her doubts were quickly laid to rest by the man. As Indu's face clouded with uncertainty, the man's smile broadened, turning into a chuckle. "From your expression, I can say that you are Sinhalese," he said, in English. "I am Tamil, but not a Tiger." He laughed heartily and then bared his teeth as if f to reassure that they were not fangs.

Then he introduced himself. "Chelliah is the name," he said. "Chelliah from Chennai. That way it is easy to remember." Then he went on to provide a short but sweeping autobiography that included an astonishing range of details. He was seventy-two years old, he said. Or was it seventy-three? He wasn't sure. He was getting forgetful these days, but it didn't really matter. He has been in Australia for nearly 40 years, all of that in Melbourne, and 25 of those he had given to the Tax Office. You could say he was almost married to the Tax office. But he was married to his wife Prasadi longer than that, nearly 45 years. A blissful marriage it was, he said, until Prasadi passed away a few years ago from bowel cancer. Thank God, his own health was fine except for creeping dementia and a slight touch of incontinence, but nothing that couldn't be checked with the flimsiest of pads.

Indu gradually relaxed as the autobiography progressed, letting out an audible sigh at the end of it. There was nothing to worry about. The man was neither a good nor bad Tamil, not even a Diaspora Tamil. Just Indian.

A few minutes later, Chelliah was sitting in their kitchen drinking sweet tea and expanding his autobiographical sketch. Indu and Kumar listened with increasing fascination while Rohan sat alternating his attention between their neighbour and his phone. He was a devout Catholic, Chelliah said. So was Prasadi. He went to the local Christian college in Chennai, and she went to the local convent not far from his home. "Sometimes I also went to the convent, but only in the night and only to see the girls," he said, chuckling. "I saw many girls before I saw Prasadi and after I saw Prasadi, I didn't want to see any other girls. Match made in heaven that was." His eyes seemed to mist over as he spoke of his wife. He was devastated when she passed away. Since then he had had a few affairs, some passionate and some non-passionate but nothing like what he had with Prasadi. Nowadays he had no energy for anything, other than the odd walk in the park and cooking. He loved cooking, he said, as did Prasadi and he promised to cook one day for Kumar and Indu. He also watched a lot of movies, he said. Crime movies were his chief interest. He borrowed movies from the library and watched them. Sometimes forgetfulness is not bad, he reminded them. He could watch the same movie after two days and remember very little.

He also told them about the neighbourhood. He was the oldest resident in the neighbourhood; he had lived there close to thirty years and he didn't want to live anywhere else. He loved his house and garden, even though the house was old and in need of repair and he was too old to do much gardening anymore. He would not be able to survive anywhere else, he believed, asserting that he was determined to die in that house, like his beloved wife.

He quickly dashed Kumar's and Indu's hopes for greater diversity in the demographics. "When I moved here, this was all White country," Chelliah said, making a sweeping gesture with his hand that seemed to move over an imaginary landscape. All those people were very nice to him and Prasadi, in those early days even inviting them to dinners and Christmas parties. There was one other Indian family that lived further up Jacob Street. But they were snooty, arrogant bastards, Chelliah said. North Indians. "As soon as they found I was from the south they didn't even want to acknowledge me," he claimed. But now the place had changed so much, he added, ruefully. Now there are almost no White families in this neighbourhood. All Indians and Chinese. Even the house Kumar and Indu had bought was previously owned by a Chinese family, he revealed. "Nice couple, with four children," he said. "Yes four! No limitation on children in Australia," he chuckled mischievously.

"Phew!" Indu said after Chelliah had left, at the end of his third cup of tea. "That was interesting! When he said 'vanakkam' like that I was a bit worried."

Kumar laughed. "I think he is lonely." he said. "Nothing to worry about."

Rohan however, immediately developed a dislike to their elderly neighbour. "Talks too much," he said. "And talks bullshit." Indu chided him and said old people are like that. They like company, and they talk a lot. She was more worried about what Chelliah had said about the neighbourhood. "Seems like we have got more of the same," she sighed.

It appeared, however, that Rohan was correct in his assessment of

Chelliah speaking nonsense. There were in fact, two White families in Park Court when Kumar moved in with his family. There were the Purics, a Bosnian family, and the Robinsons, an Anglo-Australian family. They hardly saw the Robinsons though. The four of them, Ray and Barb Robinson and their two daughters, Sarah and Rachel, lived in the first house at the top of that part of the court, on its right flank to the left of Kumar's house. They were a quiet family who kept themselves to themselves. They had been there when Kumar moved in next door, but Kumar and Indu rarely saw them except when they went out to work and returned, saying little more than "hello" and "bye" whenever they happened to see them during those fleeting moments.

This was probably why, Kumar surmised, that Chelliah disregarded the Robinsons when saying there were hardly any White people in the neighbourhood. They were hardly visible. But then, the Purics were not like that. They lived in the double-storey house right in front of Kumar's, and Edis Puric was often out and about, especially on the weekends when he cleaned and washed his van which he used in his plumbing business. Edis was in his early thirties and lived with his wife and dog and often chatted with Kumar from across the street. His wife Esma was less talkative but was friendly enough to smile whenever she saw Kumar and Indu. Unlike the Robinsons, they were very visible.

They later found that Chelliah had his own reasons to disregard the Purics also as White. They are Slavs, he said when Kumar raised the issue with him. They are not real Whites. Only the Anglos are real Whites. But only full Anglos. And having a bit of Anglo blood doesn't mean anything either, he pointed out, glancing in the direction of Andrews' house at the bottom of the court. "That man is Anglo-Indian, which means neither here nor there," he said. "He is just like Obama. Claiming to have White blood without anything to show for it."

"I told you he talks bullshit," Rohan said when he heard Chelliah's exposition on Whiteness. Kumar too seemed bewildered but did not see any point in arguing with Chelliah. They were new in that street, and Kumar was not the argumentative type anyway.

Despite Chelliah's obvious dislike for Andrews, they found him to be an amiable person. Andrews was a man in his 40s and worked as a driver for a transport company. He lived alone but did not seem to be lonely, enjoying a carefree life. Even though he always said he was trying hard to get his family to move to Melbourne from Calcutta, he didn't seem to miss them very much. Kumar and Indu soon found that the hostility between Chelliah and Andrews was mutual and went all the way back to the time Andrews' first arrived in Park Court ten years ago.

"He spoke to me only in English even though he could speak Hindi," Chelliah said, adding that he had refused to speak to Andrews until he spoke to him in Hindi. "How did you know he could speak Hindi?" Indu asked, intrigued. Chelliah said he always suspected it, but his suspicions were confirmed one day when a strong wind blew most of Andrews' clothing from the clothes line onto Chelliah's garden. "The idiot had forgotten to use clothes pegs," Chelliah sniggered, "and all his clothes, including intimate garments, were in my back yard, draped over the pot plants." When Andrews' came and asked for the clothes, in English,

Chelliah had pretended not to understand, telling him in Hindi that even though this was Australia, Andrews should remember he was speaking to a fellow Indian. Valuing his clothes more than his pride, Andrews had asked for them in Hindi. Chelliah had returned the clothes. Thereafter he had spoken to his neighbour in English, partly to be magnanimous in victory but mostly because he realised Andrews' Hindi was halting and tortuous to listen to. The tension between the two remained, Chelliah continuing to see Andrews as an arrogant fool while Andrews considered Chelliah to be a rude old man. "He has nothing better to do than poke his nose into other people's affairs," Andrews told Kumar. "The wife was the same," he added; "a match made in hell."

The Purics left the neighbourhood a few months after the arrival of Kumar's family. Esma got pregnant, and Edis Puric's company relocated to a place on the other side of the city. After that, a Lebanese family moved in to that house; Ahmed, his wife Amina, son Mahmoud and daughter Hala. Mahmoud was Rohan's age and Hala was only twelve. Ahmed ran a cleaning business, driving a big van with the words 'Hamra Cleaners' painted in big, bold letters on both sides. Ahmed and Amina did the cleaning, sometimes helped by Mahmoud on the weekends.

Ahmed was a good man. Friendly and talkative. The Purics were friendly people too, but the Purics only talked to Kumar and Indu from across the road. Ahmed often crossed the road and came to their side of the street to talk to them, and sometimes he even came into the house. And he also invited Kumar and Indu to their house often, and occasionally Kumar and Indu accepted the invitation and went in to be treated to tea and sweets. Ahmed was funny too. He was born in Hamra in Beirut where he had worked as a civil engineer, and in Melbourne, he was still working with buildings, even though he was cleaning them rather than designing them. He had lived in Sydney for years before he moved to Park Court in Melbourne. Too many fucking Lebbos in Sydney, he said when asked why he decided to move. Too many Lebbos, including family. One day he showed Kumar and Indu some photo albums in which they were able to see some of those relatives he was trying to escape from, and funnily enough, Ahmed seemed very happy in those photos which made Indu think that there must have been some other reason for him to move. Interestingly, there were also pictures of the family back in Lebanon, and Amina was seen wearing Islamic dress in those pictures. Here, in Melbourne she rarely wore anything Islamic, other than an occasional headscarf. Sometimes she was even seen wearing tight jeans when she went out.

Seeing Kumar looking at the pictures of Amina in hijab and a robe, Ahmed chuckled. "That is before marry," he said. Then he pointed to a picture of Amina with him wearing jeans and t-shirt without hijab. "This, after marry."

"That is very interesting," Kumar said without explaining why. Ahmed laughed. "Very hard to clean with Islamic dress," he said; and added with a twinkle in his eye, "jeans also more sexy."

To Rohan's joy, Mahmoud went to the same school as him. He shared Rohan's love of computer games and basketball, but unlike Rohan, he also showed an interest in actually playing sports. He played for the school footy team even though without any great aplomb, according to Rohan. He rolled more than he ran, was Rohan's wry description of his friend's playing style. And like Rohan, Mahmoud was not very studious, mathematics being the only subject he was moderately good at. He had no interest in going to uni, Mahmoud had declared. His father was grooming him to take over the business, and Mahmoud already had visions of expanding the modest cleaning business into a nation-wide empire. Apart from that, Ahmed and Amina had no great expectations of him, except that he marries a Lebanese. Like his parents, Mahmoud was also not religious. He did not even know where the local mosque was, he laughingly told Rohan, as if boasting about his ignorance. He smoked the occasional cigarette and drank the odd beer but did not eat pork, which was about the only religious thing he did. He also visited some Islamic chat rooms on the Internet, but that was mostly for entertainment, he swore. I don't know what some of those nutters are on, he often said. But they crack me up every time I talk to them. He got a buzz out of winding them up.

"You might want to be careful, Rohan admonished. The police might be monitoring your chats."

But Mahmoud simply laughed it off saying if the police were monitoring the chats, that was for entertainment too!

In contrast to Mahmoud, Hala was more studious and had set her eyes on becoming a nurse. She also had more diverse interests than Mahmoud. While Mahmoud preferred to kick the footy around or play on the computer with friends Hala played indoor soccer and went for dancing and music classes. But her most impressive activity was a project she had started all on her own. This was a fundraising project, raising money for orphaned Palestinian children. She raised funds by purchasing chocolates and selling them to kids at school and then donating the funds to a charity that sent money to Palestinian refugees. Ahmed and Amina were very proud of her. Mahmoud was too, even though he was also annoyed that Hala often pestered him for donations.

Chelliah's experience with Ahmed was predictably an unpleasant one. Finding out that Ahmed was Lebanese, Chelliah ventured to welcome him to the neighbourhood as the oldest resident and a staunch Catholic. "I don't care what they say about Muslims," he declared, after his initial greeting. He had nothing against them, and he had known many Muslims who were quite nice. Every community had their bad eggs, and there was nothing one could do about it. Ahmed listened carefully and told Chelliah that he hardly knew any Indians. "There was an Indian who used to work for me," he said, "but he was a bloody idiot." Then he turned and walked into his house. Chelliah glowered at the departing Ahmed, then turned and crossed the road to Kumar's house where he told Kumar and Indu that their new neighbour was a rude man. "Typical Lebanese," he said. "Rude and aggressive. You got to watch him."

A few months after Ahmed moved in, the Robinsons moved out. In typical Robinsons' style, all they said was "bye" when they departed. When they left, a young Timorese couple, Mark and Angela, moved in and maintained the house tradition of keeping themselves to themselves. A couple of days after they moved in, Indu managed to speak to Angela when she was returning from work in the evening but only long enough to find out their names and where they were from. They seemed to have little interest in social chit-chat and were duly left alone by the neighbours. Chelliah dubbed them anti-social recluses and vowed never to speak to them, which was meaningless, as the young couple had little interest in speaking to him or anyone else in the first place.

With the departure of the Robinsons, Andrews made a vain attempt to pose as the only White person in the court. It was a vain attempt indeed as Andrews was only a couple of shades lighter than Kumar who was fairly dark. He was firmly put in his place by Chelliah. He sneered at Andrews' pretensions and reminded him that he was neither Anglo nor Indian, only Anglo-Indian. "Even that was in doubt," he added, "as nowadays even those who have been buggered by Europeans were calling themselves Anglo-Indian." Stung, Andrews did well to hide his annoyance behind a stoic grin.

Of all their neighbours, Vivienne was the surprise package. She was already well-settled in the street when Kumar moved in. But only Vivienne and Eric. She worked in a small firm as an accountant and told everybody that she separated from her husband, who had gone back to Malaysia. She had come all the way from Queensland for the job. Eric soon became friendly with Rohan with whom he shared a passion for Xbox.

Then, one Saturday morning, not long after they moved in, Vivienne walked into Kumar's house arm in arm with another smaller Asian woman and introduced her as her partner, Lauren. As Kumar and Indu stared wide-eyed, trying to comrehend what Vivienne was saying, Rohan sat with a slight smirk on his lips, having quickly fathomed it. Vivienne explained. "Me and Lauren," she said, "partners, like husband and the wife." As Kumar's and Indu's eyes widened further as it began to sink in, Rohan clinched it.

"Lesbians," he said, nonchalantly. "They are a lesbian couple."

While Lauren giggled like a little girl, Vivienne glared at the boy, then confirmed. Yes, they were lesbians.

After they overcame their initial shock, Indu made tea, and over tea, biscuits, and cake they made small talk. Lauren was also Malaysian, Vivienne said. They had met in Queensland, but it was only now that Lauren had been able to move to Melbourne. Lauren was much smaller than Vivienne and demure, unlike her partner, and spoke very little.

"Must be the one who makes the tea in the house," Rohan quipped after they left, like a man who knew all about lesbian relationships. He soon began to refer to the two women and Eric's two mums, which Eric took as a compliment. And Rohan's cracks were not meant to hurt anyway: they were simply good-natured teasing of a mate whose company he liked.

As for Kumar and Indu, Vivienne's love life did not bother them much. Indu, however, was surprised to see an Asian lesbian couple. "I always thought they were White," she told Kumar.

"Well, now you know better," Kumar said. "There are probably Aboriginal ones too," he reminded her.

Kumar had to admit, though, when Vivienne came in with Lauren to introduce her the first time they found it very awkward. Kumar had tried hard not to gaze, fascinated, at Vivienne's hand clasping Lauren's. But they soon got used to it as they often saw the two of them walking up the road hand in hand. They turned out to be nice too, kind, and hospitable. After a while they even got used to Vivienne's feistiness, which Rohan said was the man in her driving her. But Kumar simply put it down to eccentricity. And to their great relief, they also realised very quickly that there was little chance of them being treated to anything more Sapphic than the two of them walking hand in hand.

"Why did you never tell me that you had two mums?" Rohan asked Eric one day. "You only asked about my dad," said Eric. "And I told you he had left my mum."

Chelliah's reaction to Vivienne's sexuality was very different. Before Lauren arrived, he had been very friendly, extending a fatherly watch over her. He would drop in regularly to inquire after her health and even offered to do her shopping. "Poor woman having to manage everything on her own," he had said to Kumar. Andrews went one better than Chelliah offering to do her shopping *and* her gardening, which made Chelliah call him a dirty rascal with ulterior motives. Vivienne thought they were both dirty men trying to get into the pants of a divorcee, which seemed to be the case although nobody could say what Chelliah was going to do in her pants at his age.

Quite craftily, and one might add, wickedly, Vivienne said nothing about her sexuality until her partner arrived, fending off the advances of the two men with excuses, which, despite the curtness with which they were given, dampened the enthusiasm of neither. "She is playing hard to get," Andrews said to Kumar one day with a wink and a smirk and conceded that the ploy was working. It was then that Vivienne dropped her bombshell, walking into Chelliah's house with Lauren, arm in arm, and introducing her as her lover.

"The woman even kissed the girl in front of me," Chelliah had fumed later. Vivienne didn't even bother visiting Andrews because she knew Chelliah would spread the word like wildfire, which he promptly did, on the phone, just as Vivienne and Lauren were leaving his property. Deeply embarrassed, Andrews pretended that the news didn't bother him and that unlike Chelliah's, his intentions towards Vivienne were always honourable. But Chelliah wondered why, if it didn't bother him, Andrews' voice was breaking when he told him so.

***

They may not have had a White family for a while, but they certainly had a Black family. They moved into the house to the right of Ahmed's. It was a large brick house built on a slight elevation with a spacious deck in front, which gave it the appearance of standing over the rest of the court. A Chinese family, the Wangs, use to live there and they moved out when the man, Liu, bought a bigger house in Templestowe, putting the house they were vacating up for rent. The Wangs were a lovely family with three beautiful children, even though Liu and Mei Wang hardly spoke a word of English. That was because they have spent all their lives in Australia learning to make money and not wasting time learning English, Edis Puric used to say. Nobody bothered to ask what Edis had done with *his* time as he didn't seem as rich as the Wangs and his English wasn't all that good either. Edis being a rather humourless man the irony was likely to have been lost on him anyway.

And when the Wangs moved out, the Rabulas moved in. When Rohan first told Kumar that an African family had moved in to the house in which the Wangs had lived, he first thought the boy was mistaken.

"Are they real Africans?" He asked.

Rohan nodded very confidently. "Yes," he said. "Real Africans. Black ones."

"Are you sure?" Kumar pressed, and the boy nodded again. He was sure.

"Maybe they are not Africans," Indu said. "Just really dark Indians or Sri Lankans." Kumar could see she was a bit worried. But Rohan was adamant.

"No," he said firmly. "They are Africans. I know my Africans," he declared like an expert.

"I hope they are not Sudanese," Indu had said, a worried look on her face.

"Now that is not nice," Kumar had said to Indu, but he too was a bit concerned. You heard lots of things about Sudanese people and almost all of it bad. He knew one shouldn't believe everything one read in the papers or saw on television, and he had often pointed this out to people who were saying nasty things about the Sudanese. But that was when no Sudanese were living in their neighbourhood. Now when it seemed there was the possibility of one actually living there, he also was worried. What if the newspaper reports were true? But Rohan shook his head again. "Nah," he said. "They were not Sudanese." He knew his Sudanese too.

"Then who?" Indu asked, confused. Rohan shrugged his shoulders.

"Dunno," he said. "Just African. Non-Sudanese African."

There was only one way to find out, and they went there to see them.

They were met at the front door by a large Black woman with greying hair who looked at them suspiciously at first and then smiled sunnily when they introduced themselves. She ushered the visitors into the living room where they were met by an even larger Black man with even greyer hair and an equally warm smile. Both of them appeared to be in their late fifties. They introduced themselves as Mr. and Mrs. Rabula, and Mrs. Rabula immediately began making tea.

While sipping tea and eating biscuits, they made small talk. The Rabulas told Kumar and Indu a bit about themselves. They were both retired, and their two adult daughters were both married and living interstate, one in Adelaide and the other in Sydney. They were also heavily involved with their church, something which Kumar had also gathered from all the framed biblical quotes on the living room walls. Mr. Rabula also played golf, and Mrs. Rabula played the piano. All this was fine, but the Rabulas consistently denied them the most crucial piece of information they were seeking. Frustrated, Kumar looked around to see if there was any evidence of where the new neighbours came from. But there was nothing to indicate that in the expensive furniture and what looked like some original artwork competing for the wall space with the biblical quotations. But one thing was certain. The newcomers were not

Sudanese. Who had ever heard of the Sudanese playing golf?

Finally, after a few more minutes of chit-chat, Kumar broached the subject out of sheer impatience.

"We are originally from Sri Lanka," Kumar told his hosts. "And you?"

Mr. Rabula seemed to be on the verge of revealing it when he changed his mind. He flashed his toothy smile again. "Guess," he said, cheekily. The twinkle in his eyes said that he believed they could never guess the answer to Kumar's question and that he was going to enjoy their vain efforts.

Kumar hoped Indu would not mention Sudan but Rohan, who had accompanied his parents on their visit, beat her to it.

"You are definitely not Sudanese," he said. Mr. Rabula laughed out aloud. "No, no, not at all," he protested. "Your boy is very cute," he said, turning to Kumar.

Kumar was sure Rohan would have had a go at guessing further had he known something about the geography of Africa, but his son's knowledge of African geography was as bad as Indu's and his own. He himself could think of only Nigeria, and Mr. Rabula waved it away with a pained expression. "No, no, not that!" He said, almost wincing. "Congo?" Indu asked, surprising Kumar and Rohan with her discovery of the Congo, but it only deepened the pained expression of Mr. Rabula. "Why don't you give us a clue?" Rohan asked impatiently, getting into the swing of the guessing game, and Mr. Rabula thought for a second or two and said that it was a country with a past of racial discrimination.

"Zimbabwe!" Rohan said, and Kumar knew straightaway that he had picked it up from the Television. It was only last week that there was a program on all the horrible things Robert Mugabe had done to White farmers in Zimbabwe and Kumar was disappointed that Rohan said it before he did. But Mr. Rabula stared at Rohan as if he had just sworn loudly and that his initial evaluation of him being cute had been a big mistake.

"No man," he said, in a voice strained with disappointment and frustration. "We are from South Africa."

Ahhhh! They all said. South Africa! But it was the last place they would have thought of. Kumar and Indu never thought of South Africa as a country of Black people. Apart from Mandela, the only other South Africans they knew of were White. But it also made them feel relieved. The Rabulas were definitely not Sudanese.

Then, a few months after the Rabulas moved in, Andrews moved out.

"Good riddance!" Chelliah chirped. "The pretender is gone. Hopefully, I can now have a more down-to-earth neighbour."

He never bargained for the Bogans.

FOUR

Very soon they received a full report on the Bogans from Vivienne. She seemed to be watching them like a hawk through that window every opportunity she got. She reported with the spirit of a tabloid journalist.

There were seven of them, she disclosed; two adults and five children. The man Kumar saw that first morning was the father, and he had a wife too. And apart from the two boys they had seen that morning, there was also a younger girl, seemingly in her mid-teens and another young boy about nine or ten years old. The youngest in the family was a little infant in a stroller. They all seem to be just like the man and two boys they had seen that first morning: dirty and unkempt. The father had tattoos on both arms, Vivienne said, as if revealing a terrible secret. The older boy also had tattoos on his arms and a big one on his neck.

"Does the mother also have tattoos?" Rohan asked.

Vivienne said she hadn't seen her arms yet because she was always wearing a jumper, but she had no doubt her arms were also covered in tattoos. "She look ugly," she added. "Like man. And I not surprised if even baby in stroller having tattoo also," she quipped. When Rohan suggested that it may be illegal to tattoo a baby she simply pouted and said, "if I tattoo my baby illegal, but Bogan tattoo baby, nobody cares."

"I bet they are all unemployed," Indu said gravely. "They always are." Vivienne nodded and said that is what she had heard too.

The Rabulas also agreed. This is why, Mr. Rabula pointed out, that they had so many children. "The more children you have, the more money you get," he declared with the air of a man sharing a little-known fact. Having never been unemployed, he had no idea exactly - or even roughly - how much the new neighbours could be getting as unemployment benefits, but he was certain it was substantial. They probably didn't need jobs, he opined. "Why work when you can have children?"

Chelliah, ever the inquisitive neighbour, had a very different preoccupation where the Bogan progeny was concerned. There was a big gap between the youngest child, who was an infant and the next child who was about ten years old. Why the gap? He often asked, addressing no one in particular. "Why the gap? What happened in between?" He asked, looking around, not like a man posing a question but like a magician who had just performed a clever trick and was waiting for the audience to applaud. The question made others think, but only for a few seconds as everybody quickly conceded that such irregularities were part and parcel of the Bogans' world. Only Rohan, in his inimitable style, ventured an opinion. "They probably didn't realise it," he said. "One day, like, eight or nine years after the fourth child, they must have suddenly realised they had not had a child for a while." That did not satisfy Chelliah, but as Rohan did not seem to be interested in satisfying him,

Chelliah did not take the matter any further.

Before long, they all got to see the Bogan family regularly. The man appeared to be in his late thirties, tall and wiry with a thick moustache that curled around his cheeks, and dark, bushy, unkempt hair and beard. And just as Vivienne reported, he had tattoos on both arms, which enhanced his rugged, fearsome appearance. The woman, somewhat younger, looked fleshier but quite tall with short brown hair. They both seem to be perpetually dressed in tight dark jeans and dirty sneakers and a variety of dirty tops. Sallow, pasty skin and eyes spoke of an unhealthy diet and poor hygiene, and even though the man and the two older boys were tall and looked strong, there seem to be something lacking in their physiques. It was as if they had not developed to their full potential, like trees that had only grown tall when they could have gown both tall and leafy. Their unkempt appearance also hinted at limited encounters with water. Everybody felt that if one had dared to get closer, one would have certainly experienced the smell too, but then, no one in the neighbourhood dared to go that close.

And Indu seemed to have guessed right. Both parents appeared to be unemployed. Occasionally, the man and woman were seen driving away in their beat up station wagon and, at times, the man was seen driving alone, wearing an orange hi-visibility vest. However, it did not happen very often. The older boy too was seen going out in similar attire but even less frequently. "I think they going out only to get the dole," Vivienne whispered to Indu one day when the car trundled past them while they were chatting outside Kumar's home. "And the man is wearing that orange thingy only to show that he is looking for work even though they only care about dole," she added.

"Oh, that is not very nice, Vivienne," Indu protested. "I am sure they also go and do their shopping. How else can they eat?" Vivienne simply looked at Indu as if the thought had never occurred to her.

The children seemed to have inherited their parents' habits. They roamed about in dirty clothing, their faces unwashed and hair uncut and uncombed. They did not seem to go to school much, even though every one of them, except the toddler, was of school-going age. Occasionally the older boy could be seen leaving home late in the morning, dressed in what appeared to be a badly maintained school uniform, only to return a couple of hours later. Rohan said that rumour had it that he went to a state school just ten minutes walk from the home and that there he had a reputation for being sullen and withdrawn. And when he was heard communicating with somebody, every two or three words were punctuated with an expletive, a trait that seemed common to all members of the family. Not that many people dared to speak to them, but they could be heard speaking to each other in that mixed language of expletives and ordinary speech.

If the family was unkempt, their garden was an even bigger mess. When Andrews occupied the house, he had taken pride in the appearance of the garden, growing flowering plants and keeping the lawn nicely trimmed. He had even attempted to create a little rock garden in one corner, succeeding only in creating a pile of little boulders which he industriously kept free of weeds. But his commitment to gardening was unquestionable. During the two weeks when the house had been vacant, the estate agents had made a decent attempt at keeping the grass down and the weeds controlled. The new arrivals soon changed that. The grass now grew freely, mixed with the weeds and was only thwarted by the numerous objects they left scattered about the garden. These included assorted toys, pieces of furniture, bits of wood, and all kinds of rubbish. They lay there for weeks until picked up and dumped in a different spot. Some things were never moved, like the frame of an old washing machine that stood in one corner exposed to the sun and rain. In the midst of this chaos, the grass grew, shooting freely through the scattered debris, frustrated only by the shifting of an object from its place or the introduction of a new one. As a result, the growth was uneven, much like the stubble on the cheeks of a person using a bad razor at irregular intervals, and had the same effect of presenting an unhealthy appearance. And unlike the grass, and not surprisingly, the flowering plants died, crushed by the weight of the debris and the total lack of care. The rock garden vanished, the boulders covered by a mantle of weeds and grass.

Nobody knew their names. Nobody cared - or dared - to ask. But as their neighbours desired something more specific than the generic 'Bogan' to identify the individual members of the family, they, especially the children, came up with nicknames for the new comers. The man was Father Bogan, the woman, Mother Bogan, the older boy BB (Bogan Boy)1, the next boy in line BB2, the girl BG (Bogan Girl) and the little boy simply the Little Bogan. The infant whose gender could not be determined came to be called the Infant Bogan until a suitable name could be invented.

Nobody knew where they came from, and how they moved in on that night without anybody knowing was still a mystery. An even bigger puzzle was how they managed to rent that house. It was not exactly an affluent neighbourhood, but surely the estate agents could see these people did not belong there?

"They don't really care anymore nowadays," Mr. Chelliah said ruefully. "They let anyone in now." He was not against White people, he said. He was not a racist. No, not at all. He had lived in that court when all his neighbours were White, and he had enjoyed it. If White people were to live on his street, he preferred them to be like his former neighbours who were friendly and welcoming, or like the Robinsons who kept themselves to themselves than rude Bogans with tattoos down both their arms.

FIVE

Before the arrival of the Bogans, it was Vivienne who had raised eyebrows in the neighbourhood. To some, she was an oddity and a curiosity; to others, a freak.

After their initial shock and embarrassment at discovering Vivienne's sexuality, Andrews and Chelliah had grown cold towards her. Andrews at least greeted Vivienne and Lauren with a diffident "hello" but Chelliah always treated them to a withering glare which Vivienne returned with equal spirit. Not stopping at glaring, Chelliah also tried to encourage the rest of the neighbourhood to treat the lesbian couple with contempt.

"One of the most abominable things imaginable," he proclaimed, referring to Vivienne's sexuality. "Honestly, I can't think of anything more despicable than going against what God intended for you. But I think the world has changed so much now it is barely recognisable form the world I grew up in." He, of course, had his suspicions the moment he saw Vivienne, he said. That haircut was very suggestive. But his compassion got the better of him.

"Oh, I am sure they don't mean any harm Mr. Chelliah," Indu had said. "It is not our thing, of course, but then, what can you do? We can't chase them from here. And they seem nice enough."

Kumar nodded in agreement. Vivienne and Lauren fulfilled the two criteria he expected from all people: friendly and non-violent. He too found homosexuality confronting but live and let live was his principle, especially if the people you let live did not live with you in the same house.

Chelliah was not happy with Kumar's and Indu's response, but he refrained from pushing it further.

"It must have been the heat in Queensland," he told Kumar. "The sultry, hot weather makes people give in to wanton pleasures. During the hot months in Chennai in my younger days, I too used to get a bit like that," he added wistfully.

Rohan asked if that meant Chelliah went after men when it got hotter, and Chelliah simply looked at Kumar and asked why he did not thrash this boy when he was younger and still corrigible. It was one of his constant ripostes to Rohan's butt-ins. As usual, Kumar smiled. He didn't say that he would have if he didn't love the cheeky little devil.

The Purics treated the news of Vivienne's sexuality with amusement rather than hostility, and Edis Puric, in particular, was not averse to showing that.

"Edis always looking at me like I am freak," Vivienne said to Kumar one day soon after the arrival of Lauren. "Always smiling like I am doing something funny."

The Robinsons showed little interest in the personal life of Vivienne.

They hadn't bothered to communicate with Vivienne when she was single, and they didn't bother when Lauren arrived, saying "hi" and "bye" to her too. Mark and Angela were no different. Chelliah managed to catch them on a rare occasion when they were returning from shopping one Saturday and informed them casually that some unnatural activity was taking place in the house at the bottom of the court. Mark nodded in silent acknowledgement while Angela retorted that they preferred to mind their own business. "They didn't even bother to ask what unnatural activity I was talking about!" Chelliah hissed. He felt doubly peeved that a Timorese should show such indifference. "If everybody minded their own business." he reminded Kumar, "East Timor would have never been free."

Ahmed too gave Chelliah a cold reception when the old man ventured to break the news to him. He told Chelliah he had very little interest in discussing his neighbours with the old man. "Why you not mind your own business?" he asked Chelliah much to his annoyance. But Ahmed's response to Chelliah's news was a reflection of his attitude to the man, not the news. No sooner than Chelliah left did Ahmed cross the road and go to Kumar's.

"We shudda been told by the estate agents," he seethed. "If we knew we wudda not come here at all."

"Told about what?" Kumar asked, confused.

"Them lesbians," Ahmed said, hooking his thumb in the direction of Vivienne's and Lauren's house. "If we know lesbians living here, we go somewhere else."

He stared at the two women when they walked past when he was out in the garden or on the footpath, a stare which Vivienne was only too happy to return. When staring seemed to have no effect on them, Ahmed tried ignoring them, which was a difficult thing to do, as they lived right next door and walked past his home ever so often. So he ended up avoiding them as much as he possibly could, which meant hurrying inside whenever they passed as if they were carrying the plague.

"Have you ever tried talking to them?" Kumar asked one day when Ahmed repeated his complaint about having to live next door to lesbians.

"About what?" Ahmed asked.

"Oh, about anything. I talk to them. They seem quite nice."

"You talk to them?" Ahmed asked, surprised. "About what?"

Kumar thought about it. Actually, it was Vivienne who talked to him a lot, about anything and everything, because she had come to realise that Kumar did not treat her as a freak of some sort even though he was not completely comfortable with her.

"Oh nothing serious," he said to Ahmed. "Just normal chit chat."

"I don't want no chit chat with lesbian," Ahmed said flatly. Then he was silent for a while, as if thinking deeply.

"What you reckon they do?"

"Do? What do you mean?"

"You know, lesbian. What you reckon they do? Men-men fuck, men-women fuck. What do lesbian do?"

Kumar thought for a while. He too had wondered about that but had quickly banished it from his mind because his mind was conjuring up lurid images. They were too disturbing for him and sometimes from the way Indu appeared to stare after Vivienne and Lauren he suspected that she was going through the same experience. But he didn't dare ask.

"Better not to think about it." He said to Ahmed. "I don't think it is a good idea."

Ahmed nodded. But Kumar was certain he would not stop thinking about it.

And to Ahmed's dismay, Eric and Mahmoud got on well, as neighbours and as boys. It was only a matter of time before all three boys formed a little group of neighbourhood friends, meeting at each other's homes to chat or play video games, to go to the park to kick the footy around or to sit and chat. Despite Ahmed's dislike of his mother and her partner, the boys also met at Ahmed's place, thanks to the intervention of Amina who adored Eric and found his mother's sexuality far less threatening than her husband did.

"In this country, very difficult to bring up children," Ahmed said to Kumar one day, watching Eric, Mahmoud and Rohan chatting and laughing outside Eric's house.

"They only think of themselves, not about their parents."

Kumar wanted to say that he was sure Mahmoud cared about his parents too, but he quickly realised Ahmed already knew that and was simply venting his frustration about Mahmoud having a different view of things. Kumar had no issues with Rohan speaking to Eric. He rather liked the boy. He was cheeky but polite and, like Rohan, didn't seem to take life too seriously even though he seemed to be more studious than his son.

"What you do if your son become faggot?" Ahmed asked Kumar another time.

Kumar thought for a few seconds. It was something he had thought about at times, and, like the thought of what lesbians might be doing, he had quickly banished it from his mind. He knew that if Rohan was gay, there was nothing he could do about it. He would still love his boy and wish him to be happy, but it would make life very difficult for him and his family. His relatives lived in Sri Lanka but Rohan becoming gay was entirely different from Rohan becoming an electrician. His grandmother might even have a stroke.

Seeing that Kumar was taking his time thinking of a response to Rohan's hypothetical homosexuality, Ahmed offered his own views.

"If my Mahmoud become faggot I kill him and throw him in river," Ahmed threatened, in a tone that suggested that Kumar should do the same to Rohan if the need arose.

When Kumar told Indu about Ahmed's threat, she placed both her hands on her cheeks. "That man has a temper alright," she said. "Mahmoud better not become gay."

"What river is he talking about?" Rohan wanted to know. "If it is the Yarra, he need not kill Mahmoud. Just throw him in, and he'll die of poisoning."

Kumar could not help but smile at Rohan's observation. Then he suddenly remembered something.

"Does Mahmoud have a girlfriend?"

"Not really," Rohan said. Then he thought for a few seconds. "Well, he ogles this girl who comes to the park with her dog. But that is not like having a relationship or anything. She barely notices him."

"Oh, yes I remember that girl!" Kumar said. He had seen the girl a few times, a tall, slender, blonde girl with a little dog on a leash walking to and from the park.

Kumar's recognition of the girl raised Indu's eyebrows.

"Oh, really?" She asked, somewhat playfully. "Hope *you* were not ogling her."

Kumar laughed. "Not at all!" he said. "I thought the dog was cute."

They all laughed. Then Kumar turned to Rohan again.

"Come to think of it, do *you* have a girlfriend?'

They both watched the boy closely, awaiting his response.

"Nah," Rohan said, without even bothering to look up from the phone. "I have no interest in girls."

Kumar and Indu looked at each other with concern. Rohan glanced up and seeing their worry, quickly moved to clarify matters.

"Don't worry; I am not interested in boys either."

They both heaved a sigh of relief. But Kumar was curious.

"Then *what* are you interested in?"

Rohan stared ahead at the wall for a few seconds, thinking. Then he shrugged.

"Nothing, I guess. I want to be an electrician."

He returned to his phone.

***

Eric's mum's sexuality never bothered Rohan and Mahmoud the way it bothered the adults. Mahmoud said it was sinful to be a homosexual because Ahmed had told him so, but he didn't seem to believe it. They simply treated it the same way they treated Eric's attitude to girls. Eric had declared that he was not interested in girls at this stage in his life. His two mums had wanted him to study hard and get good results before doing anything else. He was fully focused on that, to the extent of blocking out everything, unless he met a girl like Naomi Watts. Rohan and Mahmoud found it ridiculous, especially since Eric was not doing well in his studies despite all that focus and that there was little chance of him meeting someone like Naomi Watts. Eric simply scowled and said that that is exactly why he had to focus. Rohan and Mahmoud shrugged and accepted it as something they couldn't understand but had no problem with.

But they were curious about the history of Vivienne's sexuality.

"Did she give any clue when you were small?" Mahmoud asked. "You know, like, she was into women and shit?"

"Nah," Eric said. "Never."

"Can you remember your dad? What was he like?"

"Yeah, I remember," Eric said. "He was Chinese."

"We know, dumbass! You don't look exactly like Russel Crowe," Mahmoud said.

"Or LeBron James," Rohan said and laughed loudly, joined by Mahmoud.

Eric frowned and told them that he couldn't remember much of his dad apart from the fact that he was Chinese because he was very young when his parents separated. For several years thereafter, he had been alone with Vivienne. One day, when they were at a restaurant, Lauren had appeared out of nowhere and started chatting with Vivienne. That was the start of the relationship, which eventually led to Lauren moving in with Vivienne.

"Wow!" Mahmoud said. "Just like that! How did Lauren know your mum was gay?"

"I think they have a way of sensing these things," Eric said.

"Maybe they sniff the air, and they can smell other lesbians within like 500 metres," Rohan said. "Who knows?"

"Did your mum ask you if it was alright for Lauren to move in?"

Eric nodded in assent. Vivienne had hugged Eric and asked him if it was alright and she had started crying and had told him that she would never ever do anything against his wishes. Vivienne had become so emotional that it had unsettled Eric and mainly in order to put an end to the trauma Eric had consented to the union. However, he had soon found that Lauren was as loving and caring as his own mother, perhaps even more so as Lauren was always trying hard to please him.

Rohan and Mahmoud shook their heads in amazement. "I never thought your mum could be emotional in that way," Rohan said. Eric grinned. "Believe me," he said, "you don't wanna see that. Fucking painful, I tell ya."

After his father left them he had not bothered to contact them, Eric said. He didn't ask about him either. He hardly remembered him and as the man never bothred to contact him he figured that he was not worth worrying about. Besides, Vivienne and Lauren gave him enough affection for him to feel happy and content.

*****

It was with the Rabulas that Chelliah found the most receptive audience in his quest for allies against Vivienne. Before the Rabulas moved in, he had approached the Wangs, but with very little success. Chelliah's erudite assault on Vivienne and Lauren in particular and lesbianism in general was largely lost on the Wangs due to their poor understanding of English. "I spoke to them for ten minutes," Chelliah told Kumar, seething with frustration. "Ten whole minutes I lectured them about the un-natural relationship practised only two houses from them. The bloody Chinaman listened with a big grin on his face and at the end of it all, asked if I wanted a glass of water!" Surely, he said, they should enforce stricter English requirements for new migrants?

However, although they may not have understood Chelliah's sermon, the Wangs understood perfectly what Vivienne and Lauren were up to. It couldn't have been more obvious with the two of them walking hand in hand past the Wangs' house often. Liu Wang somehow found it hard to look at them when they passed. "He always turning to rose bush and looking at flower," Vivienne said, frowning. But Mei Wang was less restrained. Whenever she saw Vivienne and Lauren, she giggled uncontrollably and ran inside. "She very immature," Vivienne said, and Lauren nodded. "Like little girl," she added, shaking her head.

The Rabulas however, were far more demonstrative than the Wangs in their response to the lesbian couple down the road. When Chelliah told them about the two women, Mrs. Rabula immediately went into shock, and Mr. Rabula raised his eyes to the heavens and then started pacing up and down as if driven to distraction. After they recovered, they promised Chelliah that they would make sure that they let the two misguided women know of their displeasure, and, God-willing, make them see the light. They did it in their own inimitable style, choosing Christmas of all times to do it.

The Rabulas threw the only Christmas party in Park Court. And it was a big party. Despite his age, Mr. Rabula managed to haul a huge Christmas tree up to the front deck where Mrs. Rabula spent long hours decorating it. At least three weeks before Christmas, fairy lights began twinkling from the tree, the roof, and shrubs and trees in the garden giving the place a magical appearance. From a distance it looked as if the Rabula residence had been sprinkled with hundreds of tiny, glittering, colourful lights. And on Christmas Eve, the place also came alive with music as Rabula played old Christmas favourites as well as some of his own favourite melodies on his expensive home entertainment unit. Many of their friends, colleagues and family turned up for the party and the festivities, which started late in the afternoon, continued well into the early hours of the morning.

And they chose that night to take Vivienne and Lauren to task on their sexual preference. Vivienne was enjoying a quiet drink with Lauren, admiring the lights in the Christmas tree when Mrs. Rabula sauntered in with several of their lady guests in tow. They came and stood in a group around Vivienne and Lauren, Mrs. Rabula's friends staring at them intensely. "The moment I see her friends I know they know about me and Lauren," Vivienne later recalled. "They stare, like we suddenly come down from Christmas tree," Lauren too recounted, in one of her rare contributions to conversations. Then, while her friends continued to stare, Mrs. Rabula put her arm around Vivienne's shoulder and began talking as if she were a child.

"In our lives we all make mistakes," she said, soothingly. "Sometimes we take the wrong turn, give in to temptations, and do things that militate against what God intended for us."

Her friends nodded gravely. Then, while Vivienne stood trying to fathom what was being said, Mrs. Rabula rubbed and stroked Vivienne's shoulder comfortingly, even affectionately. Vivienne was taken aback.

"I think she is wanting me," Vivienne said later. "Wanting real bad, and I tell her, nothing personal, but I already have partner, and you know that."

Mrs. Rabula had recoiled from her in horror, withdrawing her hand as if it had been stung by something poisonous. Her friends seemed similarly shocked, some even taking a few steps back.

"I beg your pardon!" Mrs. Rabula had bellowed indignantly, bringing a few more guests onto the deck to see what was going on. "I have no such disease young lady!"

Vivienne was firing up too.

"What disease? She cried. "What disease I have? Tell me!"

Mrs. Rabula quickly calmed down. She was the hostess, and her guests were watching with interest. By now her husband had also arrived on the deck and seeing his wife in an agitated state, he quickly put a protective arm around her.

"I am talking about your lifestyle, miss, about you and your partner and I am speaking as a Christian," Mrs. Rabula said, her voice gradually assuming a gentler, even sad, tone. "It pains me to see you like this, wasting your life wallowing in sin, going against what God intended for you!"

Kumar, Indu, and Rohan arrived on the deck just in time to witness the final moments of this confrontation. They found Vivienne standing her ground, like a pugilist ready to exchange blows, glaring at Mrs. Rabula, who, for her part, was doing her best to remain civil while expressing her disgust. Lauren was seen standing behind Vivienne, apparently using her larger partner as a shield.

Mrs. Rabula continued her sermon on the deck, as calmly as she could.

"Remember, Miss, God loves everybody. He loves lesbians too," she said. "But whether He will admit you to His kingdom, now *that* is a big question."

Vivienne's response was characteristically combative.

"Why I want to go heaven if no lesbians there?" She asked Mrs. Rabula who found such impudence vulgar beyond belief.

"I have met lesbians in my life young lady," she huffed. "But I have never met a lesbian who turned her back on heaven."

Vivienne promptly turned her back on Mrs. Rabula and, hand in hand with Lauren, left the deck and the house. You can stay if you like, she said to Eric, but the boy simply said he didn't want to go to heaven if his mums couldn't, and promptly followed Vivienne and Lauren. The party continued without them but in a very subdued mood.

After that, the Rabulas shunned Vivienne and Lauren. It was clear that Mrs. Rabula also expected an apology for Vivienne's behaviour that night. Whenever she saw Vivienne and Lauren walking up the road, she would come down and wait near the gate, arms folded across her chest as if waiting for the two to apologise. Vivienne simply walked past her without even acknowledging her presence. But she confided in Indu that it was not easy.

"She standing like big black bear, looking at me like wanting to eat me," Vivienne said to Indu. "Sometimes I feel like giving her good kick up her big black Rabool-ass."

When Indu told him this, Kumar said that Vivienne had been very sensible not to give in to that temptation. But he was not certain how long she will be able to resist it.

SIX

With the arrival of the Bogans, the neighbourhood's attention shifted from Vivienne and Lauren to the newcomers as their main object of curiosity, ridicule, and hostility. But it also further complicated matters for Vivienne.

It did not take long for Vivienne's initial apprehensions about the Bogans to be realised. Ever since their arrival, the neighbourhood came to be filled with tension. This was in spite of a distinctive reclusiveness on the part of the newcomers. The Bogan family never showed any inclination to communicate with their neighbours and seem to prefer their own scruffy little world. This could have been a consolation had it not been for the fact that, in their isolation, they also showed a universal hostility to everybody else. It was as if they were deeply suspicious and wary of everyone. Anyone who dared to greet them on the street, even cautiously, during the early days of their arrival, was treated to hostile grunts and frowns. Mr. Chelliah, who once ventured to greet BB1 with a diffident "how are you this morning young man?" was treated to a stare that penetrated the depths of his soul so profoundly that he never again dared to speak to any of them again. Ahmed who once looked at BB1 walking past the house with a guarded smile on his face was also the recipient of a menacing glare followed by "What the fuck're ya lookin' at?" which left him speechless with anger and humiliation.

"I only wanting to see what he got tattooed on his neck," Ahmed said to Kumar. "And he jump at me!"

"The tattoo must be what he asked him exactly," Rohan later said to his father. "You know, 'what the fuck are you looking at?'"

Kumar frowned and told Rohan to stay away from the newcomers. "Don't you go looking at their necks!" Indu warned. Rohan simply said he had no interest in looking at them at all.

Whether they communicated or not, the mere presence of the Bogans seemed to be jarring to that little community. However, nobody felt it more than Vivienne and Lauren, who saw them daily directly opposite their house. Mr. Chelliah, who was separated from them by a fairly tall fence, had no such misfortune. He could hear them more than he could see them, but since his hearing was not the best, it didn't matter a lot if he heard them or not. Still, he could see them from his kitchen window, sitting around in their back yard, the Father Bogan and Mother Bogan smoking, sometimes joined there by BB1 and BB2. When he went into his backyard, he could faintly hear the F word and the C word being used very freely, which offended his good Catholic self to no end. But these little inconveniences could be dealt with by keeping the windows closed, the blinds drawn and avoiding his own backyard. A terrible price to pay in your own house, Chelliah said with despair but was also quick to add, philosophically, that one must learn to bend with the wind. He had learned to live with lesbians cohabiting right in front of his eyes, and after that, having Bogans next door was not such a big issue.

But Chelliah soon realised that he had to do a lot more bending when the Bogans kicked the footy around in their backyard and often kicked it into his back garden. When this happened, either BB1 or BB2 would saunter in through the gateless driveway without even bothering to ask for permission, and walked all over the garden looking for the ball. At such times Chelliah would fume silently, but not being able to do anything else, he simply sought to avoid the issue by going for a walk whenever he heard the Bogans playing football, a walk that usually ended up in Kumar's house.

But Vivienne could not do that. She could not keep her windows closed and remain indoors, could she? She had a garden to tend to and work to go to. And she had a partner and a son. Things were more complicated for her than they were for anyone else.

Trouble soon began between her and the newcomers.

It started when the Bogans realised who Vivienne and Lauren were. It didn't take very long for them to figure it out. If Vivienne's short, tom-boyish hair-do was not a dead giveaway, the fact that she frequently held hands with Lauren certainly was. Soon Vivienne and Lauren found the Bogan Boys standing around in their garden or even on the sidewalk outside their house, sneering at them when they went out for a walk or even when they were in their own garden. Lauren swore she heard one of them hissing 'lesos' one day as she went for a walk with Vivienne. Eric had a torrid time too as they seem to find the mere sight of him amusing.

They would giggle and whisper among themselves whenever they saw him.

"They seem to think I am some sort of a freak," Eric told Rohan who found it amusing.

"That is truly funny!" he said. "I don't think they of all people can afford to call anyone a freak."

That did little to appease Eric or his mums. They remained harassed, almost under siege.

Kumar felt sorry for Vivienne. Not only did she have to endure the barbs of her old neighbours, but she also had to put up with the rudeness of the Bogans. It was not a great situation to be in. He also felt sorry for Chelliah who had to leave his own house whenever the Bogans were playing footy in their backyard. It was doubly painful for Kumar as Chelliah's pain became his when the old man ended up in his house draining mug after mug of sweet tea and talking endlessly about the deterioration that was taking place in the country in general and in the neighbourhood in particular.

"But one must learn to bend with the wind," he kept saying. "Standing against the wind can break you."

Kumar sat listening, wondering how much they will have to bend with Chelliah before their elderly neighbour found another way to bend. He could think of no solution for his neighbours' problems with the Bogans. They could only endure as he endured Chelliah. He was also thankful for small mercies; that he was not living as close to the Bogans as Vivienne and Chelliah or that the Bogan Boys did not kick the ball further than Chelliah's house. He was not sure how, or indeed whether, he and his family could have endured the Bogans tramping around their garden looking for lost balls.

But the biggest loser of all this was Mahmoud. After the arrival of the Bogans, the number of people who visited the park began to diminish steadily until finally, nobody bothered turning up. One of the first to throw in the towel was Mahmoud's heartthrob, the girl with the dog. She came down to the park a couple of times after the Bogans arrived, but the Bogans were not around when she came. The third time she came, they were there, almost all of them, sitting on the front steps smoking and chatting. The girl came and saw the Bogans. As a few catcalls emanated from the Bogan steps, she entered the park, walked around more briskly than usual, and after the first round, walked straight out of the park, dragging the dog that seemed to be wondering why its owner did not complete her usual five rounds. Neither she nor her dog was seen again. Her departure devastated Mahmoud who sulked for several days. Realising she was not likely to come again as long as the Bogans were there, he even went looking for her, walking around the neighbourhood endlessly but to no avail. She was gone, it seemed, forever.

Heartbroken, Mahmoud swore never to go to the park again. It was not a hard resolution to make as since the Bogans arrived, their visits to the park too were becoming less frequent.

Then came the incident with the aeroplane.

Eric had recently purchased a remote-controlled plane which he was very eager to show off to his friends. Rohan and Mahmoud being very happy to be shown off to, they all went to the park one Saturday morning to fly it. Initially, they were reluctant to go there; the park was almost Bogan territory now. But their wish to see the plane flying was greater than their concern for any possible confrontation, and they eventually decided to be bold than cautious. To their relief, there were no Bogans about, and to their great joy, Eric quickly figured out how to work the machine. Soon the plane was airborne, circling around the park.

They were happily flying the plane around the park when the Bogan children trooped in, all except the infant Bogan. They came, they saw, and they watched. Eric and his two friends continued to fly the plane, trying their best to ignore the Bogans. But it was hard, Rohan said, to ignore someone standing there just staring at you and your plane. "You might as well try ignoring a splinter in your eye," he added.

As there was nothing they could do about it, they continued to fly their plane but without any of the enthusiasm with which they started. The Bogan children watched quietly, silently and when Rohan stole a glance in their direction, he saw them all staring with faces marked with undisguised resentment. The Little Bogan alone was following the plane with eyes filled with wonder.

Then, after a few more minutes of staring, they walked away, sulkily, muttering among themselves and casting occasional backward glances at the boys with the plane. They all went inside their house. All except the Little Bogan. He stood outside their decrepit dwelling gazing at the plane flying ever so gracefully over the park.

"I felt sorry for him," Rohan said later. "He seemed sad."

"I didn't feel sorry at all," Eric said. 'If they worked, they could have got their own plane."

Good point, Kumar thought when he heard that. Eric had bought the plane with his own money which he earned working at Woolies. Nothing prevented the Bogans from doing the same. A good shower and clean clothes could have got them a job like that easily. He remembered what Dev, the boy at work who everyone suspected of being gay, said about people like the Bogans once. "They just want to sit on their bums, get welfare and do nothing," he had said. "Just like the Abos."

The Bogans' response to the boys' flagrant display of superior possessions came the following morning. They ran up the Australian flag over their house.

And an hour later, Vivienne was at Kumar's place, complaining.

SEVEN

"I still don't see what the problem is," Kumar said to Vivienne who was becoming increasingly impatient at his attitude to the Bogans' action. This remark only annoyed Vivienne even more.

"You not see problem?" she asked indignantly, cocking her head slightly to show her irritation. "You not see problem? Why not see what they trying to say?"

"Well, what are they trying to say?" Kumar was interested to know.

Vivienne took a deep breath. "They trying to say, they Aussie and we are not. Only they Aussie. Only they!"

Kumar understood her point, but he did not understand why she was so worried about it.

"Well they *are* Aussie, aren't they?"

"And we are not?"

"Correct," Rohan butted in, drawing a look of outrage from Vivienne.

"Why? Because me not White? Lauren not White? Eric not White? Only White people Australian? At least we work and pay tax. What are Bogans doing? Sit on bum, doing nothing."

Rohan was opening his mouth to say something, probably that she was correct again, but Kumar butted in.

"You must not get too excited about these things Vivienne," he said, trying to appease his neighbour.

"I think you are overreacting."

Indu also agreed, reiterating her earlier position. This is Australia, and they can raise their flag here. No need to get upset.

But Vivienne *was* upset. They were trying to intimidate her, she said. "Ever since they come, intimidate, intimidate, nothing else," she said. "Laughing at us, staring at us, treating us like freaks. Intimidate, intimidate. All the time." Now they are trying to tell them that they were not Australian. "If not why raise flag?" She was convinced that as the Bogans were the only White people in that court, they wanted to rub that in.

"You not understand." She said finally in sheer frustration. "You not live opposite."

That, of course, was true. Kumar was not sure how he would have reacted if he lived where Vivienne lived. She lived right in front of the Bogans, seeing them daily and fully exposed to their sight and sounds and utterly at their mercy if they wished to do something more than raising a flag. But Kumar could only offer sympathy and empathy.

"I understand," he said. "It must be hard. But then, what would you have said if Indu and I lived there and you lived here?"

Vivienne looked perplexed at Kumar's question. It was clear she was not prepared to deal with such complexities and Kumar congratulated himself on so deftly side-stepping her attempt to put him on the spot. But that did not put an end to Vivienne's worrying.

"What you think we do?"

Kumar thought for a few seconds. "We do nothing." He said, gravely, like a sage. "We do nothing for now. We watch. We wait. To see if the situation gets out of hand. Then....."

"Then we still do nothing," Rohan said in a pretend Chinese accent. Kumar frowned at him, and Vivienne completely ignored the boy.

"Why you not come and look?" Vivienne asked plaintively. It was obvious that she was in earnest.

Kumar hesitated.

"Please?" Vivienne begged.

"Alright. Alright. I will come. But I don't know what good it will do." He said, getting up, sighing as he did. Vivienne beamed in delight while Indu looked on with resignation.

"We gooo. We loooook. And then we do nooothing," Rohan continued to say while checking his phone and without dropping the accent.

Kumar looked at the boy. He seemed utterly unconcerned about anything other than the video clip he was watching.

He sighed deeply. There was one more week to go before school started.

They walked down the footpath towards the Bogan's house. The mid-morning sunlight settled brightly on everything and warmed

Kumar's face. But there was a slight chill in the air. He should have brought his cardigan, he thought, as he hunched his shoulders against the cold.

One day he'd like to be free of this, he thought as he followed his neighbour down the road. This running after Vivienne when she called. But when that day was to come, he was not sure. Maybe only if they or Vivienne moved out. But then, if they moved out, they might have to keep their phone numbers or address secret. Vivienne might seek them out in their new home also. This was the price they had to pay for being the only family in the neighbourhood that treated Vivienne and Lauren with sympathy. Vivienne and Lauren were always welcome to their sympathy, Kumar thought, but he wished that did not entail missions like this.

They reached Vivienne's house from which they had a clear view of the Bogan house across the street. And once again, Vivienne ushered Kumar in quickly and took him to the room from which they could watch the Bogan House without running the risk of being seen by them. Yes, it was true. The Bogans had raised a big Australian flag on the roof of their house. And it was fluttering proudly in the breeze that was now picking up, reminding Kumar more and more of the cardigan he had left at home. He also noticed that the flag was flying upside down! The Bogan's may have raised the flag, but they had raised it the wrong way.

"They are flying it the wrong way," he said. Vivienne looked puzzled.

"What you mean?"

"It is upside down."

"It is?"

Kumar looked at her in surprise. "It is," he said. "The Union Jack should be at the top."

"What Union Jack?"

Kumar grimaced with frustration. "Never mind," he said. "But it is upside down."

Vivienne looked worried. "Well, I am not gonna go and tell them that!"

"No, no! You don't have to!" Kumar said hastily. "I was just saying."

They stood in Vivienne's front room looking at the upside-down flag for a few more minutes. No Bogan was to be seen anywhere. They were probably still asleep, Kumar thought.

"What I do now?" Vivienne asked.

"Well, they have only raised a flag. As I said they can do that. Maybe as you were saying, they are trying to show that they are Aussie to you and your son and intimidate you. But because they haven't done anything else, there is nothing you can do."

Vivienne sighed. It was obviously not the response she was expecting from Kumar.

The door opened, and Lauren poked her head out. "Hello Kumar," she said sunnily. "Good morning. Don't go yet. I make tea."

***

Kumar soon found that his advice had been completely discarded by

Vivienne. By Sunday, Vivienne and Lauren had taken matters into their own hands and responded to the Bogans' flag-raising without further consultation with him. He heard this news from Eric who came to play on the computer with Rohan.

"Mum is on the warpath," he said, beaming. "Wanna come and look?"

"What has she done?" Kumar butted in.

"Oh, nothing serious," Eric reassured him. "She raised her own flag."

"What?"

Eric nodded proudly. "Mum got me to put up our own flag on the roof."

Kumar was confused. Own flag?

"You mean the flag of Malaysia?"

"Or the rainbow flag," Rohan said and chuckled.

"Ha, ha, ha, very funny," Eric said mockingly.

"No, idiot, we also raised the Aussie flag. Mum said must show them that we are Aussie too!"

Kumar was now worried. This was not a very good beginning.

"Did the Bogans see it?"

Eric nodded again. "They sure did," he said without taking his eyes off the computer screen.

"And?"

"The Father Bogan saw it when he came out for something. He stood looking at it for a bit and then called the mother who also came out and looked at it for a bit and then they called their children who also came and looked at it for a bit like they were posing for a family photo or something. And then they all went in and after about half an hour the Father Bogan came out with a ladder, climbed the roof, and removed his flag."

"Oh, that is good! So your mum won," Kumar said, relieved.

"Oh, no!" Eric said. "He put it back, the right way up."

EIGHT

From that time onwards, the two flags flew from the two rooftops as if taunting each other. Occasionally, the whole Bogan family could be seen sitting in their porch under the flag, drinking and smoking and chatting loudly. The flag seemed to have made them louder, Chelliah complained to Kumar. He could now hear their swearing more clearly, even when he was in his kitchen. Vivienne too seemed dissatisfied with the outcome of raising a counter-flag and wondered if she should raise a bigger flag. Eric quickly shot down the idea saying he had no intention of climbing the roof again, adding, for extra weight, that if he fell and injured himself, he might not be able to do his VCE as well as his mums expected. Vivienne's response was predictable. You think I not care you are hurt? You think I care only for your Vee Cee Eee? She asked, distraught, and as she seemed to be on the verge of getting emotional, Eric quickly pre-empted it by saying he was only joking. But as an injury from falling was a real possibility. Vivienne had to shelve her plans to escalate the flag contest.

In the meantime, Mahmoud's morale, sagging after the retreat of the woman with the dog, received a sudden boost at school. The cause was the arrival of a new girl called Cynthia in his class. She had arrived from Sydney as her parents had moved to Melbourne for work. Cynthia was a plain-looking girl with a very short hair-cut and a plump body that she didn't seem to bother to get in shape. This is because she is a lesbian, someone was heard to say. They are all fat and have short hair, like boys. Cynthia however, offered no clues to her presumed sexuality. In fact she complicated everything by declaring that she was a feminist. Not just a feminist but a Black feminist.

"You are not even Black!" Naushad, a boy in Rohan's class, cried. Naushad was not the brightest spark in the class. It was only a few days before the arrival of Cynthia that he had offered an insight into the depths of his ignorance by asking in history class what subject it was that they were studying. That was after he had sat in the class for several weeks. So, if even Naushad could see that Cynthia was not Black, how could she call herself a Black feminist? But Cynthia looked at Naushad with the air of a girl who, though she had little time for fools, was simply condescending to explain out of sheer pity, and said that she was a Black feminist because she has made common cause with the oppressed Black women in the world. It made little headway with her audience though, Naushad stating again, with total confusion written on his face, and with greater confidence than before, that she was not black. Cynthia sighed and then shook her head before walking away, presumably to attend to more pressing matters than explaining her Black feminism to Naushad.

"What's a feminist, anyway?" Mahmoud asked that evening as they were sitting in Rohan's room. Rohan shrugged his shoulders. "Dunno, but I think they are supposed to be lesbians," he said, nonchalantly, the same way he would make a comment on the weather.

"I think it's like women's rights and shit," Eric offered some enlightenment. He tried to Google it but as the definition he came across was too hard to understand, they all decided to go with Rohan's explanation.

"I think they also hate men," Rohan added.

"Then they can't be lesbians," Eric said. "My mums don't hate men. In fact, they like your father."

"Yeah, true," Rohan said. But that is what he had heard.

"But no point asking her," he added. "She seems so up herself."

There was a pause. Then Mahmoud spoke.

"I think she is hot," he said, almost to himself.

That was the first indication they had had of Mahmoud's feelings for Cynthia. Both Eric and Rohan looked at each other and then stared at Mahmoud. "Are you sure?" Rohan asked. Mahmoud nodded hard.

"Yes," he said. "I think she is hot." Suddenly he seemed to be breathing heavily.

"You just like her tits," Rohan said. One of the most striking features of Cynthia was her bosom, which was ample and seemed to progress ahead of her when she walked. At Rohan's crude reference to it, Mahmoud's eyes lit up.

"Yeah, she's got a very nice pair, but it's not just that," he said. "I like her. She is a strong girl."

This was true. Cynthia had a strong personality with very strong opinions on everything, especially men. The world is run by men, she had declared. Specifically by White men, and this is why the whole world was in such a mess. Women should wake up to their plight and unite and fight to free themselves from their collective bondage. The world would be a much better place then, she assured.

It was as if she was some bad-ass gunslinger in an old Western, breezing into a town infested with evil, determined to clean it up. She walked a bit like that too, arms akimbo, as if expecting to pull out a pair of invisible guns at any moment. She prowled the corridors and the schoolyard looking for behaviour that did not meet her standards. And soon she had many victims. The first to suffer her wrath was a couple of boys who were throwing their sandwiches at each other during recess. Cynthia promptly marched up to them and ordered them to pick up the sandwiches and throw them in the bin, but not before telling them how disgusting she found the practice of having food fights. "There are millions of people who do not even get the nutrition in those sandwiches per day, and here you are throwing them at each other!" She hissed. "Girls would have never done that! I am sure it is your poor mothers who prepare cut lunches for you every morning! If they know what you have been doing with the food they prepare for you, they will have seizures!" The two boys were seen trudging away, seemingly in shell shock. On another occasion she walked up to a group of boys who made some comment about her ample bosom, speaking so rapidly and taking such purposeful steps towards them that the boys turned and ran. She was tough with teachers too. Mr. Richardson, the science teacher, received a dressing down from Cynthia for making a sexist joke in class, which made him feel like a little boy. She was not averse to taking on girls either. One day she broke up a fight between two girls and duly castigated them for fighting among themselves without focusing on the common enemy. This is the problem with women, she spat. Frittering away our energy, while the enemy gathers strength.

The area behind the canteen was one of Cynthia's favourite hunting grounds in the first few days. This was where older boys went to have a smoke or watch porn on their phones. Cynthia had no interest in stopping either of these activities. She was more keen to find out if any bullying took place. This was where she confronted Silvagni, her most notable victim. Silvagni was in the same grade as Mahmoud and Rohan and was by no means the stereotypical sadistic bully, but his rude and aggressive behaviour was sufficient to intimidate many younger kids. He was probably a proto-bully, on his way to becoming a fully-fledged one. Cynthia soon checked his rise by giving him a dressing down in front of nearly half the school during one lunch time when she found him standing over a skinny boy from Year Nine. She told him he ought to be ashamed of himself, intimidating people half his size. "Look!" She said to the audience that was gathering fast. "Look! Here is a fine specimen of White Australian manhood, scaring little boys so that he can feel bigger and better!" At the end of Cynthia's lecture, Silvagni was nearly in tears, and he promptly went home after lunch, saying he was not feeling well. He was not seen again in that school. A few days later it was rumoured that Silvagni had moved to another school where there were plenty of little boys to intimidate but no Cynthia.

The biggest problem with Cynthia was that not many people understood what she was saying. Where the hell does she get all this from? Kids wanted to know. Rohan warned Mahmoud that if ever marries her, he will have to spend most of his time Googling words. Mahmoud said he had not thought that far, but he still thought she was hot.

They were in the same class, but Mahmoud was scared to talk to her.

"I fear I might say something wrong and she will bark at me," he said to Rohan when Rohan asked him why he didn't make an effort to speak to her if he liked her so much.

"Don't worry," Rohan said. "You won't understand what she is barking about anyway."

But Mahmoud *was* scared.

He had his first and only substantial exchange with Cynthia during a class discussion on equality and housework. Their English teacher, Ms. Hughes, had brought to class an opinion piece on gender equality that had appeared in *The Age*. The discussion, which was supposed to be on the use of persuasive language, soon degenerated into a debate about gender roles, especially in the sphere of housework. Cynthia declared that both husband and wife should share the responsibilities equally. The chores should be divided 50-50, she asserted. No more, no less.

"At my home, my mum and dad both share the housework equally and often I and my little brother help them," she declared proudly, her eyes half-closed as if she was trying to visualise it.

While many others in the class agreed, Mahmoud felt it was unfair to women like his mum who loved cooking.

"My dad is hopeless at cooking and mum will not let him or me anywhere near the kitchen," he pointed out, trying to sound assertive. "And I don't want dad to cook because one day he tried to cook when Mum was sick, and it was a disaster. The whole house smelt of burnt garlic and meat for days."

While the class erupted in laughter, Cynthia took umbrage at Mahmoud's words and said it was truly pathetic how some women allow themselves to be taken advantage of. It is not so much that men rule us but that we allow them to rule over us, she said, and several girls in the class were seen nodding vigorously. Mahmoud, knowing his mum better than Cynthia, took exception to Cynthia calling Amina pathetic, and felt obliged to say that she had no idea what she was talking about.

"You don't understand our culture," he added for good measure.

Cynthia frowned, folded her arms across her chest and then declared that any culture that did not allow women to come out of the kitchen needed to be reformed and reformed fast. This led to a huge commotion. While the teacher struggled hopelessly to rein in a discussion now well and truly out of control, several boys and girls from Asian and Middle-Eastern backgrounds began to speak in defence of their cultures. Little Joanna got so excited she even began to rattle off in Tagalog. Cynthia was unfazed by the uproar. She simply shook her head in dismay and observed that perhaps reform needed to start with the school.

That evening the three boys sat in Rohan's room, chatting about the discussion in class. Since the advent of the Bogans, the boys had curtailed their visit to the park, meeting mostly at Rohan's place. It was hard to meet anywhere else; Vivienne and Lauren didn't like the noise the boys made when they met there and although Amina doted on Eric, Ahmed never really warmed to him. It made Eric uneasy. So now they met at Rohan's, to chat and to play computer games.

"That girl sounds like a piece of work," Eric said, lying in Rohan's bed, absently flicking through a magazine. "Fortunately we don't have stuck up bitches like that in our school." Rohan smirked. He said he found the idea of not finding stuck up students in a private school a bit rich. Eric smiled at the dig but said nothing. Next to him, Mahmoud sat, deep in thought.

"She is just so immature," Rohan said after a pause, like a man with decades of experience dealing with adolescents. "She thinks she can change the world even before she grows up."

"Show us a picture" Eric insisted, turning to Mahmoud and propping himself on one elbow. Mahmoud quickly took out his phone and showed Eric Cynthia's Facebook page.

"Are you guys friends on FB?"

"Nah," Mahmoud said. "I am too scared to send a request."

Eric looked at the picture. "She is fat, like a lump of lard. Big tits, though."

At the mention of the breasts, Mahmoud took a deep breath.

"I think she is hot," he said.

Eric grinned. "You just like her tits," he said. Mahmoud pursed his lips into something between a grin and a pout.

"By the way," Rohan asked Eric, "Who cooks in your house?"

Eric thought for a while as if it has never occurred to him to consider that.

"Mum does," he said, after a minute or so. "I mean my real Mum. Lauren cleans."

"I see, so it is like 50-50, as Cynthia says."

Eric thought again. "Not really," he said. "More like 40-60. Mum is very messy, especially with cooking. So Lauren cleans a lot."

"Wonder who cooks in the Bogan House," Eric said after a pause.

Rohan grinned and said they probably don't.

"I reckon they hunt the possums and birds and throw them on the fire, like in the old days."

"Nah," Mahmoud said, dismissing the idea. "They eat chips."

"How do you know?" Eric was curious. He sat up in bed.

"I seen them. I can see their house well from my bedroom window. They eat chips. Lotsa chips."

Rohan showed mild surprise, but Eric was curious.

"Just chips?"

"Yeah," Mahmoud confirmed. "Just chips."

"But who cooks the chips?" Rohan also began to show some interest now.

"Who knows? It's Bogan culture." Mahmoud shrugged his shoulders.

"Maybe if you ask Cynthia, she will tell you," Rohan teased.

Mahmoud frowned.

"I like my chips with vinegar." He said, trying to change tack. "Or with a little barbecue sauce." Eric smacked his lips.

"My mum makes them wedges and sprinkles them with green chilli," Rohan said, adding more spice to the growing discussion on chips. Both Eric and Mahmoud stared at their friend as if in disbelief.

"Who puts green chilli in their wedges?" Mahmoud rejoined.

"Mum does. Makes them taste awesome."

His friends considered his statement for a few seconds.

"Your mum's weird," Eric gave his verdict. Mahmoud seemed to agree.

"How come your mum has never given me wedges with chilli?" he asked,

"Me neither," Eric said.

"Cuz she thinks you're soft," Rohan teased. "Can't eat a bit of chilli."

Mahmoud grinned. He looked at Cynthia's picture in the phone again.

"So your mum cooks in your house too, huh?" He asked. Rohan nodded.

"Sure," he said. "Dad helps sometimes, but Mum does all the real cooking. She likes equality, but not in the kitchen."

Mahmoud turned the phone off. "See, this is what I am saying," he said as if speaking to himself. "People like Cynthia talk bullshit. They know nothing about cooking!"

Mahmoud remained hooked on Cynthia but paralysed by his fear of her to make any move. In the meantime, Eric dropped a bombshell of his own.

They were in Rohan's room chatting when Eric recounted a close encounter he has had recently. He was walking home from school one day, he said, and not far from where the street took the turn towards the park, he suddenly found himself walking behind a girl. He had not seen her until then as he was too engrossed with his phone. Even when he saw the girl, he did not give it another thought, until, hearing his footsteps, the girl had turned around.

"Guess who it was?" Eric asked with a twinkle in his eyes.

"Ummm...............Naomi Watts?" Rohan asked, tongue in cheek.

"Idiot!" Eric said. "No. It was the Bogan Girl!"

His two friends looked surprised, even shocked.

"Wow!" said Rohan. "What did she do?"

"Nothing," Eric said. "She just looked shocked. She saw me and recognised me and then quickly walked away, like she was scared of me or something."

"She was scared? Of you?" Mahmoud couldn't believe it.

Eric nodded. "She was. I am sure of it."

Rohan and Mahmoud found it hard to believe, but they were willing to accept Eric's word for it.

"This is why you shouldn't check your phone while walking on the street," Rohan said. "You bump into Bogans!"

Eric, however, wasn't interested in Rohan's pronouncement. He had more engaging news.

"But that's not the really interesting bit," he said, leaning forward as if about to reveal a secret.

His friends also leaned forward, all ears. Eric took a deep breath and made his great revelation.

"I found her kinda cute."

He winced as he said it. His friends stared at him as if unable to believe their ears. Then they burst out laughing.

"Cute? The Bogan Girl?"

Eric nodded, now steadily turning scarlet.

"What a retard!" Mahmoud said, looking at Rohan whose face showed that he agreed with Mahmoud.

"Tell us, what does she look like?" Mahmoud urged.

Eric seemed to be thinking hard. At length, he gave his answer. "Cute."

His friends laughed again. Mahmoud was rolling on the bed.

Eric was turning a deep red now.

"Have you seen her properly?" He asked, making a feeble attempt to stand his ground. But his voice sounded small. "Like, up close?"

"No," said Mahmoud. He had seen her only from a distance, and that was the only way to see the Bogans. Rohan agreed.

"Then you have no right to comment!" snapped Eric.

Mahmoud was slightly taken aback by the intensity of Eric's feelings. He glanced at Rohan.

"I think our mate is in love," he said, winking. Rohan nodded knowingly.

But he was quick to discourage Eric.

"Forget it!" he admonished. "You'd be lucky if you get to talk to her!"

"Geez guys, I only said she was cute, it's not like I want to go out with her!" Eric sounded annoyed.

"Good!" Said Mahmoud. "Cuz she will eat you alive, and if she doesn't, her brothers will!"

Eric frowned but said nothing. He seemed to be deeply regretting having revealed his discovery of the Bogan girl's cuteness.

NINE

Mahmoud may have thought Cynthia was talking nonsense regarding men and women sharing cooking duties, but he had not given up trying to get her attention. Ironically, the opportunity came by way of cooking. While he had refrained from sending Cynthia a friend request Mahmoud had not been remiss at checking her Facebook page regularly. One day Cynthia had posted a picture of a chicken dish she claimed to have cooked for dinner the previous night. 'My favourite dish: Chicken Vindaloo, cooked by yours truly,' she had captioned the photo. Over a hundred friends had liked it and there were many comments too, almost all of them congratulating Cynthia and telling her how yummy the food looked. Cynthia too had responded to her admirers, and one response, in particular, grabbed Mahmoud's attention. 'I love this dish sooooooo much,' Cynthia had said. 'Soooooooo veeeeeery much that if there is a man who can cook this to perfection, I will marry him!'

That comment touched something deep within Mahmoud. Here was a way to get into Cynthia's heart! Since the class discussion, and despite his loud pronouncements about Cynthia's ignorance, he had been thinking of impressing Cynthia by helping Amina in the kitchen and letting it be known that he had done so. Cynthia's Facebook post gave him an added incentive. Why not try his hand at helping his mum with cooking this dish? No, he thought, revising his plan immediately. He had a better idea. He will do the cooking himself.

He did not know what vindaloo was, and he didn't care. All that mattered was that Cynthia liked it. He googled the recipe on his phone, and on the way home from school, stopped at the local supermarket to purchase the ingredients. He bought the chicken breast first but getting the other ingredients was not easy; to his exasperation, he found there were too many. If finding ingredients was this much trouble, he wondered, how much more trouble would it be to cook it to perfection? But the desire to impress Cynthia was strong, almost overwhelming, so, taking a deep breath, he plodded on, picking out the ingredients one by one. It was then that he spied a bottle with the label *Vindaloo paste* in the Indian Food section. He pounced on it the way a child would on a jar of cookies. Reading the instructions on the label, he found that, apart from the chicken, the paste was the main ingredient that he needed to cook Vindaloo. The bottle came as a God-send for Mahmoud who was by now getting quite tired of hunting for ingredients. What a great idea! He thought as he gazed at the bottle. He will use the paste and cook and post pictures of it on Facebook. He will let it be known in school that he did it and that pictures were on Facebook so that Cynthia will also get to know about it. If Cynthia loves it soooooo much as she says on Facebook, there is no reason why she will not be impressed by his effort. There will be nothing in the pictures to show that he used a sauce from a bottle.

Carrying the bags of Vindaloo paste and chicken in one hand, and his school bag in the other, Mahmoud entered home announcing he had a surprise. Hala, ever the cynic, asked if he had finally found a girlfriend, but Mahmoud promptly ignored her and told Amina that he had decided to cook dinner that evening. "That is indeed a surprise," said Amina, casting a look of amusement at Hala who giggled before rolling her eyes. Mahmoud was slightly taken aback but decided to soldier on, informing his mother that he was going to cook chicken Vindaloo and he had already purchased all the ingredients. He wanted his mother and sister to go upstairs and relax while he cooked and also requested that they stay away from the kitchen for the entire duration of cooking.

Amused, yet curious, Amina took a still-giggling Hala and went upstairs, cautioning Mahmoud not to do anything silly. "I don't know what has come over you, but be careful!" She admonished. "Remember what your father did?" Mahmoud nodded and said yes, but I am not my father. It's a simple recipe, he reassured her. It is not hard to cook and won't take long.

Mahmoud started cooking. As he had expected and assured his mother, it was simple; it did not take long for him to prepare the ingredients and get the chicken and the sauce in the pot. The chicken simmered, emanating a nice aroma making Mahmoud's mouth water and his heart beat faster. He was getting closer and closer to Cynthia's heart, it seemed. But this is when things started to go wrong. Thrilled by his apparent success, Mahmoud called Rohan to tell him what he was doing. But before he could break the news to his friend, Rohan had a surprise for him.

"Did you do the home work?" He asked.

"What homework?" Mahmoud demanded, surprised.

Rohan reminded him. They had an assignment due the following day. A SAC that was an oral presentation. Mahmoud had been hoping to prepare for it that afternoon, but he had forgotten about it completely in his preoccupation with the vindaloo. Now, panicking, he forgot all about the vindaloo and taking out his laptop, immediately began to research the topic for the Oral.

When Mahmoud remembered his cooking, it was too late. The first indication that things had gone wrong was the smoke alarm, which began to bleep suddenly and loudly. He leapt out of his seat and rushed to the kitchen only to be greeted by clouds of smoke. The kitchen was full of smoke, and he could barely see the stove. The alarm continued to bleep and above the noise of the alarm. Mahmoud could hear the hurried footsteps of his mother and sister descending the stairs.

Just then, the front door opened and there stood Ahmed, returning early from work. Tired and hungry, he had arrived home looking forward to his evening meal and a rest before he returned to more work. The last thing he expected was to walk into a house filled with smoke and the screeching of the smoke alarm. By now, both Amina and Hala had also started screaming and it was nearing pandemonium.

"What the fuck is going on?" Ahmed yelled. Realising that all was now lost, Mahmoud panicked and ran upstairs, followed by Hala who let out a little squeal on the way. Ahmed rushed through the plumes of smoke to the kitchen, where, together with Amina, he managed to turn off the stove and turn up the fan. As the smoke gradually cleared from the kitchen, they found that all that was left of the chicken vindaloo was a dark crust sticking to the bottom of the pot. The initial aroma had now given way to an overpowering acrid smell.

"What the fuck is going on?" Ahmed bellowed. Amina told him in the most gentle terms how Mahmoud had tried to surprise them and cook dinner using a recipe he had found somewhere.

Ahmed was dumbfounded. "Cook?" He asked. "Cook? Mahmoud? What for?"

He called Mahmoud, but the boy stayed up, too scared to come down. Amina persuaded Ahmed to go and sit in the lounge while she ordered some food. Ahmed went and sank into the sofa, still fuming. "Cook? Mahmoud? What for? What the fuck for?" He kept muttering.

Mahmoud and Hala came down later and only when they were convinced that Ahmed had cooled down. Ahmed ordered Mahmoud in the lounge, and while he dug into a takeaway meal of rice and chicken, he began to interrogate his son.

"Who ask you to cook?"He asked a terrified Mahmoud. "I ask? Your mum ask? Why you think you can cook? Who teach you to cook? Remember what happen when I cook? You see me cook after that? You see my friends cook? Why you cook?" He fired, pining Mahmoud with question after rhetorical question. He pointed to the takeaway food cartons before him. "Because of you I have to eat this shit now. You think this is anything like your mother's cooking? Huh?"

Mahmoud shook his head. He was yet to taste the food, but he had no doubt that it would not be quite as good as his mother's cooking.

"And I don't even know if it is halal," Ahmed grunted, tearing off a big piece of chicken.

He took a sip from his coke. "Alright," he said. "Who is she?"

Mahmoud looked stunned by the question. How did his father guess? Seeing Mahmoud's surprise, Ahmed started impatiently.

"You are not cooking for me or mum. There has to be some girl. Who is she?"

Mahmoud realised there was no way he could hide it from Ahmed. He told him: it was a girl at school.

"Name?"

"Cynthia," Mahmoud said in a small voice. Behind him Hala giggled, earning a frown from Ahmed.

"Lebanese?" Ahmed asked, eyes narrowed as he tried to figure it out for himself.

Mahmoud shook his head. Ahmed's face darkened; his eyes narrowed further.

"She is a feminist," Mahmoud explained.

It took Ahmed a few seconds to fully fathom the meaning of the word. Then he glowered.

"Feminist!" He repeated. Then he growled. "Idiot, they are lesbians. Didn't you know? You like lesbians?"

Mahmoud stood, eyes riveted to the carpet. Amina had come up to him from behind and began running her fingers through his hair.

"You got picture?" Ahmed asked.

Mahmoud showed him a picture of Cynthia from Facebook. Ahmed looked at it intently, his gaze first falling on the face and immediately moving on to the ample breasts.

"Humph," he grunted. "She is lesbian. Look at that haircut. Just like that Vivienne." He pointed casually to the breasts. "Those things mean nothing on lesbian."

Then he went on to lay down the law for Mahmoud. Mahmoud was to do no more cooking in the house. Amina was the cook. Hala can learn to cook but only from Amina. And Mahmoud was to harbour no intentions of having affairs with lesbians, and he can forget about marrying anyone other than a Lebanese. "If you cook again, I kill you," he said. "And if you marry lesbian I kill you, if you become faggot I kill you also." Then he sent Mahmoud upstairs to eat alone in his room.

Mahmoud sat upstairs in his room and ate alone, humiliated by his failure. From his window, he could see the Bogans sitting on their front steps, under the Australian flag now flying in the gentle breeze that was blowing. They were smoking, drinking, and chatting. It was approaching full moon, and the whole Bogan clan sat bathed in bright moonlight. They looked strangely peaceful - and happy.

Amina came in a few minutes later and sat next to him. Stroking his head soothingly, she allayed any fears Mahmoud might have had of suffering an honour killing. "Your father loves you," she reminded him. "He has never even hit you, and today, even after you nearly burnt down the kitchen, he didn't hit you. There is nothing to worry about. He is only releasing his anger."

Mahmoud nodded. "I know," he said softly, his voice teary now.

Amina kissed him on the forehead and said better not push him though. Just to be on the safe side.

When Mahmoud told Rohan and Eric about what happened, they laughed. "Idiot!" Eric said. "You are lucky you didn't burn the house." Rohan smirked and said that it seemed Mahmoud's fate was sealed. He had to marry a Lebanese girl who could cook.

Mahmoud sighed. "Sometimes I envy the Bogans," He said. "So free. None of this bloody equality bullshit. No culture, no religion, no feminism. So fucking free."

TEN

After the cooking fiasco, Mahmoud remained sullen for a few days. He didn't go to school for a day, and when he did, he remained quiet and subdued. Rohan said that he was behaving as if everybody was looking at him and he was trying hard to remain inconspicuous. As far as Rohan was concerned, there was no reason for it. Rohan was the only person at school who knew about Mahmoud nearly burning down their kitchen to impress Cynthia, even though that did not prevent him from teasing Mahmoud about it at every opportunity.

"I hope you will stop this shit soon," Mahmoud said one day after Eric and Rohan had asked him whether he had tried any new recipes. "I have enough trouble with Hala at home."

Hala, he said, was frequently asking Amina whether it was Amina or Mahmoud cooking that day. If it was Mahmoud, she would say, giggling, she would rather have pizza than burnt kitchen - sorry chicken!

But it was not long before the boys' attention reverted to their arch enemy - the Bogans. A few days after Mahmoud's culinary disaster, the boys lost their park - and the plane - to the Bogan Boys.

After that first morning flying the plane, the boys had stopped going to the park to fly it. In fact they now rarely ventured to the park, intimidated not only by the presence of the Bogans opposite to it but also by the Bogans' raising of the flag, which everybody felt was a response to them flying the plane. But as Eric's desire to fly it was too great they had gone to another park about two kilometres away. There they had flown the plane freely, without any interruption or intimidation. But somehow, Eric felt that it was not the same as flying it in the park down their lane.

"It's a pain having to walk two kilometres to fly a plane," he said, as they were returning from plane-flying one day. "That place is full of people too and I don't feel relaxed. Besides, it is crazy to go to all that trouble when you have a park right next door."

"Yes," agreed Rohan. "You have a park right next door, but you have Bogans right next door to the park. That is why we are walking two kilometres to a crowded park to fly the plane."

Eric appreciated the logic but was not convinced. "I think we are worrying for no reason," he said. "I know the Bogans are rude and shit and they have raised that flag and everything, but come on! That doesn't mean they are gonna take our plane or beat us up?"

Rohan seemed uncertain. The looks they got from the Bogans the last time they went there was enough, he said. "I'd rather be in a crowded park ten kilometres from here than in that park with only the Bogans."

Mahmoud who had been quiet all this time now spoke in support of Eric. While flying the plane at the new park, Mahmoud had shown that not only did he enjoy flying the plane but that he could also do it better than either of his two friends. He revealed that this was because he had

had some experience with such gadgets as one of his cousins in Sydney has also possessed one. He was beginning to enjoy his time with the plane and looked forward to flying it more often. The distance to the new park, however, was a deterrent, so it wasn't hard for him to come strongly on the side of Eric. He too was tired of trudging all the way to that crowded park, he said, and he did not see the point in doing so when there was a park right next door. He also dismissed Rohan's fears of the Bogans.

"We are shitting in our pants for nothing," he said. "They can't chase us from the park. This is a free country." Moreover, he pointed out it was the Bogans who seemed to be intimidated by them the last time they flew the plane. "Remember?" he reminded his mates. "*They* left the park!"

Rohan was still not convinced, but he was not inclined to get into a lengthy argument. He simply shrugged his shoulders. "Suit yourselves," he said. "If something happens, don't tell me I didn't warn you!"

So they returned to the park, tentatively at first. The following Saturday they went there in the morning to fly the plane. Rohan too joined his friends, as he felt it was unseemly to abandon them. The Bogan Boys were seen on their front steps, watching,

but they did not come down, which confirmed Mahmoud's opinion that it was the Bogans who were intimidated by them, not the other way round. But they felt it prudent to leave after just half an hour as it was their first return to the park after months. They returned far more relaxed than when entering the park. Even Rohan felt more at ease.

Buoyed by their 'success,' the boys returned the following day. Mahmoud, being a staunch Hawthorn supporter, had also decided to don his Hawks guernsey. This time, however, things went awry. Again, the Bogan boys came out and were watching from the front steps, but after a few minutes, BB1 went inside and returned with the footy. Then, all three boys came down the steps and into the park, all three of them wearing Collingwood guernseys. Rohan swore he could hear BB1 whistling the Collingwood team song.

They continued to fly the plane, but it was clear that they were all beginning to get anxious. The Bogans were definitely not intimidated by them, and their arrival with the footy was ominous. But the boys pressed on, reluctant to leave straightaway. The plane flew, and so did the footy, and soon the boys were beginning to feel that the footy was beginning to fly after the plane. BB1 was not only tall and strong, but he also had a vicious aim which was far better than Eric's skill with the remote. Before long, Eric's hands had begun to shake, and the plane was making erratic moves above the park as if it had a mind of its own.

Now, to make matters more complicated, the Bogan Girl appeared on their front porch, dressed in shorts and a t-shirt. Even though she was far away, her mere appearance seemed to distract Eric, even more than he was distracted by the Bogan Boys. In a sure sign that his recognition of her 'cuteness' was not a passing thing, he kept glancing from the plane to the Bogan Boys and then to the girl, his gaze resting longer on the girl. As a result, the plane began to even more fitfully, as if experiencing some serious turbulence.

Mahmoud now stepped in and took over the controls. Eric later said that Mahmoud grabbed the controls, but Mahmoud was adamant that Eric was only too glad for him to take the controls. As for Rohan, he saw only the plane that was flying as if it were guided by a drunken pilot suddenly coming to life and flying more vigorously than before. When he looked down, he saw Mahmoud with the controls. How they ended up in Mahmoud's hands, he had no idea. But no matter how the controls changed hands the plane now began to move in a decidedly aggressive fashion, circling fast and the circle tightening and coming closer to the knot of Bogans in the centre of the park.

The Bogan Boys stopped kicking the footy and watched, mouths agape and eyes filled with wonder as well as anger while the plane did its rounds, occasionally coming tantalisingly low. Then, as though in a sudden desire to show off his skills with the controls and intimidate the Bogans even more, Mahmoud began to perform diving movements with the plane. The little aircraft now rose into the air and then descended swiftly towards the Bogans, and within metres from their heads, rose again to repeat the trick. Whoever he learnt it from, Mahmoud certainly had a devilish touch with the controls.

Then, the Bogans struck.

BB1 had finally had enough of Mahmoud's antics. He waited with the footy until Mahmoud performed his next dive and then, as the plane came down, he kicked the ball in one swift and deft movement, aiming directly at the plane. As the plane came down, the ball flew up to meet it. This time BB1's aim was perfect. The footy caught the plane on one of its wings, the force of the blow breaking the wing and knocking the plane off course at the same time. As Mahmoud lost control of the plane completely, it rolled and somersaulted in the air and landed in a heap not far from where the Bogans were standing. As it fell, a cheer rose from the Bogans as though BB1 had been playing in the Grand Final and had just sneaked in a goal on the siren to clinch the game.

Eric was so devastated that he did not even bother to ask the Bogans to return the plane. He stormed out of the park with Rohan and Mahmoud in tow and went straight home. He did not even look at the Bogan girl who was seen laughing and gesticulating triumphantly at her conquering brothers. He was already crying by the time he was out of the park, Rohan said later.

Rohan and Mahmoud lingered around long enough to see the Bogans carrying the downed plane into their house as if it were a war trophy. They were also singing 'Good old Collingwood forever.' BB1 carried the Little Bogan on his shoulders, and the Little Bogan held the plane aloft, pretending that it was airborne, making a noise like an airplane. The broken wing did not seem to bother him.

Within a few minutes, Vivienne was at Kumar's place.

"Why they do this?" She asked, her voice shaking. "Why they not buy their own plane? Why shoot down Eric's?"

Kumar had already had a full report of the incident at the park from Rohan. He was expecting a visit from Vivienne but not so soon.

"Why they like this?" Vivienne continued her tirade. "Why take my poor Eric's plane? Why they not get off their bum and work? Then they can buy their own plane!"

Kumar scratched his head. This was getting a bit beyond him now.

"I have absolutely no idea," he said. He wanted to ask Vivienne why she didn't ask the Bogans these questions but feared he would sound rude and insensitive.

"Why don't you ask them?"

Rohan butted in as usual. *He* obviously didn't mind being insensitive, Kumar thought.

He gazed at his son with curiosity. He had to admit; sometimes Rohan's brutal honesty and bluntness had its utility. Whatever he was reluctant to say, Rohan was more than willing to utter, and because he was still a child, he always got away with it.

Vivienne glared at the boy.

"Why *you* not ask?" She snapped. "Why *you* not ask? You also play with plane? You not ask because it not *your* plane?"

Kumar winced hoping Rohan would not say something outrageous but the boy stuck to his simple honesty.

"Me not ask because me scared of Bogan," he said without batting an eyelid.

Vivienne continued to stare at the boy as if stunned by his frankness.

"Eric also scared of Bogan," she said after a pause. "And Mahmoud also. And me and Lauren."

Kumar longed to say me too but refrained. As much as he wished to be free of Vivienne's demands he was not too keen on being seen as fearful by her. But Vivienne was not letting him off the hook so easily. She turned towards him.

"Why you not ask?"

"He too scared," Rohan said, helpfully.

"Ask what, Ask who?"

Indu came out asking. Kumar told her.

Indu's face assumed a look of sheer terror.

"*Talk* to the Bogans? Talk to the *Bogans*?" She asked. The tone of her voice complimented her expression.

Vivienne abandoned the argument. She left the house, shaking her head and muttering something about not having a real man in the neighbourhood. "If I have man he go and ask for plane," she said loudly as she walked down the drive way.

"Is that our fault?" Rohan asked cheekily. Kumar could not help but smile. But he did not like the way this whole affair was turning out.

*****

After the downing of the plane, things remained calm for a while. The boys now avoided the park altogether and it went under the complete control of the Bogans. Eric moped about the lost plane for a few days. In his frustration, he blamed Mahmoud for losing it with his reckless intimidation of the Bogans. He felt that Mahmoud was also motivated by his hostility towards Collingwood, which he has never concealed. Mahmoud admitted that it was his antics with the plane that intimidated the Bogans and that he had never thought much of Collingwood, but he vehemently denied that his intimidation of the Bogans contributed materially to the loss of the plane. He reminded his friend that the Bogans were going after the plane even before he took control of it. And couldn't it be the case that *they* hated Hawthorn? "In any case," he argued, "you would have crashed it even before they got to it, because of your ogling of that girl." Eric retreated behind a frown.

The Bogans seemed to love their conquest of the park. Now they were seen playing footy there often and generally sitting around and chatting, often smoking.

"They are also drinking in the park, sometimes in the night," Vivienne reported. "And laughing, really loudly and in a mean sort of way and I know they are laughing at us."

"How do you know they are laughing at you?" Kumar asked.

"Oh! I know these things." Vivienne said. She had been laughed at most of her life, ever since she came out as a lesbian and sometimes even before that and she knew when someone was laughing at her.

Eric confirmed Vivienne's suspicions. They were laughing at them alright.

"And they also think we all treat them like shit."

"We do?" Rohan asked. Eric shrugged.

"We don't treat them like shit. *We* are scared of them!" Rohan corrected. Eric shrugged again. "I know, right?" he said. "They have no idea!"

Mahmoud agreed. He never really liked Collingwood supporters, but no Collingwood supporter had made him feel as uncomfortable as the Bogans did. He was glad they lost only the park and the plane to them.

Chelliah however, was not so unhappy. The Bogan conquest of the park relieved the pressure on him slightly as the Bogans now spent less time in their back yard, and, as a result, their forays into his own backyard in search of the footy also diminished. As for the Bogans laughing at Vivienne and her partner, what did they expect? Unnatural acts deserve ridicule, he said like a sage.

"But that is not nice Mr. Chelliah," Indu tried to stand up for Vivienne. "People like Vivienne and Lauren are also human and have feelings like us," she reminded him. Indu found it awkward to say 'lesbians' and always used the term 'people like Vivienne and Lauren' to refer to them.

Chelliah knew exactly what she meant as he too had the same difficulty talking about the issue. He thought about Indu's observation for a minute or two as if weighing a serious proposition and finally pronounced that it was true they were human, but he vehemently disagreed with the observation that they had the same feelings as him.

The Rabulas' response was predictable for people who were comfortably removed from the immediate sights and sounds of the Bogans. "Hmmmmmm," said Mr. Rabula to Kumar, who reported the incident to him as he was returning from the shops with the paper. He sucked the end of his spectacles as if lost in thought.

"So the Bogans brought down the children's plane?" He mumbled as if speaking to himself. "Not good. Not good at all." Then he went on to caution Kumar against escalating the tensions.

"One must not allow a small issue like this to be blown up into something big and uncontrollable." He said, taking the end of the spectacles out of his mouth and shaking it in front of his face to emphasise his point. "A plane has been downed, yes, but it must not lead to retaliation."

Then he placed the glasses back over his eyes and went into his garden.

But Vivienne did not give up that easily. She went to the police to complain that the Bogan Boys had taken her son's plane. But the trip was a waste of time. She said the policeman listened to her complaint and asked if she had actually asked for the plane to be returned. Ask? Vivienne had retorted indignantly. Who wants to ask Bogans? Everybody scared of Bogans. The police officer had told her that she should first ask for the plane and if they refused to return it, then the police can get involved. There was no point in sending a police car to ask someone to return a toy plane involved in a playground dispute among children.

Vivienne came home fuming and told Kumar that the police were useless. "He not even listening properly," she spat. "Sometimes yawning and looking at watch, like he wants to go somewhere. And a policewoman coming out and listening and looking and then showing Lauren and asking if that is my daughter!"

She did not heed the policeman's advice and speak to the Bogans. That was too much of a risk to be taken for the sake of a plane she said. "I buy Eric new plane and the boys can go somewhere else and fly."

Eric was happy with the decision. He was not keen on confronting the Bogans either. Besides, if his mum was getting him a new plane, there was always the chance of getting one better than the one he lost.

***

However, although he gave up on getting the plane back, Eric could not forget it. He wondered what the Bogans had actually done with it. As they saw nothing of it after that fateful day at the park, his curiosity grew. It was as if it simply disappeared into the Bogan house, never to reappear.

"What do you reckon they did with it?" Eric asked one day. Mahmoud shook his head. "Maybe they took it apart to see how it works."

"Naaah!" Eric said dismissively. "They wouldn't have a clue."

"Yes," said Mahmoud. "But they will try to find out. I am sure they had never seen anything like that before."

"I think they will just keep it on the mantelpiece or something," Rohan said. "You know, like a trophy."

"Maybe they gave it to their sister," Mahmoud said, winking at Rohan. "As a present, from you!"

Eric's eyes lit up with anger. He started to say something but refrained. Rohan patted him on the shoulder to calm him, frowning at Mahmoud to show that it was a joke in poor taste.

Then, a day or two later, Eric approached Mahmoud with a proposition.

"You said you had a clear view of the Bogan house from your bedroom, right?"

"Mhm," said Mahmoud, guardedly.

"I was wondering if I can keep an eye on the Bogans from your window now and then during the evening. I just wanna see if I can see any signs of the plane."

Mahmoud thought for a moment. He did not mind Eric using his bedroom occasionally, but he was not sure if his friend was interested in the plane or something else.

"I could...." He began, sounding hesitant. Eric decided to help him make up his mind.

"After all, it was you who got the Bogans fired up...."

Mahmoud's face flared up at the mention of the incident.

"Dude!" he said, tiredly. "We had this conversation before..."

Seeing that the guilt card was ineffective, Eric offered the carrot.

"I have a pair of binoculars. You too can watch the Bogans with them."

Mahmoud was still hesitant, but the idea of looking at the Bogans through the binoculars appealed to him, even though Eric's use of them made his proposition sound even more like an attempt to check out the Bogan Girl than anything else. He agreed, tentatively. Maybe he too could check out the Bogan Girl and see what Eric's hype was all about. Besides, despite refusing to take the blame for losing the plane, he did harbour a feeling of guilt at contributing to it.

When he learned that his friends were watching the Bogans from Mahmoud's window through binoculars, Rohan also joined them. The prospect of seeing the Bogan girl close up appealed to him too. Soon the three boys began to engage in a new activity from Mahmoud's bedroom: Bogan watching.

But if Eric had any intention of finding out what happened to his plane, he was disappointed. There was no sign of it. The Bogans offered the boys little scope for close scrutiny anyway, as when they were home, they spent most of their time in the backyard which was not visible from the window. The park too was out of sight. Whenever they came to the front yard, however, the boys studied every movement of the Bogans with the keenness of wild life enthusiasts observing the habits of rare fauna.

It soon became clear that Eric had little interest in the plane. He was happy for Rohan and Mahmoud to watch the Bogan Boys, but as soon as the girl came out, he wanted the binoculars. Then he kept using them until the girl disappeared inside. This frustrated his friends, who also wanted to get a good look at her.

One day, out of sheer exasperation, Mahmoud snatched the binoculars from Eric when the Bogan Girl was out. As Eric fumed, he gazed at the Bogan house where the girl and the two older boys were sitting outside, chatting. The two boys were smoking.

"That's the girl you said was cute?" Mahmoud asked, eyes still on the binoculars.

Eric nodded, slightly, still annoyed with Mahmoud for taking the binoculars away.

"Looks like a mouse," he said, handing Rohan the binoculars. "Oh, really, Eric!" He said, shaking his head.

Rohan too had a good look at the Bogan girl and seconded Mahmoud's opinion. She looked like a mouse.

"Maybe," Eric said, already regretting confiding his feelings in his friends. "But she is a cute mouse."

Both Mahmoud and Rohan stared at their friend in disbelief. Then they burst out laughing. Eric turned scarlet.

"I can't believe this!" Mahmoud said. "What do you see in her? She looks like a bloody plank. All straight and narrow!"

Stung by the comment Eric pursed his lips, the colour on his face now a deep red.

"Better a plank than a lump of lard," he hit back, with an obvious reference to Cynthia. Mahmoud started at the dig but did not retaliate. Realising the Eric had been rattled Rohan intervened.

"You are not serious, are you?"

Eric gazed at the darkness outside, thinking. He himself seemed to be wondering whether he was serious or not. Rohan decided to help him.

"Forget it, mate," he said. "You have a better chance of finding what happened to the plane than ever talking to her."

"You will be like them Romeo and Juliet," Mahmoud brought a literary example to support his opinion. "Killed by their parents. For love!"

"Romeo and Juliet killed themselves, you dumbass!" Eric sneered at his friend's ignorance. Mahmoud was unmoved. "Same difference," he said. "They died. If you are not careful, you will also get killed, by Father Bogan or the Bogan Boys."

Eric winced at the unpleasant thought. Rohan now moved to raise a more practical issue.

"What about your studies? Aren't you supposed to be focusing seriously on studies without thinking about anything else?"

Eric nodded. "Like I said, I am not thinking about going out with her, not right now anyway," he said. "Maybe after VCE, who knows?"

Mahmoud and Rohan exchanged glances.

"Forget it, man!" Rohan admonished again, this time more firmly. "VCE is not until next year. We'd all be lucky to survive the Bogans until then."

Eric knitted his brows. When he realised the Bogan Girl was cute, he did not expect this drama.

The door to Mahmoud's room opened, and Amina came in with a tray of fried chicken, chips and three bottles of coke. She said something to Mahmoud in Arabic.

"Mum says to eat before the chips get cold."

They began eating the food, looking over their shoulders at the Bogan house now and then to see if there was any movement there.

"This is halal chicken, right?" Eric asked.

"Yeah."

"How do you make 'em? Mum has eaten some once, and she is crazy about 'em."

Mahmoud shrugged his shoulders. "Dunno," he said. "Mum makes 'em. I'll ask her."

***

The Bogan watching came to an end in dramatic fashion. Rohan first dropped out as he has had enough of Bogan watching and because he felt he had also seen enough of the Bogan girl. Mahmoud too felt the same and preferred to join Rohan playing computer games. Seeing Eric looking crestfallen at being abandoned, Mahmoud offered him a deal. He could still watch the Bogan girl, he said, but not for too long and without letting his father find out. "I am doing this for you," Mahmoud said, "but if my dad finds out," he warned, "you and I both will be in trouble." Eric's desire to see the Bogan girl was far greater than his perception of the threat from Ahmed. He nodded to show he understood.

Eric engaged in solitary Bogan-watching for a couple of nights. Amina, not realising what he was really up to, and believing that he was only interested in finding out what happened to the plane, was happy to let him do it, bringing him drinks and snacks. Then, on the third night, things suddenly went awry. Eric was so engrossed in his activity that he did not even hear Ahmed coming up the stairs or see him parking the van in the street and entering the house. Then there was a knock on the door and thinking it was Amina bringing him some refreshments, Eric said, "come in" absently. Then the door opened, and he heard Ahmed's deep bass voice asking something in Arabic. Panicking, he quickly stood up, closing the curtains but overturning the chair in the process just when Ahmed turned the light on.

Seeing Eric standing against the wall near the window like a rabbit caught in a torchlight, Ahmed froze.

"What the....." he started. "What you do here?"

Eric saw the little head of Hala peeping from around Ahmed's ample torso.

"Watching Bogans," she offered cheekily and ran away tittering.

"Watching Bogans?" Ahmed repeated, as a question. "What for?"

He reached the window in three steps, and parting the curtains slightly, looked out. He saw the Bogan girl sitting outside their house and then looking down, saw the binoculars in Eric's hand.

"I see," he said, knowingly. "Turn the light off!" he ordered Hala, who had reappeared. Then, as the room sank in darkness, he grabbed the binoculars and placed them to his eyes.

"At least you like girls," he muttered as he did so, an obvious dig at Vivienne. But as he watched, his face changed rapidly in to a grimace.

"She looking like Mickey Mouse!"

Eric had no interest in Ahmed's views of the Bogan girl. He was already on the way out, making use of Ahmed's preoccupation with the binoculars to sneak his way around him to the door. Then he ran out and dashed down the stairs, passing a bewildered Amina who was coming up the stairs with a bowl of chips for him. He heard Hala giggling from somewhere and Ahmed firing a parting shot from the room.

"You just like your mother!" He bellowed. "Weirdo!"

Then Ahmed came down the stairs, taking the bowl of chips from his wife and playfully swatting her on the shoulder. "And my wife is spoiling them," he said as he made his way to the kitchen for his dinner.

Eric did not stop until he reached Rohan's house, where he found the boys playing video games. They were eating their own bowl of chips, with green chilli!

Rohan and Mahmoud listened to Eric's brush with Ahmed and burst out laughing. Mahmoud was worried about what Ahmed might say to him, though. "I hope he'll forget," he wished.

"I don't think I will watch Bogans from your room again," Eric said as if he had a choice. "Too much trouble to go through for a girl I may never be able to speak to." His friends nodded to show they approved.

Eric took a handful of chips and began eating them. "Hey, this is awesome!" He said. "I could eat this all day!"

Eric's Bogan watching ended with that. Mahmoud returned the binoculars with a message from his father: if he caught Eric watching the Bogan Girl from his house again, he would attach the binoculars to his eyes with super glue. Eric was so intimidated by the threat that he asked Mahmoud to keep it. Mahmoud refused, assuring his friend that Ahmed's bark was worse than his bite, but he also warned Eric to play it safe, just in case Ahmed decided to bite.

Thereafter the three boys began to meet at Rohan's place very regularly to play on the computer, to the great dismay of Kumar and Indu who found the noise level and the general clutter increasing beyond their comfort levels. They didn't mind having the boys around, and Indu certainly didn't mind feeding them, but not as regularly as they had to, especially when both Mahmoud and Eric had got hooked on her wedges with green chillies.

"Don't Eric and Mahmoud have other things to do than playing on your computer? Come to think of it, don't *you* have other things to do?" Kumar asked one day when Mahmoud and Eric had left.

"I have," Rohan said. "But I prefer to play on the computer."

"Then why don't you at least go and play at Mahmoud's house or Eric's house for a change? At least now and then."

"I could," Rohan said. "But their parents don't like it when we make a lot of noise."

Kumar sighed. They have spoilt this child, he realised. Chelliah was right. They should have thrashed him when he was young. Then they were living in Sri Lanka, and the law would have been on their side. Now they couldn't. This was Australia, and the boy was too big to be thrashed. It was their sheer love for the boy that had prevented them from thrashing him then, and it was their sheer love for him that allowed them to put up with his nonsense now. But at least he was not committing any serious misdemeanours that he knew about. Didn't smoke, no drugs, not much of a party goer. Not much of a goer of anywhere to be frank. He and Indu will have to settle for that. That would be so much better than some other alternatives he could think of. Besides, if the boy's threat to become an electrician worked out, then he might actually come good himself.

Relatives will always say this and that, Kumar concluded, but as long as those relatives continued to live in Sri Lanka and didn't come to live in Australia, it didn't matter.

ELEVEN

After the incident with the plane and the Bogan conquest of the park, tensions showed little evidence of abating. They seemed, if anything, to be rising.

Interestingly, now the Bogans appeared to be focused on Mahmoud as their main adversary. Whenever Mahmoud was around, they stood in their garden or at the entrance to the park staring at him, watching him, menacingly, as if waiting for an opportunity to strike. This was not surprising. It was Mahmoud who flew the plane so close to the Little Bogan doing the dive bomber routine. And it was probably Mahmoud, with his height and stouter frame, who must have appeared as the leader of Park Court boys. It was as if the Bogan Boys had marked him as the person to be brought down a peg or two.

Poor Mahmoud was also in Vivienne's sights. A few days after the incident with the plane, Eric mentioned to Vivienne in passing that it was actually Mahmoud who had been flying the plane when it was struck by BB1. Vivienne, predictably, was furious.

"That boy losing my Eric's plane," she said to Kumar. "He take remote from Eric. Then he provoke Bogan and Bogan kick ball at plane.

He trouble maker," she hissed. "That Ma-mood. Big trouble maker. And rude also, like father."

Things deteriorated for Mahmoud - and Ahmed - very quickly. Not long after the downing of the plane, Ahmed's cousin Abasi visited them from Sydney. It was not a visit that thrilled Ahmed since Abasi was one of those people he had moved to Melbourne to avoid. But as it was difficult to move any further to avoid them after they came to Melbourne, and family being family, Ahmed reluctantly agreed to host Abasi and his family, which included four children. The oldest of these, a boy named Hamid, was a year older than Mahmoud and like his father Abasi, an overbearing and obnoxious person. And just as his father resented Abasi's company, Mahmoud found little pleasure in having Hamid around.

Mahmoud's discomfort neared panic proportions when Hamid, in his characteristically haughty fashion, came out one morning wearing a Sydney Swans guernsey and announced that he was going to the park to kick the footy around, implying that Mahmoud was to follow. Hamid's declaration placed Mahmoud in a quandary. If he did not follow his cousin, he would seem rude and inhospitable; telling him not to go because there were Bogans nearby was awkward. And going to the park when the Bogans were around could be dangerous. So in order to bolster his confidence and sense of security without appearing to be rude and weak, he appealed to his neighbourhood friends, Eric and Rohan.

"Would you like to kick the footy around with me and my cousin Hamid?" He asked Eric on the phone, the plaintive tone in his voice obvious. But unfortunately for Mahmoud, Eric had little enthusiasm for a return to the park, and unlike Mahmoud, he had no difficulty in turning down the invitation.

"You fuckin' crazy?" he asked. "The Bogans will kill ya!" Taken aback by the intensity of Eric's response, Mahmoud looked at Hamid, hoping to see any signs of his cousin changing his mind but Hamid was waiting impatiently, tossing the ball from one hand to the other. Sighing, Mahmoud called Rohan.

"Go to the park?" Rohan asked, shocked.

"Yes," Mahmoud said in a small voice.

"I can think of less painful ways to commit suicide," Rohan said. "And you'd be staying away from that park too if you know what is good for you!"

Mahmoud felt lost and abandoned. His friends' response only made him feel even more anxious, but unlike his friends, he had no choice. His bossy cousin was pacing about restlessly, waiting for him to accompany him to the park. He also seemed to be increasingly curious about Mahmoud's phone calls and the look of worry that clouded his face progressively after each call. He had to go before Hamid became too suspicious. The unavailability of his friends was not likely to be a good excuse. So he trudged behind Hamid, crestfallen, hoping that the Bogans would not notice their presence or leave them alone if they did.

That, alas, was wishful thinking. No sooner had they started kicking the footy around, than the Bogans walked in, this time only BB1 and BB2. Both were dressed in their Collingwood guernseys and had brought their footy with them too. As Mahmoud watched with trepidation, they began kicking the footy around, all the while casting menacing glances at them, particularly Mahmoud. Even Hamid, not the brightest spark around, quickly realised that the Bogans were a little bit more aggressive than he would have wished and he said so to Mahmoud in Arabic. Mahmoud, happy to see his cousin had had a glimmer of the situation, was only too willing to encourage him to leave, but Hamid being also an egotistic character, refused, saying loudly - in English - that this park was theirs as much as it was anybody else's. He continued to kick the ball towards a tense and nervous Mahmoud who dropped it more often than he held on to it.

Very soon, the Bogans raised the ante. They started kicking their footy towards Mahmoud and Hamid as if to intimidate them. A few verbal taunts were also heard, especially about the poor footy skills of Swans and Hawks supporters. The ball passed dangerously close to them a few times and once Mahmoud had to actually duck in order to avoid being hit on the head. Even Hamid began to get anxious; his aim with the ball became increasingly erratic. Sensing that things were about to get out of hand, Mahmoud pleaded with his cousin in Arabic. Let's get out of here, he said, his voice trembling with anxiety.

Hamid finally seemed inclined to yield, but before he could make a move, the Bogans struck. BB2 kicked the ball high in the air towards Hamid and as Hamid watched as if transfixed by the sight of the ball descending towards him, BB1 ran up and took a mark, kneeing Hamid in the back in the process. Hamid, a slightly built lad in comparison to either of the BBs, fell to the ground and in the shock and pain of the collision lost all pretensions to toughness. He began to cry, and Mahmoud had to escort him from the ground. As they walked out, they heard the Bogan Boys laughing and BB1 saying something about weak Muzzies who couldn't take a knee in the back.

When Ahmed heard what had happened, he and Hamid's father went to the park to confront the Bogan Boys, but by then they were gone. Then they heard catcalls, and when they looked, they saw all the Bogans sitting outside their house jeering at them. Father Bogan was even giving them the bird, and when Abasi made as if to charge them the Father Bogan mooned him to the great merriment of the rest of the Bogan clan. Ahmed, Hamid, and Mahmoud had to restrain Abasi and steer him towards Ahmed's home but not before Abasi vowed - fortunately in Arabic - to bring his two brothers and their sons the next time from Sydney so that they can teach the Bogans a lesson.

Everybody agreed that this was a serious escalation.

"Maybe the Bogans want to drive us all out of this court," Mr. Rabula said when he heard about it. But he also did not approve of Hamid's father's tactics.

"We do not do things like that in this country, man," he said. "We stand up to these people, yes. We fight back, yes. But not with violence."

"How are you gonna do that?" Rohan asked.

Mr. Rabula said passive resistance was the way. Civil disobedience.

"How is civil disobedience gonna work here?" Rohan wanted to know.

"Oh, you simply refuse to give in." Mr. Rabula said as if that was the simplest thing to figure out. "Keep going to the park. Keep playing. Show them you are not scared."

"That is fine for you to say," Rohan said. "You don't play in the park."

Mr. Rabula looked at the boy and then at Kumar. "When your child was younger, you should have thrashed him soundly," he said. "If you did, he would not be this impudent."

Kumar simply grinned. He was now quite accustomed to Rohan's impudence and public reactions to it. Besides, he also felt that his son had a point. The Rabulas were pontificating about something that hardly bothered them.

Mr. Chelliah too was all for non-violence. Fighting fire with fire only creates a bigger inferno, he said. He lost no time in trudging out his well-worn philosophy. You must learn to bend with the wind, he said, perhaps for the huindreth time since the arrival of the Bogans. Standing against the wind can break you. I hope you don't mean we should turn the other cheek? Eric asked, almost toungue in cheek, and Chelliah said that was certainly not an option. The Bogans will simply keep slapping until you have no cheeks left. But you must bend with the wind, he reiterated. Standing against the wind can break you.

Kumar sighed. The Bogan wind was certainly picking up and he hoped it would not acquire the force of a gale. There was no question of bending with a wind like that; it would simply sweep them away.

As for Ahmed, he had mixed feelings about the whole incident. He did not mind Hamid getting a knee in the back at all, not so much because he had anything against the boy but because he was convinced that the son's painful experience would keep the father away from Melbourne for the foreseeable future. Ahmed knew Abasi well and had no doubt that his threat to return with his two brothers was only pure bravado.

"He only pretending to charge Bogan because he knows that I am gonna hold him," he later confided in Kumar. "Maybe I shudda let him go, and get smashed by Bogan," he said rather ruefully.

But at the same time, the new aggressive attitude of the Bogans also unsettled him as, according to Mahmoud, it was directed at him as much as Hamid. That wasn't a good omen.

TWELVE

No one was more shaken by the confrontation with the Bogans than Mahmoud. He was not overly concerned about Hamid getting pushed around, but he knew very well that it might well have been he who would have got the knee in the back - or worse. It made him feel jittery; even walking up the street now became a challenge for fear of the Bogans lurking around. His friends agreed. "That was just the two Bogan Boys," Eric reflected. "Imagine what the father is capable of?"

"I don't want to get into any fights with them," Rohan declared categorically. "I can't even run fast."

Eric agreed. He could run fast, he said, but the problem was whether he could run fast enough. The Father Bogan may not be able to do much running due to his limp, but the two older Bogan Boys seemed to be pretty good runners. It wouldn't take long for them to catch him, he was certain. Mahmoud was of a similar opinion. He felt that all of them together would not be enough to handle the Bogan Boys, especially if the Father Bogan also decided to join his sons, which was very likely. He also revealed, for the first time, that he had been speaking to his Internet chat buddies about the issue.

"You are crazy!" Eric said. But he was also curious.

"What did they say?"

"Oh, some stupid thing about Muslims being pushed around all the time because they are Muslims, and how we should stand up to them to defend our faith and culture." This time, Mahmoud said, he didn't even find them funny, only annoying as he had talked to them in search of a practical solution to their problem and received nonsense in reply.

"You *are* crazy!" Eric repeated. Rohan agreed.

"We need to think of something that works," Eric observed. Rohan said it would be good if it worked without causing them any pain.

That was when Mahmoud made his great revelation. He had a plan to put the Bogans back in their box, and maybe even take the park back, he said. A plan that would not cause them any harm. In fact, they didn't even have to be part of it.

"What do you mean?" Eric asked, intrigued. Rohan's eyebrows arched.

"I mean, we don't do anything. We get someone else to do our job for us."

Rohan and Eric stared at Mahmoud as if to see if they could detect any signs of Mahmoud joking. But the boy seemed to be in deadly earnest.

"Who do you have in mind?" Rohan asked.

Mahmoud smiled and waited for a couple of seconds before he revealed the name.

"Jimmy," he said, grinning cheekily.

At the mention of the name Rohan's face lit up, his lips curling into a cautius smile.

"Who the hell is Jimmy?" Eric asked.

Jimmy was one of the African boys in Rohan's and Mahmoud's school and the only African boy in their class. He was tall, quite athletic and like most Africans, very dark. Although only seventeen, he had the face of a man, a man who was perpetually embattled. He also had the whitest set of teeth which, when set against the lines of worry on his face, gave him the impression of a boy who, despite all his troubles, had managed to keep his teeth dazzlingly clean. His real name was Jimiyu, but the last two letters quickly dropped out of his name when other kids at school began to say it. Jimmy made a feeble attempt to protest, saying that his name had a meaning which was "born in the dry season." But his school mates cared more about convenience than meaning. It was a cute name, they said. Really cute, but hard to pronounce. So, whether born in the dry season or wet season, Jimiyu became Jimmy.

An equally difficult task was to make kids understand where Jimmy came from. Even though he was originally from Uganda, everybody considered him to be Sudanese. As far as many kids were concerned, all Africans were from the Sudan; it was as if they had this image of a huge Sudanese continent to the west of India. This exasperated their English teacher Miss Hughes so much that one day, suspending the teaching of English for one period, she did a geography lesson. It was a fiasco. She brought a huge map of Africa and showed the students where the Sudan was and where Uganda was. She also showed where other African countries were, such as South Africa and Nigeria. She allowed the students to study the map for fifteen minutes and then, folding it, distributed blank maps of Africa with only the borders of the countries marked. Mark Sudan and Uganda on the map, she asked the kids. Not one of them got it right. Half the class had written Sudan where Uganda was and the rest, although they had written Sudan in the right place, had written Uganda somewhere else. Even Cynthia got it wrong, writing Uganda on the Democratic Republic of Congo. Embarrassed, she blamed it all on White colonialists who had made a mess of Africa's natural borders. Naushad's Uganda appeared in the Indian Ocean. After that, Miss Hughes gave up teaching them geography. Jimmy remained Sudanese.

Although Jimmy had a temper, he preferred to vent it on the footy field than in ordinary life, except on one occasion when he took exception to a boy asking which gang he belonged to. Jimmy punched him, just once, but hard enough for the boy to get a black eye. The Ugandan got suspended, but the incident cemented Jimmy's reputation as an African gang member. Interestingly, he seemed to grow to like it, as it raised his stature at school. Everybody preferred to cut him a wide berth and comments about Sudanese gangs were now made only behind the back of the temperamental African.

But what made Mahmoud favourable to enlisting Jimmy's help was the fact that the African was also good friends with him. Mahmoud functioned as an unofficial math tutor to Jimmy. Mahmoud was moderately good at mathematics, but Jimmy's mathematics was close to pathetic. Strangely, only Mahmoud seemed to know how to explain math to Jimmy, so the two became good buddies at school.

Rohan, however, was somewhat sceptical about Mahmoud's idea.

"Jimmy is good," he said, "the kind of guy the Bogans would be intimidated by. But what are we going to get him to do? We can't certainly ask him to beat them up? "

"No," said Mahmoud. "We don't get him to beat them up but only to intimidate them. You don't have to beat someone up to intimidate them," he said with a smirk. "Remember what Cynthia did to Silvagni?"

Eric was happy with the idea. He wouldn't mind if the Bogans were beaten up if it could be done without implicating them. But he too agreed that intimidation didn't necessarily mean beating up someone. Just scaring would do. He had heard about what Cynthia had done to Silvagni. He was very happy for someone to shake up the Bogans like that.

"Why not get Cynthia then?" Rohan asked, half tongue-in-cheek.

"The Bogans will kill her," Mahmoud said, concerned for his heartthrob. "Besides," he said, adding a more prosaic element to his reasoning. "We can't get a woman to do a man's job."

"Ok," Rohan said, still undecided and unconvinced. "But how is he gonna scare them?"

Mahmoud and Eric thought for a few moments. "Dunno," Mahmoud said at length. "But I am sure it can be done."

Rohan grinned, raising his eyebrows slightly. He was still not convinced.

"Why don't we ask this Jimmy person?" Eric suggested. "Tell him about our situation and let him decide."

Mahmoud and Rohan agreed: tell Jimmy their problem and let him decide how best he can help them. It relieved them from the responsibility of making the decision.

They met Jimmy at the local MacDonald's. Mahmoud knew Jimmy was fond of burgers and to get him in a mood favourable to their request they asked him to choose any meal he liked. Jimmy seemed a bit taken aback by the generosity - and the responsibility - but quickly warmed to the task to choose a quarter-pounder. a large serve of chips, and a large coke. Mahmoud made the order and looked at his friends only to realise that they were waiting for him to pay. Shaking his head, Mahmoud pulled out his wallet and paid, making his own order in the process. "You guys order your own shit," he hissed to his friends as he stepped aside, adding in a lower tone that he expected them to share the cost of Jimmy's meal.

They all sat around a corner table. For the first two or three minutes, Jimmy was all concentration, focused on demolishing his meal. He bit off large pieces of bun, meat, and salad and chewed them ravenously, eyes riveted on the rapidly diminishing quarter-pounder. In between bites, he absently pulled out fingers full of fries and stuffed his mouth with them, consuming the drink in the same casual manner. The three boys from Park Court watched with undisguised fascination, wondering how Jimmy managed to maintain such a wiry physique while having so ferocious an appetite for junk food.

After finishing about half the burger, Jimmy leaned back in the chair, apparently to take a rest from his attack on the meal. As he took a deep breath and cast his eyes around, he suddenly seemed to become aware of his eager audience. He grinned embarrassedly and then leaned forward in the seat.

"Sorry man," he said. "My bad. I could easily eat ten of these, and when I do, I forget everything. I am so hungry." He looked at the remainder of the burger lovingly and then pulled out a few chips which he stuffed into his mouth. The boys watched, their fascination now gradually giving way to the apprehension that Jimmy might want to eat more burgers to assuage his rampant hunger before he was ready for them.

"You were saying you had a problem with some neighbours, huh?" He turned to Mahmoud who nodded in assent.

"Tell me about 'em."

Mahmoud told him about the Bogans. He told Jimmy how the Bogans had come into their neighbourhood and behaved in a threatening manner, making everybody afraid. He told him about the plane and added some spice of his own by saying that the Bogans had kicked the ball at the plane without any provocation and later even threatened to break Mahmoud in half if he ever came to the park again. He had attacked his cousin without any provocation and threatened to hurt all of them if they went anywhere near the park.

"We want our park back!" Mahmoud said by way of concluding remarks. His two friends nodded vigorously in assent.

Jimmy smiled like a godfather hearing the woes of his family. He took a long drink from his coke and seemed to be weighing his options.

"Too easy," he said at length, and then let out a loud burp. "Bogans are no big drama for me. I have dealt with them in our hood. They are shit scared of Africans. I will only have to take a nice stroll in the park a couple of times for them to see and I swear they will stay inside for two weeks!" He chuckled as he finished off the chips.

The Park Court boys were overjoyed. "That's fuckin' awesome!" Eric cried. "Thank you!"

Even Rohan grinned.

"No sweat bro, you know I will do anything for you. You are my teacher, my saviour," Jimmy flashed his brilliant smile and reached out to squeeze Mahmoud's hand. Mahmoud blushed; it was not certain if it was due to the obvious reference to his mathematical skills or Jimmy squeezing his hand.

"If you do this and get us our park back," Mahmoud said, overcome by gratitude. "We will treat you to the best Burger meal ever!'

Both Eric and Rohan nodded but quickly checked themselves as they remembered the way Jimmy had demolished the quarter-pounder. Mahmoud too seemed to have regretted his offer no sooner than he had made it.

Jimmy seemed delighted. "Thanks, man!" he said. "You guys are so cool." Then, ominously, he looked at the list of meals above the counter.

"Tell you what," he began, "I will have a cheeseburger now if ya don't mind, and we can negotiate the big meal later."

Mahmoud, now totally regretting speaking too soon, looked at his two friends. Rohan and Eric looked at each other.

"Just a cheeseburger. No drink," Jimmy helped them with decision-making.

Sighing deeply Eric went to the counter and ordered a cheeseburger.

While munching on the cheeseburger, Jimmy laid down some conditions for his services. He needed to see the Bogans first. He had to know who he was dealing with. He also needed to see the neighbourhood to see what it was like, especially the park. "I am a professional," he reminded them, brushing a bit of cheese from his mouth. "I need to know everything about the job."

"Fair enough," Mahmoud said. "You can come and have a look one day in the evening, when the Bogans are there."

"Nah," said Jimmy. "Won't work. I want to see them without them seeing me. Like spying on 'em, you know?"

The boys looked at each other. How were they going to do that? Suddenly Eric perked up.

"Oh, Mahmoud's bedroom has a great view of the Bogan House" he said. "We used to spy on them from there."

Mahmoud kicked Eric under the table, but it was too late. Jimmy had decided to accept the deal.

The following Saturday evening, Jimmy came to Mahmoud's house. It was with the greatest reluctance that Mahmoud had agreed to let Jimmy spy from his bedroom window.

"I don't want him in my house," he had declared while discussing the issue at the MacDonald's.' For greater secrecy, they had decided to meet there to talk about Jimmy's mission.

"Why?" Rohan asked, somewhat teasingly. "You don't like Black people?"

"Don't be silly!" Mahmoud said. "If I didn't like Black people, why should I teach Jimmy math? And you are kind of Black too, and you are at my house every so often."

"Then what's the problem?"

"It's Mum and Dad," Mahmoud said.

"Why? Don't *they* like Black people?" This time it was a serious question from Rohan.

Mahmoud seemed unsure about that. "Not really, But you know, they watch the news..."

"Oh, you think they will think he might be with a gang?" Eric asked.

Mahmoud nodded.

"Don't be fuckin' crazy!" Eric chided. "He is just one guy. Not a gang."

"That makes little difference to my parents," Mahmoud assured. And he reiterated that they watch the news.

"Then what do we do? We have to show him the Bogans, and your bedroom is the best place." Eric seemed worried.

Mahmoud thought for a while. "Mum takes Hala for math help on Saturday evenings," he said. "We can ask Jimmy to come then. He can come when it's dark so that nobody else sees an African sneaking into our house."

His friends agreed. Saturday evening it was to be.

"Why does Hala have to go for math help?" Eric asked as they were leaving. "Aren't you the math genius?"

Mahmoud frowned. "She needs proper help," he said.

Jimmy agreed to the plan, and the following Saturday when Amina was away with Hala, he came in. Mahmoud had turned off all the lights to make it even darker outside, and having watched Jimmy's shadowy figure approaching Mahmoud had been ready near the door to whisk him in.

"I like this," Jimmy said as he stumbled up the dark stairs, nearly slipping twice. "Like a fuckin' movie."

Upstairs, they sat at Mahmoud's bedroom window with the binoculars. As usual, the Bogan Boys were out, BB1 and BB2 sitting on the front steps, smoking. BB1 was wearing his Collingwood guernsey. They were having a nice chat, and occasionally their raucous laughter could be faintly heard.

Jimmy surveyed the scene for a few seconds. "They are Bogans alright," he said. But ominously, his face seemed to change as he watched them.

"That all?" He asked without taking his eyes off the binoculars.

"Oh, no!" Eric said. "These are just the two older boys. There is the father and another younger boy.”

Jimmy seemed to be thinking hard. “Father is a big guy?”

“Yeah,” Rohan said. “Tall and strong. And tattoos down both arms.”

“Jimmy grimaced. “And the other boy. How big is he?”

“Not so big,” Mahmoud said. “But very cheeky and rude.”

“Yeah, Bogans are like that,” Jimmy said. “And you said there is a girl too.”

“Yeah, the girl is rude too, and bigger than the small boy,” Mahmoud said. Eric frowned at the reference to the girl but said nothing.

“But she is cute,” Rohan added quickly, more tongue in cheek to tease Eric than for Jimmy’s information. Eric blushed, clearly resenting the sudden diversion in the discussion.

“And the mother is big too and very aggressive,” he quickly added, keeping things on track.

Jimmy was looking increasingly less confident now than he was when he arrived.

“You gonna do this, right?” Eric asked, seeing his changed demeanour.

“Sure,” Jimmy said, but without a great deal of conviction. “But I need to think about this, you know, there are more Bogans than I expected and they are quite big.” He looked at the Bogans again. “Let me get back to you in a couple of days. I will do it, but I gotta think of a good strategy, you know?”

The boys agreed. Jimmy was taken aback by the sight of the Bogans, they realised. But they hoped he would not back down.

His surveillance finished, Jimmy got up to leave. He began to descend the stairs in darkness as Mahmoud was still reluctant to turn the lights on. Jimmy was fine with that. "Don't sweat man," he said. 'This is way too cool."

But it was not cool. Jimmy, who was the first one descending, kept missing the steps and swearing loudly each time he missed a step. "Easy, easy man" Mahmoud whispered but Jimmy, now quite exasperated by the unexpected level of difficulty in descending the stairs, seemed determined to reach the level ground as quickly as possible. "Climbing was not this fuckin' hard," he even muttered. And the more he tried, the more he missed.

When he sensed that he was very close to the floor, Jimmy made a dash for it, literally, jumping from the step he was on to the floor below to avoid negotiating the steps in between. Later he said that he could even see the floor in a shadowy form. But whether he saw it or not, he landed first on the last step and that too, at an awkward angle. He made a desperate attempt to grab the balustrade but missed it completely. His knees buckled and Jimmy collapsed in a heap on the floor, a loud expletive escaping his mouth.

At that very moment, the front door opened. Later, Mahmoud, who was coming down close behind Jimmy, said that he could hear the lock turning from outside and he was trying to grab Jimmy by his sweater. But that was not to be, and Jimmy was already on the floor when the door opened. In the open doorway, bathed in the light of the streetlamp were Amina and Hala. Hala's class had finished early, and Amina had brought her home.

They did not bargain for what awaited them. Jimmy, totally oblivious to the return of the two females, hit the ground with a thud, but being Jimmy, he did not allow the mishap to dampen his spirits. He rolled as he hit the ground, and rolling several times, like a movie stuntman, he athletically sprang to his feet near the doorway, right in front of Amina and Hala. Seeing the two females, he was taken aback but recovered quickly to smile, flashing his brilliant white teeth.

It was not clear who screamed first, Amina, or Hala. But it was only Amina who fainted, collapsing in a heap on Hala who tried hard to support her mother, without collapsing herself. Jimmy, realising what had happened, quickly came out of his stunt-man mode to lend a hand, his strong arms taking over from Hala's little ones. As the rest of the boys quickly gathered around Amina who was now lying on the floor, Hala tried to turn the light on.

"Close the door first!" Mahmoud ordered. Hala obeyed. Soon, the hall was bathed in bright light, and they could see Amina lying motionless, as if dead. And Hala could see Jimmy more clearly too, as he was bending over Amina, trying to figure out if he had killed her or simply paralysed her with fright.

"Who is this?" Hala asked Mahmoud.

"Jimmy," Mahmoud said as if making the most casual introduction. "Jimmy, from school."

"He is here for math help," Eric added quickly.

Jimmy seemed less interested in introductions than in attending to his victim. He bent down and quickly began administering CPR to the prone Amina.

"What is he doing?" Hala asked.

"I think he is trying to revive Mum," Mahmoud said, not quite sure if that was what Jimmy as doing.

"Yes, I am," Jimmy confirmed his actions.

"I hope he knows what he is doing," Hala said, and Jimmy looked up at her long enough to sneer.

"Yes, I do. I have learnt this at our footy club."

True to Jimmy's words, Amina soon began to show signs of revival, coughing and moaning. Jimmy got up and looked at her like a doctor surveying a patient.

"All good!" He said. "Give her some water later on." He turned to the boys. "I gotta run," he said. Then, without waiting for any farewells, he opened the door, looked around the darkness outside, and ran.

Rohan and Eric thought they should stick to the story about Jimmy coming for math help, but Mahmoud disagreed. She would get very upset, he said. "And if Dad finds out Jimmy was in the house, he will go crazy, and my mum always tells Dad what happens, and Dad always tells her."

"Like 50/50" Eric dug. Mahmoud frowned.

They agreed to tell Amina that she had actually seen one of the boys in the dark and fainted out of fright. They made Hala also promise not to tell anything about Jimmy to Amina or Ahmed. The girl promised, but with an ominous look of mischief on her face. Amina seemed to go with the explanation even though she had her doubts. "But why keep the lights off?" She asked, and Mahmoud said they were watching the Bogans and they didn't want them to see. But you don't turn *all* the lights off when you watch the Bogans? Amina asked, and Mahmoud rolled his eyes.

"Geez, Ma! Relax! We forgot!"

Amina was happy with the explanation. Ahmed, when he heard the story, was livid. He was annoyed that the boys were still watching the Bogans from his house, as Mahmoud's story suggested, but he was furious that Amina had fainted due to their antics. He fumed for a few minutes and added another one to the list of things Mahmoud should avoid if he wished to remain alive: hurting Amina. Then he laughed good-naturedly.

"One day when I am your age, I bring girl into house, and I am trying to sneak her out of the house. My mother come home from shopping and she getting a fright. But she never faint." He laughed again.

"So you were fooling around a bit at our age?" Mahmoud, now relaxed, asked. Ahmed got a twinkle in his eye. "Oh yes," he said. "A lot!" Then, seeing a smirk appear in Mahmoud's face, he quickly put his foot down. "And every one of them was Lebanese! And none of them feminist lesbians!"

THIRTEEN

The following day Jimmy approached Rohan and Eric and, to their great relief, reaffirmed his commitment to their cause. He allayed any fears the boys may have had of him reneging on his earlier commitment. On the contrary, he seemed eager.

There was, however, a caveat.

He will do it, Jimmy said. But he couldn't do it alone. "Them Bogans are big," he said. "Bigger than I expected, and there are a few of them." He needed help.

"*We* can't help you!" Rohan said. "We want *you* to help us, not the other way round."

Jimmy smiled and said he understood the conditions of his assignment perfectly. He will find the help, he said. He knew two or three big African lads who were willing to come. But there was one small issue. His friends will have to be paid.

"I am doing this for you guys, out of friendship," Jimmy assured. "You, Mamood, are my good mate, my math genius. But my mates are not your mates, and they are pretty short on money. Besides, two of these guys are also die-hard Pies supporters, and when I told them that the

Bogan boy was wearing a Collingwood guernsey, they were a bit reluctant. So they will need some reward to encourage them."

"How much?" Rohan asked, worried that the little money he had saved might be drained into this dubious project.

Jimmy thought for a few moments. "How much can you guys offer?" He asked, his eyes narrowed.

The boys looked at each other. "We have to talk this over," Mahmoud said. Rohan and Eric too looked worried at Jimmy's proposition. "We need to see how much we can afford."

"Take ya time," Jimmy said, trying to appear nonchalant. "It's ya problem."

The boys went outside and conferred. It was agreed unanimously to offer $ 50, to be shared equally between the three. They returned and reported to Jimmy

"Fifty is all we can offer," Mahmoud said. Jimmy thought for a few seconds.

"Let me check with my guys," he said, getting up. He walked out and was seen making a call with his mobile. He returned presently, not looking very happy.

"Not enough," he said. "My mates say they wipe their asses with fifty."

Mahmoud scrunched his face at the insult. He was furious that Jimmy showed such scant respect for their offer. "Fifty is all we can offer," he said, trying to sound firm. Eric and Rohan also looked at Jimmy in dismay.

But Jimmy was unrelenting.

"I know, man," He said, trying to sound sympathetic. "If it was me alone, I would have done it free of charge. I know how much you have helped me," he said, looking at Mahmoud. "But it's my mates. As I said, my mates are not your mates."

He sighed deeply and started as if getting ready to leave. It seemed he had given up on them.

"Wait!" Mahmoud pleaded. He gestured to his friends to follow him outside.

"We gotta keep him," Mahmoud said. 'We all want this done, don't we?"

Rohan looked undecided. "How much more we gonna pay?" He asked. "I don't have so much money." Eric was happy to continue with Jimmy. But he was also concerned about the rising expense.

"He should be doing this for free," he said. "Considering you are helping him with math and shit."

"I know," Mahmoud said, crestfallen. "But as he says, it's not his decision."

Reluctantly, they decided to double the price and stick to it.

Jimmy seemed happy. "I am sure my mates will be happy," he said. He didn't even call them this time which made the boys feel that it was his idea all along.

"Next week, I will be there," Jimmy promised, standing up and shaking hands to seal the deal.

"I will come with the boys and we will go to the park and wait for the Bogans."

"What are you gonna do?"

"Wait and see," Jimmy winked.

"I hope he is not gonna cause a lot of trouble," Eric said on the way home. "If my mums get to know I am involved in this, they will kill me."

"My parents won't kill me," Rohan said with confidence. "But they will not be happy, and I will feel bad if they are not happy."

"How do you think I feel?" Mahmoud asked. "My dad will definitely kill me."

But they all felt that it was now too late to pull out of the deal.

Then Mahmoud made a revelation. He told his friends that, unlike them, he was already suffering due to Jimmy's involvement.

"How so?" Eric wanted to know.

"It's Hala," Mahmoud said. "She is threatening to tell Mum and Dad what happened that evening if I don't pay her."

Rohan and Eric grinned. "The little shit!" said Eric. "How cheeky!"

"I know, huh?" Mahmoud said. "Like, this morning, as we were getting ready to go to school. She said there were some really nice doughnuts in the school canteen and she would like to have one. I said she could buy one with her own money and she says she needs that for her lunch and besides, unlike me, she is not earning. I said then she needs to get a job, And she asks very sweetly, 'now what was the name of that African boy?'"

Rohan and Eric laughed. Mahmoud frowned.

"So you paid up?"

Mahmoud nodded.

"I had to." He said. "If Dad finds out he will kill me!"

***

As promised, Jimmy turned up with his boys on Thursday. The day was chosen because, that day, Amina was away helping Ahmed, and Hala was going to a friend's place to be picked up by Amina and Ahmed on their way back from work. They were not expected till around nine in the night. That, they all thought, gave Jimmy and his mates more than enough time to do their job and disappear.

There was much haggling to be done before that though. Jimmy wanted half the money paid before the action and half after. The boys were reluctant.

"We don't even know what you gonna do?" Eric said. "It is unfair for us to pay upfront without knowing."

Jimmy scowled and said they were going to intimidate the Bogans as requested. The tactical side was to be left to his boys. "If you don't like it, we will call it off," he reiterated. The Park Court boys relented.

A bigger issue was who was to accompany the Africans to the park. Jimmy insisted that one of the boys should come with him to the park and be with him. "How else are the Bogans gonna know I am working for you?"

The boys looked at each other as if thunderstruck. They had never bargained for this. Accompany Jimmy and his friends and be seen by the Bogans in their company? That seemed suicidal. "But not so dangerous if the Bogans think I got your back. And I can always return with my boys,"

Jimmy reminded. "You do want your park back, don't you?" he asked, pointedly.

Mahmoud wasn't sure if he wanted the park back anymore. But things seemed to have gone too far now. So he agreed, reluctantly. He will come to the park, he said. But they would appreciate if the Bogans are scared off the first time and there was to be no need for further visits from Jimmy. The other two boys nodded vigorously. They couldn't afford 100 dollars each time they got help, they reminded Jimmy. And they wanted no violence.

Jimmy laughed. "Don't fuckin' worry!" He said. "We are not gonna bash them." But, he added ominously: unless in self-defence.

They paid the fifty dollars the day before. On the day, around 5.45 pm, Mahmoud went to the park. As it was getting closer to summer, the Bogan Boys usually came there around 6.30 and kicked the footy around or just sat and chatted. Jimmy was to arrive with his friends around 6, and they were to sit and chat with Mahmoud in plain view of the Bogans. Eric and Rohan were to keep an eye on the Bogan house from Mahmoud's bedroom window.

"I have a bad feeling about this," Rohan said as they climbed the staircase. Eric nodded. "But nothing we can do now," he said. "Wait and see and hope it all goes well."

They waited, getting text messages from Mahmoud every minute or so, updating them of the situation. They were all tense with anxiety. Where the fuck is this guy? Was the most common refrain.

Jimmy finally turned up around five minutes past six. He had four other African boys with him; three seemed bigger than Jimmy and the fourth fairly small. They walked past Mahmoud's house chattering loudly in their language, striding confidently after Jimmy towards the park.

"They're on their way!" Eric texted Mahmoud.

The two boys could see only half of what happened thereafter, as they could not see the park from Mahmoud's window. They could hear Jimmy's friends' loud voices and received one hurried text from Mahmoud: "Cunts fuckn loud." There were no Bogans in sight.

Then, around 6.25 the door to the Bogan House opened and out stepped BB1 and BB2, in customary gear. BB1 was carrying the footy. They walked down the drive way nonchalantly, like they always did, chatting casually.

"Bogans are coming!" Eric texted, his palms already sweaty.

There was no response from Mahmoud. This, they learned later, was because Mahmoud was too preoccupied watching the Bogans come down the driveway. Rohan and Eric only saw the Bogans walking down, chatting and laughing. It seemed that the Bogan Boys had not seen the Africans.

Then they suddenly came to a halt in their tracks. They had spotted the Africans! They stood rooted to the ground as if they had seen a ghost. BB 2 whispered something in his brother's ear, and BB 1 whispered something back.

"Game on!" Eric said. His voice quivered.

The two Bogan Boys stood watching the Africans for a minute or two and then turned around. They walked back, slowly, casting glances over their shoulders as if guarding against sudden attack. Then they disappeared into the house. Within moments the whole Bogan clan came out and stood on their porch looking at the park.

"I think they're scared to go down," Rohan said. "Just like we were when they were in the park."

"Jimmy did it then!" Eric said, triumphant. He slapped Rohan on the back. His phone chimed. It was Mahmoud texting.

"See that?" Mahmoud asked.

"Yup," texted Eric.

"Fuckn awsum," texted back Mahmoud.

The Bogans stood watching, not daring to enter the park while the Africans were there. BB1 had even sat down on their front step as if prepared for a long wait until the Africans left. Rohan, however, had a bad feeling that it was not over yet.

He was right. Suddenly they heard a siren, and soon a police car and a divvy van arrived at the bottom of the court, coming to a screeching halt in front of the park. Several police officers got out of the vehicles and walked hurriedly towards the park.

"They called the cops!" Eric said under his breath. "The bastards!"

They could now hear a loud commotion from the park. People were shouting and swearing. Soon, two policemen were seen dragging one of the African boys by his top and then pushing him into the divvy van. He was followed by another two officers bringing another African. The Africans appeared to be protesting loudly, even flailing their arms about.

"Oh, my God!" Eric said. "They are arresting them!"

"Yes," said Rohan, placid as usual. His main concern was whether Mahmoud too would be hauled away for whatever the Africans were being taken away for.

By now the Bogans too had got animated. Evidently elated by the way things had turned out, they advanced down the driveway, jeering. "Awww, look at that!" A male Bogan voice was heard to say. "Fucking pigs having a fight with the monkeys!" Raucous laughter followed.

By now the police had pushed all the Africans - Jimmy included - into the divvy van. Curiously, Mahmoud was nowhere to be seen.

"Where the fuck is he?" Eric wondered aloud. Rohan too seemed to be getting uncharacteristically agitated now.

On the street, things were heating up. A policeman had taken exception to the 'pig' remark and was engaging in a loud argument with the Bogans. Other policemen were trying to pull him away, as the man seemed to be threatening the Bogans with physical violence. The commotion ended when an officer threatened the Bogan family with capsicum spray, and the Bogan clan retreated, but not before Father Bogan had bared his buttocks yet again.

Rohan and Eric quickly went downstairs and up to the gate. By now the whole neighbourhood seemed to be out, anxiously watching the drama at the bottom of Park Court. Chelliah was seen peering from behind his wall, and Kumar and Indu were standing outside their gate. Vivienne came out with Lauren and stood hand in hand, staring at the police struggling with the Africans and the Bogans. Mr. Rabula was also out but watched from inside his garden, craning his neck over their front wall. The commotion was so great that even the normally quiet Mark and Angela made a rare appearance, coming out to stare for a minute or two at the police vehicles and the knot of people near the park before disappearing into their house.

Eric waved at Vivienne to show he was alright. Rohan did the same with his parents. They waved back and signalled them to get back in Ahmed's house as if they were also in danger of being bundled into the police van. The boys were only too glad to beat a hasty retreat. They returned to Mahmoud's room and waited anxiously for their friend.

The police vehicles left. Moments later, Mahmoud slunk into the house and reported.

The Africans had arrived on time, but they had not dispelled Mahmoud's anxiety.

"My first time with so many Africans," he said. "And they were fuckin' loud. One seemed much older, the uncle of another guy there, according to Jimmy, and he smelled like he'd been partying all day. I felt shit scared." He seemed to be still trembling from the experience. Then the Bogans had come, and seeing the Africans, they had stood staring and walked away. "I can just imagine," Mahmoud said. "They must have been scared. I know I was scared, and those guys were on my side!"

Then the police had arrived and behaved aggressively, asking the Africans what they were doing in that part of town, and the Africans had asked if there was a law against being on any part of Melbourne. Or is it a Black thing? One of them had asked, and one of the cops had warned him not to play the race card. But you are the one playing the race card, the older man had said. You are playing the race card talking to us as if we have broken the law just because we are Black. Then all the Africans had started talking together, and the police had decided to end the argument by hauling them all away.

"That's pretty extreme," Eric said. "Yeah," Mahmoud said. "Good thing I wasn't Black or I would have been taken away too."

"How'd you managed to escape?" Rohan asked.

"I just stood aside and pretended I didn't know them," Mahmoud said. "I was quiet too. The cops didn't even look at me."

"Why look at you when they have Jimmy and his friends to look at," Rohan said, scowling.

"I felt really bad though," Mahmoud said. "The way they just hauled them away, for nothing. What will they do to them? And what will Jimmy think of me now?"

"They will probably release them after scaring them," Rohan said, "And Jimmy will be pissed-off with you, but he will come around."

"Will the cops come for us now?" Mahmoud was worried. "What if Jimmy tells them the whole story?"

Rohan shrugged his shoulders. "I guess we tell them we know nothing about it and stick to the story."

But Mahmoud didn't seem convinced. His face was marred with worry.

"We should have called Cynthia," Eric said after a pause. "She would have just barged in to the Bogan House and scared the shit out of all of them."

Rohan agreed. "At least she wouldn't have got arrested," he said.

"Fifty dollars gone!" Eric said.

"Fifty dollars plus Jimmy," Mahmoud reminded.

"I can't believe the bastards called the cops!" Eric said, shaking his head. "They can't handle Jimmy's friends, so they call the coppers!"

***

The police never came for the boys. Either Jimmy had not told them or the police didn't believe what Jimmy told them.

And it was not the Bogans who had called the police. That night, during dinner, Kumar revealed that it was actually the Rabulas who had done it.

"I saw the Sudanese walking down, and I said to myself, I have watched the Bogan menace threatening this neighbourhood, and I will not let the Sudanese do the same. Mark my words, Bogans will be nothing compared to the Sudanese!"

"They are not even Sudanese!" Rohan said. "Africans. But not Sudanese! And even if they were, what is the big deal?"

"How do you know all this?" Indu asked. "And what is your involvement in all this?"

Rohan told them. Kumar and Indu looked at each other in disbelief.

"You have done an idiotic thing!" Kumar said. "Are you trying to turn this neighbourhood into a war zone?"

Rohan said that never occurred to him. All they wanted was to intimidate the Bogans.

Indu gasped, and Kumar rolled his eyes.

"And you didn't think intimidation would not end in some big fight?"

Rohan said nothing. He was staring at his plate.

"I am glad the police came," Indu said. "Those boys looked like real ruffians. I am sure they are from one of those gangs."

"They are not gang members!" Rohan said, his voice rising with indignation. "They are just African. The cops wouldn't have taken them if they were not Black. They did nothing to the Bogans who were calling them names."

Kumar stared at his son. Indu gasped again and placed her palms on her cheeks.

"Oh my god!" She exclaimed. "You silly boy! Don't you watch the news?"

Ahmed was also infuriated by what had happened. Unlike Rohan, Mahmoud had refrained from telling his parents the truth. But Ahmed guessed that something must be up because he had heard that Mahmoud was also in the park when the Africans were arrested.

"What you doing there?" He asked. Mahmoud said he had seen the little Bogan taking something that looked like Eric's plane and dumping it there and he had waited till the Bogan left to go and see if it was actually the plane. Then the Africans had arrived.

Ahmed didn't seem to believe the story. He found it hard to believe that the Bogans would throw the plane away. "And how come the

Africans turn up suddenly?"

Mahmoud shrugged his shoulders. "Dunno," he said. "Maybe they came to see the Bogans."

Ahmed knew something was not right, but as he didn't know what it was, he let it drop, but not before giving Mahmoud a severe warning that if he ever found out that Mahmoud had something to do with what happened, he will face severe consequences.

The biggest winner was Hala. After the incident with the Africans she approached Mahmoud and suggested that they settle upon a fixed weekly amount and then, to help Mahmoud with the decision, she set the price herself: twenty five dollars. That would really help the poor Palestinian orphans, she had said, a doleful expression on her face. Why the sudden hike in price, Mahmoud had asked, his face scrunched in dismay, and Hala said the previous price was for one African. The new one was for four.

As Rohan had predicted, Jimmy and friends got released pretty soon. There was nothing to charge them with. Jimmy was also convinced that the two boys who were Collingwood supporters had also helped their release by singing 'Good Old Collingwood forever' when thrown in a cell, which had caused someone in the adjacent cell to start singing the Richmond song in a loud, drunken voice. The singing competition had got so out of control that the police had thrown them all out with a warning not to cause a disturbance again. The boys were pleased, but they were also shaken. At school, everybody got to know about the arrests but not the story behind it. As Jimmy's reputation as a gang member grew by leaps and bounds, children kept their distance from him. Only Cynthia seemed sympathetic. She had rarely paid Jimmy any attention in the past, but now she suddenly discovered him and approached him with offers of solidarity. The patriarchal state is also a racist state, she told him and added that they must fight together for freedom because your liberation is tied to mine, and vice versa. Jimmy told her to piss off. The problem with people here, he was heard to say, is that half of them want to throw us in prison and the other half wants to save us. Nobody wants to help us.

He did not speak to Mahmoud for days.

"That is better than beating you up," Eric said as they had all feared that might happen. Mahmoud nodded. He was relieved too. He had feared Jimmy and all his friends would catch him after school and beat him up.

But it was not long before Jimmy began talking to Mahmoud again. Underneath all that bravado, he was still a child. And his math was atrocious.

FOURTEEN

Not long after the incident with the Africans, Ahmed had his spirits lifted.

One Sunday morning, he came to Kumar's place, beaming from ear to ear. There was a spring in his step. His whole body language spoke of a joy he was impatient to share.

"Don't tell me," Kumar said. "The Bogans are leaving?"

Ahmed made a sweeping, dismissive gesture with his hand. "Baahh!" He spat. "Forget the Bogans. Who cares for them! I got better news."

Then he shared the good news. Amina is pregnant, he said, his voice quivering with excitement.

Kumar raised his eyebrows. Even Rohan looked up from his phone.

Ahmed nodded proudly. "Yes, man," he said. "Pregnant. All confirmed. Baby coming in June."

Kumar badly wanted to ask why they decided to have another child after so long but resisted the temptation. It was at times like this that Rohan's lack of tact was invaluable. And the boy did not disappoint.

"Why?" He asked, glancing up from his phone. "Why now? You are not happy with Mahmoud and Hala?"

Ahmed stared at Rohan for a moment as if in disbelief. He then turned to Kumar and explained. "I am very happy with Mahmoud and Hala. Very happy, thank you very much. But I am thinking, they must have company, and I also like to have one more child, maybe another son."

Rohan gazed at him, wide-eyed, head slightly cocked, as if his question has not yet been answered. Ahmed glanced at him and then continued to explain, to Kumar.

"And we been trying, many times in the past. But no luck. Finally Allah is blessing us."

Rohan quickly uncocked his head and returned to his phone, satisfied.

"Well, that is very good news," Kumar said. He called Indu.

"Amina is pregnant," he said, and Indu assumed the same expression Kumar had when the news was broken to him.

"They been trying many times," Rohan explained. "Only now Allah blessing them."

This time, both Ahmed and Kumar stared at Rohan but the boy simply returned to his phone, totally unmoved by their incredulity. Indu quickly moved to create a diversion by offering Ahmed a coffee which Ahmed politely declined as he had some work to do that morning. But he would definitely come back later, for a longer chat, he promised as he got up, giving Rohan another cold stare as he did so.

They went outside, chatting. Ahmed was talking non-stop about all the plans he had for the child. They had done the tests to find the gender of the child, and it had been confirmed that it was a boy. Ahmed was over the moon about that. He had even decided on a name for the boy: Abdul.

It was approaching hard rubbish day, and a heap of old furniture and other discarded items lay on Kumar's nature strip. Ahmed looked at the pile and shook his head in disbelief.

"Lot of shit here, man," he said. "You are throwing away good stuff."

Kumar wanted to say it was just stuff they did not need, but then he noticed the speaker set that belonged to Rohan on the heap. He had bought him a new set recently as the old set was too powerful and the whole house shook when Rohan played music on it. Rohan had not been unhappy to lose the old speakers because they shook his room more than they shook the house, and, as he put it, he was not really interested in going deaf at seventeen. But Kumar had not expected to see the old set thrown out like this. It could have fetched a good price if he had advertised on Gumtree or eBay. But that was not Rohan's style. As soon as he got something new, he threw the old one out. And sometimes it wasn't even something old. Kumar remembered how his son once wanted to learn to play the guitar. Kumar bought him one, only to find Rohan losing interest in the instrument in a couple of weeks and landing the guitar in the hard rubbish dump. When asked why he did that, he had simply shrugged his shoulders and said he just didn't need it, because he had realised that he was pathetic at playing it.

He wondered what the Bogans might have thrown out. Maybe they threw out Eric's plane, he thought. Maybe Vivienne should get Eric to look in their pile. After dark.

He looked at Ahmed's house and saw only a small pile.

"You don't throw out much, obviously."

"I don't." Ahmed said. "Only my wife. She is always throwing stuff but as soon as she throw from front door, I take in from back door," he chuckled. Then he noticed the speaker set.

"Good speakers you are throwing out," he said, ruefully.

"You want them?" Kumar asked. Ahmed looked longingly at the speakers and then glanced apprehensively at his house. "Maybe not. If I take, might end in my pile because Amina is in cleaning mood." He smiled at the house and waved. "There she is," he said, continuing to wave and smile. "Watching from the window."

Kumar looked sharply at Ahmed's house, but he couldn't see anyone. But he didn't doubt Ahmed's word. Ahmed probably knew his wife very well.

Ahmed stopped waving and turned to Kumar.

"Why throw it out anyway?"

"It's not me," Kumar confessed. "It's my son. He does what he wants."

Ahmed nodded gravely as if he understood Kumar's pain. Then he glanced at Kumar's house as if remembering something and placed his face closer to Kumar's.

"Just asking," he said. "You are Boodhist right?"

"Yes."

Kumar said, although not with much conviction. He had never been a devout Buddhist. As far as he was concerned, Buddhism was something he and Indu had been born with, like their limbs and lungs and the colour of their skin. Their devotion did not go beyond visiting the local temple in Melbourne infrequently. Even that had come to an abrupt end about two years ago after Rohan was banned from the place. A new Chief Monk had arrived at the temple, and during his first sermon, Rohan had started laughing uncontrollably at his sing-song voice, causing a major distraction and prompting the priest to issue what was akin to a Buddhist Fatwa on the boy. If that boy comes anywhere near the temple again, the monk had hissed at Kumar after the sermon, I will strangle him personally using my own robe. The threat thrilled Rohan to no end as he hated having to sit without being allowed to use his phone for more than an hour. But it also dampened whatever enthusiasm Kumar and Indu had for temples. They became plain, non-temple-going Buddhists.

Ahmed nodded gravely, then regarded Kumar with narrowed eyes as if searching for something in his face.

"In your religion there is nothing against children not listening to parents, butting into parents' conversations, children being cheeky?"

Kumar was embarrassed by the question. But only a little. He was now quite accustomed to other people's reaction to Rohan's cheekiness even though he had never really got used to it himself.

"Mmmm..." he said, smiling weakly, trying to think of an answer. Ahmed relaxed his attitude, shook his head, and patted his friend's back as if he understood Kumar's difficulty. "Wait here," he said and hurried up to the pile of rubbish outside his house and picked up something. He came back to Kumar. He had a DVD in his hand.

"I give you this DVD by famous Islamic scholar. All very good stuff. Help you have meaningful family life. You watch and show your son also." He patted Kumar's shoulder again. "In your own time. No pressure," he said before turning away.

"Obviously you don't want it," Kumar said, glancing at the DVD. It carried the portrait of a man in traditional Islamic dress with his hands raised as if delivering a sermon. *The Best of Dr. Ashrafi*, the title read.

Ahmed laughed. "Oh, I already know what is in it," he said, winking. "But you don't." Then he waved and walked towards his house, the spring in his step now very pronounced. This was the happiest Kumar had seen him since he discovered Vivienne's sexuality and since the Bogans arrived.

But if Ahmed had thought that his wife's pregnancy could help him forget the Bogans, he was badly mistaken.

"Because of you Ahmed thinks I should become a Muslim," Kumar said to Rohan when he returned to his house. But Rohan was not interested. He was peering out of the window, preoccupied with something outside.

"What are you looking at?"

Rohan shooooshed him.

"The Bogans!" He whispered.

Kumar was intrigued. Rohan could see the Bogans from here?

Rohan sensed his father's curiosity. "They are here," he whispered again. "Outside. BB1 and BB2. Checking out our hard rubbish."

Kumar quickly went up to Rohan and peered out. Yes, they were there alright. BB1 and BB2. Checking out their hard rubbish.

Soon Indu joined them. "What are you looking at?"

"Bogans," whispered Kumar. "BB1 and BB2. Checking out our hard rubbish."

Now all three of them stood at the window, peering out, all three of them tense. Outside the house stood the two Bogans, decked in their trademark dirty jeans, sneakers and sweaters, going through the rubbish in the pile. This was the first time they had seen them so up close. The older one had brown hair that danced around like a mop on his head, and the younger one had shorter dark brown hair that was equally unruly. Their skin looked pallid, and the tattoo on the older boy's neck made him look older than he probably was. And they could see what the tattoo said too: AWSOM. But despite their unkempt and unhealthy appearance, they both looked boyish. Maybe if they were put under a shower and dressed in nice clothes they would have looked very different, Kumar thought. Almost as normal as Rohan. And they would have probably learned to spell too.

The Bogans were obviously on a rubbish hunt. BB1 carried a plastic garbage bag that seemed to be already quite full. Now they fossicked through the rubbish on Kumar's nature strip in a leisurely manner as though they had all the time in the world and didn't care whether people were watching them or not. They pushed the furniture around, turned over the broken flower pots to see if there was anything under them, and put their hands through the hole in the laundry bucket as if to check whether it was really there. BB2 sat in the old recliner and put his feet up on the pile of rubbish and posed like a lord and BB1 laughed and slapped him around the head playfully. BB1 then picked up the flat screen monitor with the cracked screen and gazed at it with disappointment.

Then they saw the speakers. Kumar sighed as the Bogans' eyes lit up at the sight of the speakers. They looked good even from here, he thought. His son had much to learn from Ahmed, if not about Islam then about frugality.

The Bogans were now admiring the speakers as if they had found treasure. *Wow!* BB2 appeared to mouth, and his brother seemed to agree. They cast a quick glance at Kumar's house before BB1 picked up one speaker. BB2 took the other.

"I thought I told you not to throw away the speakers," Indu whispered. "You did," Rohan whispered back. "But I don't need them."

Then the Bogans spied something else. They put the speakers down, and BB2 picked up a pair of shoes. It was not hard for Kumar to recognise Rohan's old Nike pair.

"You threw the Nikes too!" Indu whispered, swatting her son gently on the head. Rohan shrugged his shoulders.

BB2 tried the Nikes on. He seemed thrilled with the result.

The Bogans now walked away, happy with their acquisitions. They both walked like Ahmed, with a spring in their steps. BB2 wore the Nikes but still carried the old pair which he had placed on the speaker he was carrying. BB1 carried the other speaker, and the garbage bag slung over his shoulder.

"See!" Indu said, her voice still a whisper even though the Bogans were out of hearing now. "They don't throw away things like you do!"

"'Course they don't!" Rohan retorted, frowning. "They're Bogans!"

Kumar cancelled his plan to tell Vivienne to look for Eric's plane on the Bogan's nature strip. Somehow he felt that there was little chance of finding it there.

But now he had another concern. The Bogans had taken the speakers. He knew they were powerful. They caused a headache even when Rohan was playing music softly. This is why he had bought him a new pair that was not as powerful but good enough to satisfy Rohan's needs as regards volume. Now the Bogans had the speakers in their hands, and there was no guarantee, Kumar thought sadly, that the Bogans would be playing their music softly.

FIFTEEN

It did not take long for Kumar's fears about the speakers to be realised. It happened a couple of days after the Bogans had picked them up. Kumar was watching the news on television in the evening while Indu made some tea when, suddenly, a terrific boom shattered the calm of the evening. Kumar found himself almost thrown off the sofa while in the kitchen, Indu dropped the kettle, spewing boiling water all over the floor. Boom followed boom, and now stunned and bewildered, Kumar jumped out of the sofa and rushed to the kitchen, only to run into Indu who was rushing out, both of them nearly slipping on the water Indu had spilled. By now, Rohan who had been in the shower had also joined them, a towel around his waist and the water dripping from his body adding to the puddles on the floor. Meanwhile, the booms continued, now joined by other loud noises that seemed to be competing with the booms and struggling to form a pattern of noises. It took them a while to realise that it was, in fact, loud music and once they realised that it was not hard for them to figure out who and what was behind it. It was the Bogans, and they were using the speakers Rohan had thrown out.

From that day onwards, Park Court was treated to the sound of thunderous music coming from the Bogans' house – metallic concoctions of sound punctuated with heavy, booming drum beats. It was a noise of the most horrible kind, and only the Bogans seem to think it was music. It shook the walls, rattled window panes and threw tea and coffee out of cups and mugs.

Nobody in the neighbourhood could concentrate on anything. Locked doors and windows were no protection against the invasion of the booming beats. Even worse, they sent everybody into fits of ill-temper and irritation. Perfectly normal, calm people went crazy, losing their temper at everyone and everything. At Kumar's house, Indu yelled at Kumar and Kumar yelled back at her, for reasons unknown to either of them. Even the normally placid Rohan became irritable, dropping his phone on the table and pacing up and down the house muttering to himself. Sometimes he was even heard to mumble profanities which Kumar and Indu had believed he had lost interest in uttering years ago, and ominously, now the obscenities seem to be coming straight from the heart.

But when the stereo was finally turned off, things changed equally dramatically. Everybody heaved sighs of relief, and people who had been irrational and on edge for the last hour or so reverted to being perfectly normal human beings. Kumar apologised to Indu and Indu apologised to Kumar while Rohan simply returned to his seat and phone. It was as though the world that had suddenly started turning in the wrong direction had finally found its bearings and returned to its normal motion.

"I think you have made a huge mistake!" Kumar told Rohan the first day of the music, after the din had stopped and he had just finished apologising to Indu who was wiping off the coffee she had spilled on the table.

"A *huge* mistake!"

"Let's hope nobody knows that it was the one we threw away," Indu said. "We will become the bad people around here."

Kumar was not too sure about that. He remembered Ahmed waving at Amina, who was looking, he said, out of the upstairs window. If Amina had been looking out of the window, she must surely have also seen the Bogans taking the speakers from the nature strip. And if she saw it, she was likely to tell Vivienne.

Kumar was right. Two days later, Vivienne was at their door.

"Thank you very much," she said mockingly. "For giving Bogan speaker. We can all sleep well now."

Kumar tried to explain that they had not actually *given* the speakers but as far as Vivienne was concerned, leaving them on the nature strip was as good as giving the speakers to them.

"Thank you very much," she said again, this time even making a slight bow to emphasise her sarcasm. "Now thanks to you me and Lauren arguing. For first time in our life." She went home in a huff.

The tensions continued to mount. The Bogans continued playing loud music, at all odd times, usually, sometimes well into the night. It was always music with heavy, thunderous beats and little else. It shook the neighbourhood, rattling windows and people alike. On the nights the music was on, few people slept.

One Saturday morning, after a night of particularly thunderous beats, Vivienne came to Kumar's house looking as though she had been run over by something heavy.

"It's terrible," she said. "This noise. Terrible. They are trying to kill us. No sleep all night. No sleep!"

Kumar tried to console her. Not much sleep here too. He assured her. Not much sleep at all.

"What kind of music are they playing?" Vivienne wanted to know, and Kumar looked at Rohan who shrugged his shoulders and said it was very hard to tell with all the noise. If they turn it down, maybe he might have an idea.

But the most significant consequence of the musical assault was the least expected. The music caused so much distress to the neighbourhood that it brought even the usually quiet and private Mark and Angela out of their house. Until now the Timorese couple had shown very little concern about the Bogans. They lived the furthest from the Bogans, and the chances of them being intimidated by them were remote. Therefore their attitude to the Bogans seemed to be no different from their attitude to lesbians living down the road; it was simply not their business. They had shown mild interest in the arrest of Jimmy and his mates but nothing more than that. But the music changed that. The thunderous noise it made now travelled freely and frequently to their little haven, and unbeknownst to the rest of the neighbours they had been disturbed and disturbed deeply, so deeply that they found it hard to mind their business anymore. One evening, during the usual Bogan musical broadcast, while Kumar stared blankly out of the window grasping the rails desperately as if he wanted to break out and run somewhere quiet and peaceful, he saw the young couple walking hurriedly down the road towards the Bogan house. Even in that state of disorientation, Kumar could recognise the significance of the moment and quickly called Indu, who was heard rattling dishes in the kitchen. As no verbal communication was possible above the din Kumar wrote on a piece of paper:

"Mark and Angela going to tell Bogans to shut up."

This he held it up to Indu who read it and put both hands on her cheeks in despair. Then together, they waited anxiously near the window to discover the outcome of their quiet neighbours' bold venture. Observing his parents strangely preoccupied with something in the midst of the mayhem, Rohan also sidled up beside them. Seeing the piece of paper, he recognised its import and decided to join his parents, not with the apprehension of a sensitive viewer anticipating a distressing scene on Television, but with the eagerness of a spectator at a bullfight.

They did not have to wait too long in suspense. A few minutes after Mark and Angela had walked past their house, there was a sudden spike in the noise level of the Bogan music signalling that their mission was a failure. Of the fate of their intrepid Timorese neighbours, there was no sign. Kumar and Indu were beginning to get anxious, and Rohan was becoming impatient when suddenly they saw the Timorese duo walking briskly up the road back towards their own house. They seemed to be walking back much faster than they walked towards the Bogan house. Mrs. Rabula, who had also witnessed the retreat of Angela and Mark, said later that she was certain Angela was crying.

Much later, when the music had finally stopped and when everything had returned to normal, Mahmoud recounted in vivid detail what had occurred. He had seen it all from his bedroom, he said, his eyes twinkling with excitement.

"The two little Teemorese walked down the hill like they were going to war," said he, chuckling. "They looked like they were gonna rip the Bogans apart and they walked up the driveway like they were racing each other to be the first to do it." He shook his head as if still unable to believe what he saw. "Then they stand outside the door and knock and knock and no one comes out. No wonder. Who can hear someone knocking on the door with that racket going on? But the Teemorese are not gonna give up easily. The man starts banging on the door really hard and finally, the door opens and guess who comes out? Father Bogan! But here's the funny thing. He opens the door and looks out but 'cause the Teemorese pair is so short he doesn't see them at first. Then he looks down and sees them, and he jumps like he's seen a mouse. It was fuckin' priceless!"

Rohan and Eric thought as much, and they were sorely disappointed that they had missed it.

Mahmoud continued his recount.

. "Then the Teemorese say something to Father Bogan, and he can't hear him at first. Then he says it again, probably very loudly and Father Bogan jumps back and looks at the two of them like he can't believe his ears. Then he steps outside, yelling at the Teemorese and out comes BB1 and Mother Bogan also, then together they keep yelling at the Teemorese and walking towards them and the Teemorese are just backing up towards the gate."

"Wow!" Said Eric.

"Yeah it was fuckin' awesome," Said Mahmoud. "And this is the best part. They keep backing up to the gate, and at the gate, Father Bogan pretends like he's gonna jump them. The two of them turn around and run out like two scared little children."

"They weren't running when they went past us," Rohan said.

"They stopped after they ran a few meters and turned back and saw that the Bogans were laughing at them and not chasing."

"That's so funny!" Eric said. "So fuckin' funny!"

They sat in silence for a few minutes, savouring what has happened. Finally, Rohan spoke.

"But I guess that means the music will go on."

Mahmoud thought for a few moments. "Yeah, that's true," he said.

"That's not funny."

That was the last anyone saw of Mark and Angela. A couple of days after their ill-fated foray to the Bogan House, a 'For Lease' sign appeared on their property. A few days later the sign remained, but in addition, a chain and a padlock appeared on the gate. It seemed that the Timorese couple had moved out as stealthily as the Bogans had moved in.

Their departure rattled everyone. They may have been reclusive, but at least they hadn't bothered anyone. And their fate was seen as a bad omen. Regardless of whether they had shown courage or stupidity in taking on the Bogans, their retreat from the neighbourhood seemed like a sign of terrible things to come.

"I hope we won't all have to move out of here eventually, to avoid listening to music we can't even recognise," Mr. Rabula said to Kumar. "We love this house. It cost us a fortune, and after what has happened, we will not be able to get a good price for it even if we move."

Kumar nodded. The 'For Lease' sign outside the house where Mark and Angela had lived didn't seem to be attracting any prospective tenants. It was hard to say if people who wanted to rent it had come and fled after hearing the Bogan music as the Bogans played their music mostly in the afternoon, but Kumar had a bad feeling that word might have already got out that Park Court was rapidly turning into a little hell for its residents.

"Why don't we complain to the police?" Indu asked one evening after the music had stopped, seemingly for the day, and she had made a fresh cup of tea for Kumar to compensate for the one she had spilled during the musical interlude.

"Surely they can't do this. We have rights."

Kumar thought that a good idea too. But before calling the police, he spoke to his friend Asela. Asela had been to school with him in Sri Lanka and had arrived in Australia long before Kumar and Indu. Kumar was accustomed to considering Asela as a fount of wisdom, mainly because of the fact that he was doing very well as a GP. He had always been full of sound advice even though Indu had considered him to be full of other things too, a perception that Kumar was becoming more inclined to share after Asela moved into Wheelers Hill a few months previously. Their new house was not big, but the affluent status of the suburb seemed to have made Asela and his wife Pushpa behave as if their small three-bedroom house was a country estate. Their whole outlook changed. Asela sold his Subaru and bought a Mercedes and Pushpa discarded much of their old furniture in favour of new, more upmarket table and lounge settings that matched the plush carpet and curtains. They also employed a gardener to trim the lawns and weed the flower beds, a job which Asela had been perfectly capable of doing by himself at their previous residence. The most significant change, however, was in his political allegiance. Asela and Pushpa had been staunch Labor supporters ever since their arrival in Australia, but after their arrival in Wheelers Hill, they suddenly discovered the virtues of the Liberal Party. Asela defended it by saying that he had always been a small 'l' liberal. With the change of suburbs, he had merely changed his Ls.

"No point asking them for advice," Indu said when Kumar told her of his intentions of consulting Asela. "They will only tell us what a wonderful area *they* live in." Besides, she reminded, it was Asela who had advised them to buy this house, saying it would be a good investment. "See where that landed us!" She lamented.

But it was not his fault that the Bogans moved in, Kumar pointed out. Asela was a good adviser, but he could not predict the future. But he too felt that Asela was likely to play up the advantages of living in an area like Wheelers Hill. Still, he asked. He had no other advisers.

Asela was pleased to see his friend, and while Pushpa made some coffee, he took Kumar to their little balcony. As they were climbing the stairs, he placed a finger to his lips.

"Shhh," he cautioned. "Revantha is studying," he said, almost under his breath.

Kumar grinned and nodded to show that he understood, and demonstrated it by walking as if he was treading on eggshells. Revantha was Asela's son. He was Rohan's age, but unlike Rohan, he wanted to be a doctor.

Up in the balcony, Asela closed the doors to keep the noise out. "I told you Revantha wants to do medicine, right?" He asked Kumar and Kumar nodded. He didn't say Asela had said it so many times, almost every time he met Kumar.

"Rohan still wants to be an electrician?" Asela asked, showing his friend to an ornate wickerwork chair with a plush cushion on it. Kumar nodded again as he sat down. Asela nodded gravely as he took his seat.

"Each to his own. Follow your heart is what I say. Electrician jobs are not like those days. They pay well if you are good at it."

Kumar wanted to say yes, but as he was not sure how good Rohan was going to be as an electrician, he refrained. He also didn't say that it didn't really matter to him how good an electrician his son would become as long as he had a decent income. He did not think Asela would understand.

From the balcony, they had a clear view of the street below. As it was early evening on a weekday and residents were driving in from work. Their cars seem to match the houses and Kumar's red Mazda, though not exactly old or decrepit, looked out of place among the new shiny BMWs and Mercedes. The cars seem to go well with the houses, and Kumar wondered if they all bought their cars after they bought their houses, like Asela. Maybe they all voted Liberal too, he thought.

Asela saw him looking down the street and smiled in the same knowing way he did when he had shown Kumar the house and the balcony the first time he visited the house, soon after he and Pushpa had bought it.

"Nice view, huh?" he asked again as he did on that day, and Kumar smiled and nodded, just as he had done then.

After some small talk about the weather and work, Kumar broached the subject of the newcomers to his neighbourhood. Asela listened attentively to Kumar's story. And as Kumar mentioned each escalation in tensions between the Bogans and the rest of the neighbourhood, his face grew increasingly worried. He shook his head and made clucking noises with his tongue. Finally, when Kumar had finished his tale of woe, he turned and called out to his wife.

Pushpa came out on to the balcony with the coffee she had made.

"Some Bogans have moved into Kumar's street," Asela announced.

Pushpa quickly placed the mugs of coffee on the coffee table without bothering about coasters so that she could place her hands on both her cheeks in dismay.

"Oh my God!" said she. "How long now?"

"A few months it seems."

Pushpa shook her head in disbelief. "How are you coping?' She asked, placing a concerned hand on Kumar's shoulder.

Before Kumar could answer, Asela replied.

"With great difficulty. Apparently, there is a lesbian couple also living down that street."

"My!" Pushpa had to sit down now.

"And some Lebanese Muslims who are fighting with the Bogans."

Pushpa reached over and touched Kumar's hand.

"You can't let this go on Kumar," she said. "You must move."

Kumar looked at Asela and saw that his friend was studying him with hooded eyes.

"I too think you need to move," he declared. "That, of course, may not be easy. You have to think very carefully about your options, which may be limited."

Kumar sat bewildered by the horror he had caused in Pushpa.

"From what I hear, Bogans are moving into many suburbs," Asela continued. "I heard recently that even Glen Waverley has a few now. Only a few places like Toorak, South Yarra, and Wheelers Hill are safe from them."

"Well, there may be some here too, God knows," Pushpa interjected. "Maybe even lesbians. But everybody keeps themselves to themselves around here. Till very recently I thought our neighbours were White, but only last week I found out they were Asian. Japanese."

"But Japanese aren't called Asians anymore you see," Asela said, with the air of a teacher correcting an errant pupil.

"Well, what are they called?" Kumar asked. For a moment he forgot his own predicament. This was indeed new to him, and he badly wanted to know. Pushpa too seemed to be somewhat perplexed.

"Well, just Japanese. Not Asian, not White but Japanese," Asela said. His tone suggested that it was too profound a subject for him to even consider explaining to Kumar.

Pushpa, who had been temporarily stalled by her husband's exposition on Japanese identity, now returned to her theme.

"Everybody here is quiet and peaceful. I am sure even if Bogans come here, they will be very different."

"Bogans can't afford these prices, Pushpa! Don't be silly!" Asela said, raising his voice slightly. Then he turned to Kumar. "Let me have a think about it. You definitely need to move out, but then, what is your budget?" He asked with narrowed eyes and a painful grin as if he already knew what Kumar's budget might be.

By now, Kumar had lost all interest in the conversation. He finished his coffee and stood up. "Let me have a think about it," he said. 'I will get back to you once I have made up my mind." Asela rose with him, but Kumar bade his goodbyes on the balcony and walked downstairs alone.

As he was descending the stairs, he heard Pushpa's voice. "My! Coffee mark all over this table. I might have to put a cover to this." He didn't hear whether Asela agreed with her or not.

When Kumar told Indu about the conversation, she shook her head and reminded him that she had warned him.

"No point asking them anymore," she said. "Too up themselves now. Ask someone else, someone who can understand. Don't you have anybody at work? Someone White?"

***

On Monday Kumar spoke to David, his manager at work. David was Anglo-Australian, the only Anglo-Australian in his department. He was in his early sixties, nearing retirement and already playing the part. He worked more like a man winding down than a man continuing with work. He spent his lunchtimes out in the sun, reading the newspaper and drinking a cup of tea which he made in the kitchenette and usually drank from a cup with a saucer. Lately, he had taken to puffing on a pipe too. In his suit and tie, cup of tea, his newspaper and pipe, he looked every inch an English gentleman even though he was half Irish. He had been Kumar's boss for years and had a reputation as a good listener if not always a good source of advice.

So on Monday during lunchtime, Kumar approached David. He sat next to him on the bench and opened his lunch box of rice and curry. Then he opened his heart.

"We have very noisy neighbours," he told David. "They are so noisy that we can't sleep. What can we do?"

David looked at Kumar and then sniffed the air. "What's that?" He asked. "Curry?"

Kumar looked around and then realised that David was referring to the food in his lunch box.

"Oh, yes!" He said. "Chicken. Want to try some?"

David glanced at the curry in the box and waved it away. "No, thanks," he said. "I have had my lunch, even though that looks very appetizing."

"Thank you," Kumar said, flattered. "Now, about the neighbours..."

"Ah, yes," David said. "The noisy neighbours. I know. It is not easy. Not pleasant. The worst thing that can happen." He puffed on his pipe. "Tell me, have you tried speaking to them about this?" He asked, looking sideways at Kumar.

"No," said Kumar. "We haven't ever spoken to them."

David looked at him with surprise, and Kumar explained. They are not the kind of people we feel comfortable speaking to, he said. Then he went on to describe the neighbours he was speaking of. He was careful not to call them Bogans or White. As David was also White, he didn't know if he might be offended if he called his White neighbours Bogans.

David listened and nodded.

"Bogans, hey?" He said at length. Kumar was slightly taken aback by his observation but did well not to show it. He nodded.

"Then you have to tread carefully," David said. "Perhaps it is the police you should be speaking to the next time it gets out of hand."

He returned to his newspaper.

Kumar came home and told Indu what David said.

"Don't be silly!" She said. "If you call the police, it will only make the Bogans madder."

But somebody did call the police. The following Friday night, a police car drove in and parked outside the Bogan house, and Vivienne said she saw two policemen going into the house. Then the music stopped. Vivienne heaved a sigh of relief. Then the cops left and the Father Bogan emerged and poured out his outrage in filth for about ten minutes, and went in. Then the music started again, louder than before.

The following day, Kumar told David what happened. David looked mildly alarmed but then shrugged his shoulders. "Best not to push it, he advised. "From what you say, they sound quite aggressive, maybe even violent. Best not to push it."

"Then do you think we should continue to suffer like this?" Kumar asked, trying hard not to sound petulant, and David asked him if he had heard of Perfect Homes? No, Kumar said. He had not heard of Perfect Homes. He was about to ask what David meant when David explained.

"It's a Real Estate Agency," David said. "My sister's son Garry owns it. His surname is Holmes so he's got a nice little play with words going in the name," he smiled mischievously. "They advertise a lot of properties. Prices are coming down, Garry tells me. This is a good time to buy."

Kumar came home dejected. This was not working. The Bogan problem was bigger than he had anticipated, and it showed every sign of becoming bigger. Maybe Asela and David were right. They should move, as Mark and Angela had done. Indu was ambivalent on the subject. She felt sad, leaving the street in which she had lived for five years. It also meant having to postpone their trip to Sri Lanka which they had planned for early next year before Rohan started his VCE. They had not been back for three years now, and their parents were longing to see them, especially Rohan whom they loved dearly.

But then, there had never been anything like the Bogans for the last five years.

The noise the Bogans made, however, was likely to disrupt Rohan's studies in the crucial final year. Even if the boy was not much of a student, any disruption to even the little studying he did had the potential to undermine whatever mark he could get. He might not even become an electrician and end up checking out groceries at the local Woolies. That would be a terrible come down for a child who had once wanted to become an astronaut.

As for Rohan, he wasn't too keen to move as he did not like leaving his friends, but not going to Sri Lanka was an appealing prospect. Even though his grandparents adored him and he loved their adoration, the boy also found their constant queries about his studies and what he hoped to become when he grew up too irritating. During their last visit to Sri Lanka, they had been constantly on his case, and during the last three years, the questioning had continued over the phone whenever they called Sri Lanka. They had no idea he was hoping to become an electrician; many times he had felt like telling them, but Kumar and Indu had told him that that would break their heart. So, he always told them whatever came to his mind; micro-biologist, aerospace engineer, software development manager and his original favourite, astronaut. Rohan told his grandparents whatever he thought would sound dignified enough to their ears even though his parents advised him to stick to one profession. Rohan was certain the interrogations would continue if they went next year, probably more intensely, now that he was so close to finishing school. He didn't mind waiting another couple of years to visit.

But, he warned his parents; Remember, there are Bogans everywhere. If they can come here, they can come anywhere. It reminded

Kumar of what Asela had said. They are even in Glen Waverley. And Glen Waverley was not even a suburb that came within his budget.

Maybe we should give it a bit longer and see what happened, Indu said. Maybe after their Sri Lankan trip, after Rohan's VCE. Maybe things will get better. The Bogans will settle down.

Kumar agreed. Or they might also get worse he thought. He hoped they wouldn't.

SIXTEEN

But things did get worse.

The music continued, and so did the Bogans' war with Ahmed. Now the boys hardly even looked at the park. Hala rarely got out of the house except to go to school. Ahmed continued to be thrilled by the prospect of Abdul, but he was also worried about the discomfort to his family. The music got to him too and more than once he threatened to go and rip the cords out of the speakers.

"I shudda taken them when you offer me," he said to Kumar. "And take and throw in bin. Now bloody Bogans making everybody deaf!"

Things got a bit more serious when BB2 started to skateboard on the sidewalk outside Vivienne's and Ahmed's houses. He went up and down every afternoon during the week and morning, afternoon and evening on the weekends, the wheels of the skateboard clattering on the sidewalk irritatingly. Amina, Vivienne, and Lauren were extremely reluctant to go out when the boy was trundling up and down the sidewalk on his board. Interestingly, BB2 did it only on that side of the street and only outside Ahmed's and Vivienne's houses.

"One day I am gonna catch that bastard and break his two legs,"

Ahmed threatened one day after the Bogan boy had spent nearly the entire weekend skateboarding along the sidewalk. "He's soon gonna bump into one of us."

"Just ignore him," Amina advised. "He will grow out of it soon and then it will be all over."

Ahmed simply scowled and said he better stop it soon or he will finish it for him.

As the situation was escalating, like Kumar, the boys also sought enlightenment from a higher authority - Cynthia.

Mahmoud had also been speaking to his Islamic group again. There was much sympathy, Mahmoud said, but little of practical importance. "They want me to start becoming more religious," he said. "Go to the mosque every Friday, start praying, like five times a day, start growing a beard." How is that going to stop Bogan music? He had asked. When you embrace your religion more fully, the answers will come to you automatically, they had said.

"That is too much to suffer for, to get rid of Bogans," Mahmoud said. He will consider that if all else fails.

So they spoke to Cynthia.

They met at the same McDonald's where they had first pitched their proposal to Jimmy, sitting around a table in the same corner. Cynthia had agreed to meet at the McDonalds only if she was not required to eat anything as she was boycotting McDonald's. The boys had wondered why but had not pressed it too much as they were happy with her attitude. They remembered well how much it cost them when Jimmy was there.

Cynthia sat and looked around nervously. "If any of my mates from our feminist group sees me here, I will be in trouble," she confided. "They'd think I am here to eat." But she also kept looking longingly at the burgers the boys had ordered.

"Have some," Eric offered some chips. Cynthia declined. "Not in this life!" she spat.

"Suit yourself," Eric said and stuffed a handful of chips in his mouth. Rohan smirked and did the same. Only Mahmoud was not touching his food. He was staring at Cynthia's breasts.

As Mahmoud was otherwise occupied and Rohan seemed too busy with his burger, Eric described the Bogans to Cynthia. Cynthia listened carefully to Eric's description and nodded gravely at the end.

"Sounds like good recruiting material for the Fash," she said.

"Who's Fash?" Rohan asked through a mouthful of chips and bun.

"Fascists"

"Who's Fascists?"

"Oh, I know!" Eric intervened. "It's like Hitler and that Italian dude. They liked to march with them big Swat-sticka flags, and they hated the Jews."

"We never learned that," Rohan said, showing more interested in his coke than in the Fascists. He glanced at Mahmoud for confirmation, but the boy was too busy staring at Cynthia's breasts.

"That is because you go to a shit state school," Eric teased through his chips. Rohan playfully sneered and smirked at Eric's banter, but Cynthia fixed him with a menacing glare.

"Well, I guess his mummy and daddy can't afford the exorbitant fees of a private school," she shot back, a mocking lilt in her voice. As Eric smarted from her retort, Cynthia declared that as far she was considered they were all ignorant idiots. "Fascists are right-wing nut jobs who want to bring the world under the control of White males and keep everybody else down. They are violent and authoritarian. They try to recruit people from lower socio-economic backgrounds like your neighbours."

Rohan and Eric looked at each other. At the mention of Hitler, Mahmoud looked up from Cynthia's breasts.

"My dad says, if Hitler was around, Israel would not be getting away with all the shit they are doing."

Cynthia stared at Mahmoud as if unable to believe her ears. Her face turned scarlet from rage.

"What a stupid, idiotic thing to say!" she almost cried, drawing the attention of some people in nearby tables. "The way to deal with Israel is not to exterminate the Jews, you moron!" She raised her eyes to the heavens and rolled them in frustration. "Why are you people so ignorant and tribal?"

Wilting under Cynthia's verbal assault, Mahmoud appeared to shrink. His shoulders slumped, and he seemed to slide down in his seat as if trying to make himself smaller and inconspicuous. Feeling sorry for their friend, Eric and Rohan came to Mahmoud's rescue by bringing the discussion back to the original topic.

"The Bogans are very much like the Fash you talk about, but we don't really know what they think," Eric said. Rohan nodded.

"We have never spoken to them."

"Idiots!" Cynthia sneered, then rolled her eyes again. "Never occurred to you that perhaps you should speak to them?"

Rohan and Eric shook their heads. "Nah," Eric said. "Never. They don't look like the people we wanna talk to."

"Oh, my god!" Cynthia shook her head in frustration. "What imbeciles. You know their names so that we can check them on social media?"

Again, the two boys shook their heads. "How can we know their names if we don't talk to them?" Eric asked, almost triumphantly.

Cynthia rolled her eyes again. "Any pics?"

Again, a vigorous shake of heads from the boys, followed by a heavy sigh from Cynthia. She took her phone out and started flicking through it. Eric and Rohan waited expectantly. Mahmoud had straightened slightly in his seat, and his eyes had returned to Cynthia's breasts.

"Here," Cynthia said after a minute or so. She took her phone out and showed them some pictures in her photo gallery. "Here are some pics of the local Fash some of my mates in the Left have taken. Are your neighbours in any of these?"

The boys looked at the images. They were pictures of mostly young and middle-aged men in angry moods, shouting or jeering at something or someone off-screen. Many of them were dressed like the Bogans, and some had tattoos. Many had beards too, like Father Bogan.

"Very hard to say," Eric said. "They all look the same to me." Rohan nodded his assent.

Cynthia glared at Eric for a moment and then sighed again before putting the phone away. It seemed she had given up trying to enlighten the boys. But she was still on the Bogans' case.

"Will you be able to snap some pics of them?" She asked. "Then I can show them to my mates and see what they come up with."

Again the boys looked at each other. "We can try," Eric said. "But only from a distance. We don't want to go anywhere near them."

Cynthia was satisfied with that even though she was still unhappy with their attitude. "Alright," she said, getting up. "Do it ASAP. The sooner I get them, the sooner you will get some feedback," she said, like a teacher talking to a pupil about an assignment. The boys got up, Rohan having to pull Mahmoud by his collar to get his attention. Eric stood to attention, and gave Cynthia a salute and said "yes Mein Fuhrer." Cynthia almost opened her mouth to retaliate but only managed another sigh of frustration.

As the boys walked off Mahmoud tarried. He was staring after Cynthia's back as if mesmerised.

"What's wrong?" Rohan asked.

"Wait here," Mahmoud said, and before Rohan or Eric could say anything, he ran after Cynthia. He was seen handing her something and then, while Cynthia looked after him in bewilderment, came back briskly. Rohan and Eric could see that he was blushing.

"What the hell was that about?" Rohan asked. "What did you give her?"

"A card," Mahmoud said, smiling sheepishly. "It was her birthday today. I saw on Facebook."

"You cheeky little shit! What did you say in the card?" Eric was curious.

"It's private," Mahmoud said, but in the face of repeated coaxing and driven by his own desire to share his act of daring, he quickly revealed all. He had written a lengthy message about how much he admired Cynthia's courage and strong personality and how much she longed to see her each day at school. He cherished her friendship and her ideas and was very keen to know more about her. He would consider it a great privilege, he had said, if she could go to the movie with him the following Friday and to a place of her choice for a meal afterwards. In anticipation of a speedy reply, he had also inscribed his mobile number at the bottom of his long, romantic message.

"You forgot to mention the tits," Eric said. "But nice message. Very romantic."

"Hope you spelled everything right," Rohan said. Mahmoud nodded. He had first typed everything and spell-checked it and then copied it on to the card.

"Wow!" Eric said, shaking his head in amazement. "That is so fucking sweet! You are

really in love with her, aren't ya?"

Mahmoud nodded, glowing.

"I think you are very brave," was Rohan's candid observation. "Going against your father's wishes, risking your life."

At the mention of Ahmed, Mahmoud stopped glowing, but as the appreciation of his bravery began to sink in, the glow returned, with renewed vigour.

"I wonder if I should slip something in the Bogans' letterbox," Eric muttered, almost to himself. His friends looked at him in disbelief.

"Still thinking of her?" Mahmoud asked, now quite perky, lips curving into a smirk. Eric grinned. Rohan laughed.

"Don't be silly!" He snapped. "We don't even know if she can read!"

Eric reddened.

Cynthia's response came within ten minutes. The boys were nearing home when Mahmoud's phone chimed, signalling the reception of a message. Mahmoud had been holding it in his hand all the way from McDonald's, in anticipation of the message.

Mahmoud looked at the message. As he read it, the glow on his face disappeared, gradually giving way to a dark cloud.

"What does she say?"

Eric asked, impatient.

Mahmoud showed them the message.

"Dear Mahmoud," Cynthia wrote. "It was sweet of you to have given me the card with your beautiful message. As much as I admire your forthrightness in approaching me in this fashion, I regret to inform you that I am unable to comply with your request. I fear that our values, ideas, and cultures are not mutually compatible and that I will never be the humble, compliant partner you crave. I wish you luck with your future endeavours."

Rohan and Eric looked askance at each other and then at Mahmoud.

"Who the fuck writes like this?" Eric asked.

"Cynthia does," Mahmoud said.

"Sounds like some fuckin' job rejection," Rohan said. Eric agreed.

"Any idea what she is tryin' to say?" Mahmoud wanted to know.

"I think she is trying to say that you guys don't match," Eric said.

"I get that," Mahmoud said, frowning. "Kinda. But what is that shit about culture?"

"Um..., I think she is trying to say that your views are different because your culture is different..."

"Cuz I am Muslim??" Mahmoud asked, the glow returning to his face, but for a different reason.

"Yup," Eric said, agreeing with Rohan. "Muslim and Lebanese, I guess."

Mahmoud was indignant. "What the fuck!" He cried. "I am not the Muslim she thinks I am! You know that!"

"Well, yes," Rohan agreed. "But *she* doesn't know that."

"Those idiots in the chat groups even think I am a Jew pretending to be Muslim!" Mahmoud continued his lament. "And she thinks I am Muslim! What the fuck!"

Rohan patted Mahmoud on the shoulder.

"Everybody wants me to be Muslim. I can't be the Muslim they want me to be!" Mahmoud continued muttering. He kept shaking his head in disbelief.

"Best to be yourself," Rohan advised like a seasoned counsellor. "Look at me. I want to be an electrician and no one is gonna stop me from that."

"Or be like my mums," Eric advised. "I don't mean you should be gay or anything like that. But you know what I mean."

But by now, Mahmoud was not hearing what his friends were saying. His mind seemed to be somewhere else as he continued to shake his head and mutter softly to himself.

***

When they reached home, they were met with chaos. A small knot of people was seen gathered close to Ahmed's house which, they quickly realised, consisted of Ahmed, Amina, Hala, and Kumar and Indu. Opposite to them, outside the Bogan home, were arrayed the entire Bogan clan, except the infant Bogan who was probably asleep in the house. Kumar, Indu, and Amina were desperately trying to restrain Ahmed who was letting forth a tirade in choice Arabic at the Bogans who seem to be paying them back in the same coin, except in English. Looking around they also saw Chelliah peering at the commotion from the safety of his garden. Vivienne, Lauren, and the Rabulas were nowhere to be seen, but it was very likely that they were watching.

"What's going on?" Mahmoud asked. Ahmed shook his fist at the Bogans and fired another burst of Arabic before responding to his son.

"Bastards who don't even own their house telling me to get out of their country!" He hissed. "And not even the big ones. The little rascal telling me go back to my country!" He shook his fist again across the road drawing a round of jeering from the opposition.

Ahmed would have spent another few minutes on his verbal assaults had Amina not reminded him that he had to start work soon. That sobered him up quickly, and he immediately got into the van and drove off, but not before he shook his fist again at the Bogans whose ranks seemed to be bristling with middle fingers.

When Ahmed had gone, and the Bogans too had drifted back into their house, Amina explained what had happened.

That day, a Saturday, BB2 had been skateboarding since lunch-time. Ahmed had been cleaning his van outside, and the boy had been going up and down, skateboard clattering and making Ahmed wait for him to go past each time he wanted to go inside the house or come out to the street to his van. Eventually, Ahmed had snapped and confronted the boy.

"Why you do this?" He had asked, standing on the sidewalk, arms spread out in sheer exasperation. He was about to go to work, and BB2 had just come teetering down the sidewalk on his skateboard, missing him by inches. He stopped just in time and looked at Ahmed as if he had been asked a rude question.

"Do what?" He asked, one foot on the skateboard and the other on the pavement.

"Going up and down like this. Like a lunatic."

BB2 had stared at him as if he couldn't believe what he was hearing. Then he spoke.

"This is not your fuckin' sidewalk," he had hissed. "You don't like it, go somewhere else."

"This is my house you bastard!" Ahmed had growled, shaking his fist at the boy. "You don't tell me where to go!"

BB2 was undaunted. "*This is my country* you fuckin' Arab!" he had yelled. "You go back to yours!"

Stung by the insult, Ahmed stood staring at the boy. Then he vented his outrage in choice Arabic, making as if to pounce on the boy at the same time. Lacking the courage to stand his ground in the face of Ahmed's verbal assault and what appeared to be the preparations for a physical attack, BB2 made a tactical retreat letting loose a hail of expletives of his own. The shouting brought the other Bogans out of their house, and BB2 was quickly provided with a safe haven in their midst. Then, the whole Bogan family advanced towards Ahmed, who quickly realised that he had bitten off more than he could chew. Mercifully, Amina, Kumar, and Indu had come out and formed a protective circle around Ahmed who, emboldened by this support, had increased the volume of his abuse while being careful not to venture out of the safety of his wife and neighbours. That was when the boys came home.

They all went inside their respective homes. When it was clear that Ahmed was not likely to return in a hurry BB2 returned to the sidewalk with his skateboard. While the rest of the Bogans kept a watchful eye on him from the front of their house, he skateboarded well into the night to the sound of their thunderous music.

Then, things really began to spiral out of control.

SEVENTEEN

The first sign that things were spiralling out of control was the appearance of the swastika. The morning after Ahmed's confrontation with BB2, Rohan received a text from Eric: "Big-ass swat-sticka outside Mamood's house!" Rohan promptly went to see and found that Eric was right. There was a big swastika drawn on the sidewalk right in front of Ahmed's driveway. The words 'Muzzies fuk off!' were also written underneath that. He quickly returned home and reported to Kumar and Indu. Someone had certainly drawn a big swastika in front of Ahmed's house and written in big letters, 'Muzzies fuk off!'

"How do you know it is a swastika?" Kumar asked as he came out of the house to see for himself. He was surprised that Rohan knew what a swastika was because he never thought the boy knew anything other than the names of cars and basketball players. Rohan said he had seen his classmate Naushad drawing it on the books of a boy named Retinger and he had asked Naushad what it was. Naushad had said it was a swastika and that Jews didn't like it.

"And is this Retinger Jewish?" Kumar asked. Rohan laughed. "No," he said. "But Naushad is a dickhead, and everybody knows it."

Kumar winced at his son's expletive but said nothing. He was too keen to find out what Rohan was talking about. To be sure they found Ahmed standing outside his house staring at something drawn on the sidewalk. Mahmoud stood beside him, his shoulders hunched, his hands in the pockets of his shorts, his face scrunched. Ahmed saw them and grinned painfully.

"Some dumbass has drawn a swastika here," he said. "And it is all wrong."

Kumar looked at the drawing. Yes, someone had drawn a swastika and written 'Muzzies fuk off!' He could also see what Ahmed meant. The swastika was drawn facing the wrong direction.

"What's wrong with that?" Rohan asked. Kumar explained.

"That is exactly how Naushad was drawing them too," Rohan said. "Maybe Naushad came here and did it," he suggested.

"Don't be stupid," Kumar said. "Why on earth would Naushad want to do that? And why would he want to write 'Muzzies fuck off' when he is a Muslim himself?"

Rohan laughed again. "You don't know Naushad," he said. "He is a dickhead!"

But Ahmed was not laughing. He simply told Rohan not to swear in front of him, and Rohan grinned and nodded. Kumar too frowned at his son, then patted Ahmed's shoulder to console him.

"I don't give no shit about the swastika," Ahmed said. "I am no fucking Jew. It's graffiti I am worried about." Kumar patted him on the shoulder again.

"I am so sorry this has happened, Ahmed," he said. "I hope the bastard who did this gets what he deserves."

"I know the bastards who done it," Ahmed muttered, as if speaking to himself. "What I don't know is which Bogan bastard done it."

Seeing them all gathered there, Eric also joined them. The previous night had been windy, and a small branch had fallen across their wall and Vivienne, ever conscious of the state of her garden, had sent Eric out to remove it. It was then he saw the drawing, he said. As soon as he saw the swastika he had gone inside to text Rohan, attending to the branch only after that.

"Maybe if you tell the police they will come and check," he advised Ahmed.

"Now, how are they gonna do that?" Ahmed wanted to know.

"Maybe they will ask each Bogan to draw a swat sticka on the sidewalk," Eric suggested. "And they will see whose swat sticka is the nearest to the first one that was drawn."

Ahmed shook his head, clucked his tongue, and said no, that is not going to work. "Police are fucking pathetic," he said. "They will come and take a picture and take notes and go away and nothing will happen." Besides, he didn't want his sidewalk littered with more swastikas and graffiti because the cops want to check who has drawn the swastika. "I don't want no fucking cops dealing with this," he grunted. "I will do it myself."

"Fuckin' awesome!" Eric said, obviously relishing the possibility of a confrontation between Ahmed and the Bogans, especially after the disappointment over Mark and Angela. Ahmed frowned.

"Yes," he said. "It will be when I am done with them." He then glared at Eric. "And no need to fuckin' swear!" He reminded Eric too. "Sorry Mr. Ahmed". Eric apologised, a cheeky grin on his face. "My bad."

Kumar too gave Eric a glare, in order to remind him of his manners but he was more worried about what Ahmed might do. He feared that his furious neighbour might not beat a hasty retreat as Mark and Angela had done. He noticed that Mahmoud was not looking very happy either. The boy kept staring at the swastika and the graffiti. His face lacked any expression, but he seemed to be deep in thought. Maybe both father and son together might decide to take on the Bogans, Kumar thought, with consequences nobody could foresee.

"I will help you scrub it off," Kumar offered, but Ahmed was happy to do it himself.

"Thank you, but I can manage," he said, casting ominous glances in the direction of the Bogan house.

By mid-morning, the word had spread that the Bogans had drawn a swastika and scrawled graffiti all over the sidewalk in front of Ahmed's house. Vivienne and Lauren came out of their house, walked hand in hand up to the graffiti, and then asked Ahmed who had just appeared with Mahmoud, carrying a bucket of water and a scrubbing brush, if it was an Islamic sign. The question only made Ahmed nearly explode with indignation. He controlled himself, however, and began to scrub the sidewalk, ignoring the two. The Rabulas came by, gazed at Ahmed scrubbing the graffiti, clucked their tongues and went away, while Chelliah came and stood quite still and waited till Ahmed finished scrubbing, offering advice, but not doing much else to help. He moved away only when Ahmed reminded him that he needed no advice with cleaning as he was a professional cleaner. Chelliah simply crossed the road and went into Kumar's house and told Kumar that he had no idea Ahmed had a Jewish background.

Eric and Rohan joined Ahmed and Mahmoud outside their house and helped their friend to clean the graffiti. They did it in complete silence. Their initial chatter had gradually disappeared, largely because they realised Mahmoud was utterly subdued and dejected. His mood had become darker than the day before when he received Cynthia's rejection message. Fortunately, no Bogans came out while Ahmed was scrubbing the graffiti. Kumar was worried that they might come out while Ahmed was outside scrubbing, but strangely, they remained indoors.

"Must be tired from all the graffiti work," Rohan said when he finally returned after finishing the cleanup. The idea cheered his father considerably. If the Bogans had come out while Ahmed was out with his brush and bucket, Kumar thought, anything could have happened.

Ahmed did confront the Bogans but in a way far worse than Kumar had feared. For the rest of the morning, he stood outside the house or prowled around his front garden waiting for a Bogan to appear. There was not a sign of any Bogans for several hours and then finally in the afternoon, the Little Bogan, for some unfathomable reason, decided to try his brother's skateboard outside Ahmed's house. Either he was not aware of what his family had done to Ahmed's sidewalk, maybe he just didn't care. He simply sauntered down the sidewalk with the skateboard, which was half his size, and started skateboarding.

Ahmed, who was skulking in his front yard, heard the noise and pricked up his ears. He quickly came out on to the footpath just in time to see the Little Bogan hurtling towards him on his skateboard. Seeing him riding his skateboard so nonchalantly over the sidewalk, that had been so recently vandalised by his family, Ahmed's rage mounted. He grabbed the boy by the collar, pulled him off the skateboard and began shaking him, much to the boy's terror. He shook the Little Bogan like a rag doll and pushed him to the nature strip before sending him off with a message which amounted to a declaration of war.

"Tell your fucking parents," he said, "Ahmed staying here and not moving."

That evening the music started early and was the loudest it had ever been. In between songs, one could also hear loud swearing. Everybody expected the Bogans to make a mass invasion of Ahmed's home, but, apart from the swearing and the louder than usual music, the Bogans did not retaliate.

"Maybe they are more restrained than we thought," Kumar said to Indu.

Rohan disagreed. "I think they are planning something," he said. "I don't think they will leave it at that."

Rohan was right. The following morning there was another swastika, bigger than the previous one, drawn not on the sidewalk but on the street in front of Ahmed's house. It was still facing the wrong way, but now everybody knew for certain who was doing it. It was not Naushad.

Everybody waited breathlessly for Ahmed's explosion, but it didn not come. According to Rohan, he had simply walked out of the house, looked at the swastika, and gone inside muttering to himself. Soon, he returned with the bucket and brush and began scrubbing the graffiti, still mumbling. Mahmoud was nowhere to be seen. Rohan had tried to get Mahmoud on the phone, but he was not responding, and when Rohan went to see him, Amina told him that Mahmoud was in his room and didn't want to be disturbed. Eric had met with the same response.

"Mahmoud is in 'shut down' mode," he reported. "Hope it is only temporary."

"It's the rejection from Cynthia," Rohan said. "He can't take it."

Eric was not too sure. "Don't forget the swat sticka," he reminded. "I think that is what did it."

Rohan was adamant that it was the rejection letter from Cynthia that sent Mahmoud into depression. "Remember," he said, "he nearly burnt down their kitchen for her and went against his father's death threat."

Eric laughed at the mentioning of Mahmoud's cooking fiasco. "I had almost forgotten about that," he said. "He shudda told her. Maybe even sent a piece of the burnt chicken."

They both laughed. But they both also knew it was not funny.

When Rohan told Kumar about Cynthia's response to Ahmed, Kumar felt sorry for the boy. "Poor kid must be devastated," he said. He put Mahmoud's depression down to both Cynthia's rejection and the

Bogan's graffiti attack. "He must be thinking his religion is the issue."

But Indu was quick to take Cynthia's side. "She must be worried," she said. "With all the news about terrorism and bombs and suicide attacks. Sometimes I am also worried. You never know with them."

"But we know Mahmoud is not like that," Rohan reminded her. Indu agreed. But does Cynthia know him? She asked.

Rohan now revealed Mahmoud's cooking debacle to his parents. Kumar and Indu found it very amusing but also sweet. However, Indu also thought that it added weight to her argument. "See!" She said. "Now, does that girl know about how foolish he has been for her?"

"I think it is called prejudice," Rohan said.

"What is?"

"Judging someone without knowing that person. That is what my English teacher said."

"Pity you can't pay attention to everything she says," Kumar quipped. "Your English marks could have improved so much!"

Rohan grinned. "However," he pointed out, swiftly bringing the conversation back to the original topic, "we are not entirely sure why Cynthia rejected Mahmoud. We think it had something to do with his culture and background, but because of the weird way in which she writes and talks, it is difficult to know exactly what she is on about."

Then it was for the best, both Kumar and Indu said. Nothing worse than a partner who talked nonsense.

By evening, however, the situation was getting more serious. Around five o'clock, Vivienne and Lauren dropped by to tell Kumar that they were hearing disturbing noises from Ahmed's house.

"He is swearing loudly and is saying 'Allah' all the time," Vivienne said, shaking her head. "This is not good, not good at all."

Kumar explained to Vivienne that Muslims say 'Allah' frequently because that means God in Arabic. "There is nothing to feel alarmed about," he assured.

Rohan agreed. "Whenever Rhonda who has a big backside and sits in front of Naushad in class, leans over to speak to her friend Marika," he said, "Naushad starts panting and whispering 'Allah, Allah,' but I don't think he means the girl any harm."

Vivienne, however, was determined to be alarmed and looked at Rohan as if to ask since when he became an expert on Islam? Lauren grabbed her partner's hand as if the frequent mention of Allah was making her dizzy. The two of them did not leave until they were satisfied that they had communicated the full extent of their concerns to Indu and Kumar.

"I am also beginning to get a bit worried now," Indu said after Vivienne and Lauren had left. "Ahmed has always been a bit aggressive."

Kumar tried hard to reassure her. There was nothing to worry about. Ahmed was simply trying to vent his anger. "Wouldn't you be angry if someone drew a swastika in front of our driveway and wrote abusive things?"

Indu thought for a few seconds and said she found it hard to imagine a swastika in front of their house. Rohan offered to help her by drawing one outside the driveway. "Then you will know how you feel," he said with a smirk.

"Don't be silly!" Indu snapped at her son. "This is not funny!"

***

Indu continued to worry. But her worry was nowhere near Vivienne's and Lauren's. Although things quietened down after that, they remained on edge. Vivienne also brought further information about some of the things Ahmed has promised to do to the Bogans.

"Not very nice," she said. "All cutting and burning. It makes me wonder if what they say about them is true."

"What is true about who?" Kumar asked.

"That they - Muslims - are violent people," Vivienne said.

"You mean like terrorists?" Rohan asked. Vivienne frowned.

"I did not say that," she snapped and then reminded Kumar that children should not butt into adults' conversations.

Kumar told Rohan to go away and play with the computer, and the boy went away and started playing with his phone while his father advised Vivienne to calm down.

"It is just Ahmed being angry," he said. "I am sure if we can hear what the Bogans are saying we will hear some very disturbing things too."

Vivienne said this was exactly the point. The Bogans were now sitting around in the park next door and saying all kinds of horrible things they would like to do to Ahmed and his family.

"They think we also with Ahmed." she said. "They say we all treat them like shit and the Arab and the Lesos think they own this place.

Sometimes they talking about doing horrible things to us and Ahmed together. And this all Ahmed's and Mamood's fault," she added. "It is Mamood only flying plane at little Bogan and Ahmed only starting fight with Bogan. And anyway Ahmed never liking me and my Lauren. Even Eric he not like."

Kumar winced as he realised the growing complexity of the problem. He felt sorry for Vivienne and Lauren, but Vivienne's reasoning left him bewildered. He could not imagine what Ahmed was going through. All he knew with any certainty was that he didn't want to be in the shoes of any one of them.

But contrary to Vivienne's apprehensions, Ahmed did not do anything violent. The response, when it came, was bizarre indeed. A couple of days after Vivienne's frantic visit, Kumar was leaving his house on his way to work in the morning when he saw something fluttering from Ahmed's rooftop. Looking closely, he realised that it was a flag. A Pakistani flag.

Intrigued, he quickly crossed the road and went to Ahmed's house and rang the bell. Ahmed opened the door, bleary-eyed after late-night work.

"What is going on?" Kumar asked. "Why is a Pakistani flag flying from your rooftop?"

Ahmed stared at Kumar as if he was not sure if he had heard it right.

"Pakistani flag? From my rooftop?"

Kumar nodded. "Yes," he said. "Pakistani flag. From your rooftop."

Ahmed came outside and looked up. He saw the flag and seemed even more surprised than Kumar. "What the fuck?" He spat. "Who fly Pakistani flag from my rooftop?"

Kumar looked at Ahmed as if to say that Ahmed was the best person to find out.

Ahmed shook his head. "I am sure it's that bloody Mahmoud. Ever since that swastika he not himself." He promised Kumar he would find out. Mahmoud was still asleep having stayed up late helping Ahmed with his night work. Kumar nodded. If it was Mahmoud who raised the flag, the boy must have been working very late indeed.

Later that evening Kumar found out that it was, after all, Mahmoud who had done it. Ahmed and the boy were at work, but Rohan filled him in with everything. He had managed to get through to Mahmoud during a rare break in the boy's wall of silence.

"Mahmoud's gone nuts," Rohan said. "He wants to show the Bogans that they are proud to be Muslim."

"But why the Pakistani flag?" Kumar was curious.

Rohan laughed. "Mahmoud couldn't find any other flag with the Islamic moon and star thingy," he said. "So he just used a Pakistani flag he borrowed from someone."

"Why on earth would that boy want to do that?" Indu asked, bewildered. "Amina told me he never went to the mosque!"

"I think the boy has gone crazy," Kumar surmised. Rohan thought otherwise. "I think he has decided to become Muslim after all," he said.

"But this is not a good way to become Muslim," Indu said. "Father is threatening Bogans and son is flying foreign flags. Not a good sign at all."

"What else did Mahmoud say?" Kumar wanted to know.

"Nothing much," Rohan said. "He said he had been thinking a lot. I asked about what but he didn't say anything. Just hung up."

Kumar was worried; the situation seemed to be truly getting out of hand. The following morning he spoke to David again, and David said very gravely that it sounded very bad. An alarming escalation in tension, he said, gently chewing the stem of his pipe. Alarming indeed. As for Mahmoud raising the Pakistani flag, he had only one word: radicalisation. Clearly, the boy has become radicalised, he said. He needed to be watched closely. He took a puff from his pipe and then shook his head.

"This is the problem with these Muslims," said David, betraying a rare flash of irritation. "They take their fucking religion way too seriously, and it is so easy to get them radicalised, even the nice ones. Now take that fellow Ayub in the Planning Department. Very nice man, a very good planner too, but before he joined they had a lot of fun in that department. People were free to say anything, crack any joke, and everybody laughed. The Chinese laughed the loudest at the Chinese jokes. But once when someone asked Ayub if there is any halal pork he got very upset and sulked for a whole day. Ever since then everybody has been very careful not to say anything to offend Ayub. I am sure this Ahmed and his son are also a bit like that; very serious-minded and can't take a joke."

But drawing a swastika on the side walk and writing "Muzzies fuck off!" is not a nice joke, Kumar pointed out in the humblest of tones. But

David simply folded his arms across his chest, cocked his head and asked whether Kumar considered that a reason for a boy to be radicalised. Confronted with such profound reasoning, Kumar could only retreat into a timid smile that David accepted with a gentle nod. Then he took another puff from his pipe.

"Have you had a look at that Real Estate Agency yet??" He asked.

"No, not yet," said Kumar, smiling sheepishly. "But I will do that soon."

David shook his head in disappointment. "Don't put it off," He advised. "Check Perfect Homes. And watch that boy."

"Is anyone watching Ayub?" Kumar was keen to know.

"Anyone?" David asked, rolling his eyes. "The whole Planning Department is watching Ayub!"

When Kumar told Indu about David's admonition, she was not impressed. "How does he expect us to watch Mahmoud?" She asked. "Spy on him with binoculars or follow him around?"

"Maybe we shouldn't take what David said literally," Kumar said. Maybe what he said was to keep an eye on the boy, see if he is acting strangely."

"How are we going to do that from here?" asked Indu.

Kumar looked pointedly at Rohan who was sitting close by and listening to their conversation, alternating between checking his phone and looking up at them. Seeing the expression on his father's face, Rohan flatly refused to have anything to do with it.

"Mahmoud is my mate," he said. "I don't spy on mates. Besides," he added, "it would be hard to spy on him as he is keeping to himself. Even at school, he is not mixing with anybody now, just checking his phone or staring blankly at something which nobody else can see. And by the way, he hasn't been to school much since the swastika incident."

"Have you tried contacting him at home?" Kumar asked.

"Yes," said Rohan. He and Eric had both been trying to contact him on his mobile but had received no answer.

"What is he checking on the phone?" Indu wanted to know.

"I don't know!" Retorted Rohan, his voice rising. "And I am not going to try finding out. Mahmoud is my mate."

Eric later confirmed what Rohan said. Mahmoud was acting strange. Yes, he was not responding to his calls either, and no, he too had absolutely no intention of finding out what he was checking as Mahmoud was his mate too. But he had his own problems.

"My mums are also acting strange," he said to Rohan when he came to play Xbox with him.

"Ever since Mahmoud's dad went bonkers, they too seemed to have gone bonkers, talking about doing all kinds of horrible things to Ahmed." He wondered if they too had become radicalised.

Indu laughed. "Don't be silly, Eric," she said. "Whoever heard of people like your mum and Lauren throwing bombs or shooting people?"

That didn't seem to ease Eric's mind. He had no concerns about his mums throwing bombs or shooting people, he said. But he had never seen them like this, and it was worrying him.

One person who was greatly disappointed by Mahmoud's

withdrawal was Jimmy. He was missing his math tutor. A few other people tried to teach him, but Mahmoud's teaching methods had made such permanent inroads into Jimmy's psyche that it was difficult to free him from the fixation. He felt helpless. It was so unfair, he was heard to complain, that Mahmoud makes him his student and then abandons him. Rohan tried to tell him gently that Mahmoud seemed to have abandoned everybody, not just Jimmy. But Jimmy was only concerned about his abandonment by Mahmoud. Nobody cares about us, he kept saying. Nobody wants to help us.

Cynthia seemed oblivious to Mahmoud's depression. At first, she had seemed somewhat curious as to why he was skipping school so often, but she soon lost interest. Rohan overheard her saying something about fragile male egos to someone which Rohan guessed was probably her verdict on Mahmoud. She was more focused on her new feminist school magazine called 'Femination' which she was hoping to launch in the New Year. The rumour was that she was the editor as well as the sole contributor. At first, a large number of girls had been willing to contribute, eager to let their voices be heard, as Cynthia had promised. But when they realised that Cynthia had her own ideas about what they should say in their voices, they lost interest, leaving Cynthia to carry on alone, which she did with gusto.

Things continued to deteriorate. A few days after Mahmoud had raised the Pakistani flag, Amina came to see Indu. She was sobbing. Kumar thought at first the Bogans had stuck again. He was wrong.

"It's not Bogans," she said, sniffling. "They are bad, yes, but it's those two."

"Those two who?" Indu wanted to know.

"The two Chinese women next door," Amina said. "They say nasty things about Ahmed because after Ahmed start fighting with Bogans their life become hell."

"What do they say?" Kumar asked.

"They saying horrible things," Amina said. "Oh, yes! How people causing unnecessary problems by being violent and aggressive. The little one even ask me why I not stay in Sydney, and why we always have to fight. And the big one say why we not go back to where we come from," she whined. "I not tell Ahmed half the things they say. If he know he will get very angry, and I not know what he do."

"Maybe I should speak to all of them," Kumar said to Indu after Amina left.

Indu rolled her eyes. "What do you think you can do?" She asked Kumar. "And who do you think you are? Obama?" She frowned. "Forget talking to these maniacs. Maybe we should now seriously consider looking at new houses."

Rohan butted into their conversation to say that he was not really keen on moving as he didn't want to leave his mates. But he'd already looked a bit on the Internet, and he had found that if you were willing to move away from Melbourne, you could get really big houses, some even with swimming pools. But then, he said, the farther you went, the greater were the chances of meeting more Bogans. Indu thought awhile.

"Maybe," she said at last. "The Bogans aren't so bad after all, considering what these other people are doing."

The situation continued for a week or two with no change. Mr. Chelliah was also now weighing in on the side of Vivienne and Lauren. It seemed that dissatisfied with Kumar's moderate views on the issue, the two of them had gone to see Mr. Chelliah and the Rabulas. Chelliah was only too happy to oblige.

"The Bogans are bad, yes I know," he said to Kumar one evening, gazing at the Pakistani flag fluttering from Ahmed's rooftop, drinking his second cup of sweet tea. "But this guy sounds positively dangerous." He had seen and heard enough, he said. From the day they came, he has had his suspicions. That man was always loud and obnoxious, he said. But lately, he has become even louder. He too had faintly heard something like the cry of 'Allah' a couple of times when he went out to put out the garbage. And now they had raised a flag, and the Pakistani flag to boot.

"It gets my blood boiling as an Indian each time I see it," he said. "If I had the agility and the strength I would have climbed the roof and pulled it down myself. It is a pity there is no one man enough to do that around here," he said, looking pointedly at Eric and Rohan. Rohan simply said he lacked the agility, the strength or the desire to do something as dangerous as that. Eric, who was visiting Rohan, said he had previous experience climbing roofs because it was he who had raised the Australian flag over their house in response to the Bogan's flag-raising at his mum's request. But on that occasion, he was climbing his own roof. Climbing somebody else's roof could be something altogether different, especially if Ahmed was in such a foul mood.

The Rabulas received Vivienne and Lauren with caution. There had been minimal contact between them since the Christmas party, and their relationship had been one of glaring (on the part of the Rabulas) and ignoring (Vivienne and Lauren). Indeed the first reaction of the Rabulas when Vivienne and Lauren turned up was to glare at them, and the first impulse of Vivienne and Lauren was to turn around and walk away. But their desire to seek allies in the struggle against Ahmed was stronger than their urge to spite the Rabulas, so Vivienne and Lauren bore the glares with grins and revealed the reason for their visit. At first, the Rabulas made a pretence of listening to their tale of woe with indifference. But it so happened that Ahmed's outpouring of rage had also travelled over the fence to them, and they also were alarmed by it. It didn't take much for the Rabulas, therefore, to join hands with their former enemy.

"In the interest of the peace in this neighbourhood we shall forgive and forget that act of impudence on Christmas night," Mr. Rabula said to the accompaniment of spirited nodding from his wife. "Your concern is our concern because we are all residents of this neighbourhood, and like you, we too share a fence with the man in question. We shall fight this gathering evil together and defeat it," he declared.

Vivienne understood little of Mr. Rabula's grand pronouncements, but she felt that she and Lauren had won the Rabulas over to their side, especially when Mrs. Rabula offered them tea and biscuits. Mr. Rabula shook their hands, and Mrs. Rabula even gave them each a light, cautious, peck on the cheek in parting. Vivienne badly wanted to say that she was also willing to forgive and forget but her instincts told her that having taken one step forward in her struggle, it would be unwise to take two steps back.

They all came together to see Kumar and Indu to canvass their support for some joint action to defend the neighbourhood from what Mr. Rabula called 'rising Islamic extremism.' Over tea, coffee, biscuits, and cake, they denounced Ahmed, one after another and sometimes, all together.

"I know not what you think," Vivienne said, "but I think this Ahmed is up to something."

Very gravely, Chelliah nodded his assent. "I believe so too," he said, reminding Kumar that he had warned about Ahmed as soon as he arrived. Ahmed was a typical Lebanese, he said, rude, loud and aggressive. But he was more worried about Mahmoud.

"The boy is definitely showing signs of radicalisation," he said. "We must stop the fool before he does something more than raising somebody else's flag on top of their roof."

Mr. Rabula agreed. He was by no means a racist, but there was something about Muslims that made him feel uneasy. "You can take the Muslim out of the Middle East, but you can't take the Quran out of the Muslim," he said with the air of a man who had just made a profound revelation.

"And at least Bogans are Aussie," Vivienne chirped. Lauren nodded.

"This is Aboriginal land," Rohan butted in from his seat near the dining table, and Mr. Rabula shook his head in exasperation.

"Young man, don't you have school work to do?"

"Holidays," Rohan said and went on playing with his phone. Mr. Rabula frowned and looked at Kumar for some support but seeing Kumar's face marred by a bigger frown, sighed and gave up.

But it was not enough that they came to see Kumar. They wanted Kumar and Indu also to join them in doing something about Ahmed. Kumar was somewhat taken aback by the extent of his neighbours' alarm. He was not sure if it was necessary for him to share their sense of outrage, to the same extent. When Kumar appeared indecisive, they looked disappointed.

"Maybe you are also with him," Vivienne said, pouting. Lauren nodded her total agreement. "Maybe you also take his side," Vivienne added in a petulant tone and Lauren nodded again, more vigorously this time. The Rabulas and Mr. Chelliah said nothing, but they had disappointment written all over their faces.

"I think we should persuade this Mr. Ahmed to leave this neighbourhood for the sake of peace," Chelliah proposed after an awkward pause. Kumar was not sure if that was the solution. He wanted to say that he was himself thinking of leaving the neighbourhood for the sake of his own peace, but he did not. He wanted to keep it a secret until everything was settled.

"I will speak to Ahmed and see what I can do," he said, rather like a politician trying to appease his restless constituents. His offer calmed the group but only for a moment.

"When?" Vivienne wanted to know. "And what are you going to say to him?"

Mrs. Rabula was curious, too. Kumar parried the questions with a vague, "Let me think about it," which didn't seem to satisfy anybody. But they agreed to give his powers of persuasion a chance. "Our hopes rest on your shoulders," Mr. Rabula said as he left and Vivienne and Lauren looked at Kumar's puny shoulders without much confidence.

But before Kumar could speak to Ahmed, the Bogans struck again. One night a brick was thrown in through the front window of Ahmed's house, very nearly hitting Amina. Glass scattered all over the carpet, causing a serious safety hazard. Ahmed came outside and poured out his wrath, again in choice Arabic, which was lost on everybody, including his family, due to the loud music from the Bogan house. Then, Ahmed called the police.

The police came and spoke to Ahmed. Everybody went to Ahmed's house, forming a small crowd around him. Ahmed stood on the street, shaking his fist at the Bogan house, continuing to pour his venom out in Arabic. Amina came out and tried unsuccessfully to move him indoors. Strangely, Mahmoud was nowhere to be seen. When Kumar looked up, he saw the silhouette of the boy standing near the window in his room, staring at the Bogan house with his hands folded across his chest.

The police tried to calm down Ahmed, but they soon realised it was impossible without stopping the Bogan music. One of the cops went to the Bogan house and ordered them to stop the music. The Bogans turned down the music and then they all came outside. Seeing them, Ahmed attempted to charge them. The police restrained him, but they couldn't stop him from continuing his tirade.

"Will you shut up!" One of the policemen said, at length. "And tell us what is going on!"

That was a useless request as both Ahmed and Father Bogan started talking at once. So the request had to be modified to 'one at a time,' which also had little effect for both Ahmed and Father Bogan assumed that they had the first go. An officer had to introduce a further refinement to the request by pointing to Ahmed, who seemed the most agitated, and saying, "you first!"

Ahmed resumed his tirade, but this time in English. Gesticulating wildly, and shaking his fist frequently at the Bogans, he went on to explain how he was getting ready to go to work, and Amina was watching TV when a large brick came flying through the front window and landed only inches from Amina.

"A few more inches and my wife getting hurt," he said. "And if my wife getting hurt you getting hurt," he said, shaking both his fists at the Bogans.

The Bogans hit back without any reservation.

"We did nothing ya crazy Arab cunt!" Father Bogan shouted back. "You think we have nothing better to do than throw bricks at ya fuckin' window?" BB1 yelled. The Mother Bogan also said something, but it was completely lost in the cacophony of the Father Bogan, BB1 and BB2 all shouting at once.

"Then you think brick falling from sky?" Ahmed sneered.

"Maybe it fell from your ass!" BB2 yelled back. "We couldn't fuckin' care where it fell from, nobody here never threw nothing!" Father Bogan reiterated.

Vivienne joined the fray. "It's they you should be worried about," She said to a young policeman, hooking her thumb in the direction of Ahmed. "They provoking them, all the time."

Lauren nodded, joined by Chelliah.

"I never provoked nobody!" Ahmed screamed. "They are crazy! Fucking crazy lesbians! It's the fucking Bogans doing all this, playin' loud music, drawing swastikas and now throwing bricks! It's them! It's them!"

The Bogans had had enough. "Stay away from us you Arab cunt!" Father Bogan warned before he led the Bogan clan back into the house. "Or we'll rip ya nuts off!"

Ahmed again made as if to charge the whole Bogan family but was held back by a cop.

EIGHTEEN

Everything gradually fizzled out. The police left, after warning both parties. This was not to the liking of Ahmed who thought he had nothing to be warned about. The Bogans spent much of the night playing their music, and Father Bogan was heard to swear loudly in between songs.

It was a couple of days later that the truth about the brick was revealed. Eric was playing some video games with Rohan one evening and, pumped up after winning a few, confided in Rohan that it was actually he who had done it, at the instigation of his two mums.

"That's a shit thing to do to a friend," Rohan said.

"Yes, and no," said Eric. "It was a shit thing to throw a brick through my friend's window, yes, but if I had not done it, my mum would have done it anyway, and if she had done it, she would have definitely hit Mahmoud's mother."

Rohan wasn't convinced by Eric's logic. "You tell that to Mahmoud!" He shot back. Eric, increasingly remorseful, begged Rohan not to tell anyone, least of all Mahmoud. Rohan promised but added that he wasn't sure if Mahmoud didn't already know. He was seen looking out of the bedroom window during the commotion on the street, and it was possible that he saw Eric sneaking in and out of the garden. Eric seemed to shudder at the thought but said nothing.

Rohan's promise to Eric was short-lived. He broke it by telling his parents at the first opportunity.

"What on earth is happening to this neighbourhood?" Indu asked in horror. Kumar shook his head in disappointment. "Start checking real estate agencies on the Internet," he advised her. I think we have to move. Fast."

He wondered if he should speak to Vivienne, but that would mean betraying Eric and Rohan. Perhaps he should speak to Ahmed, he thought, and tell him that he had very reliable information that the brick was thrown by someone other than the Bogans. But he decided against that too, realising that Ahmed would quickly put two and two together and immediately work out who the brick-thrower was. Given the state Ahmed was in, his behaviour was very unpredictable.

Kumar spoke to David again.

"I would appreciate your advice on a personal problem I have, David," he said. "What should I do if I knew that someone I know has done something bad to someone else I know, if the information had been revealed to me in confidence, but I still thought the identity of the culprit needed to be revealed?"

David looked at him in confusion and said it would be a lot easier if Kumar could break the story down into smaller sentences. Then he would be able to make himself understood. A problem with people whose first language is not English, David said, is that they try to say too many things all at once without any consideration for the overall meaning. When Kumar obediently broke his question down into shorter sentences, David looked less confused but offered very little help. He simply took out his wallet, fossicked through the contents and pulled out a business card.

"That's the place. Perfect Homes," he said, offering the card to Kumar.

"Take it," he urged. "Think of it as a gift. Use it wisely."

It was now getting close to Christmas. Kumar and Indu were looking forward to the big party at the Rabula's again. Disappointingly, they received no invitation. Only a card from the Rabulas, dropped in their letterbox, wishing "Merry Christmas."

"I think they are not happy with our efforts with Ahmed," Indu said.

"Seems so," Kumar agreed. "But what can we do? We can't get dragged into their fights."

"It is a pity we can't see that Christmas tree," Indu sighed.

Rohan wasn't disappointed. "It's the most boring party ever," he said. "All grown-ups, talking rubbish they probably don't understand themselves." As for seeing the Christmas tree, there was nothing to worry about, he assured. "It's such a big-ass tree you could see it from the street."

It was also Park Court's first Christmas with the Bogans, and everybody was wondering what they would be up to. But they were surprisingly quiet. Even the music stopped. Kumar wondered what might have happened to cause such a change. Then he realised that Christmas was not an easy festival to celebrate. With five children and the parents seemingly unemployed, it must be hard, and at Christmas time, the Bogans probably felt it more than at other times. He remembered BB1 and BB2 fossicking the rubbish and the glee with which BB2 had picked up Rohan's old Nikes. Suddenly, for the first time since they arrived, he felt a tinge of sympathy for them.

On Christmas Eve, Kumar and Indu stood on the veranda, watched fairy lights twinkling at the Rabulas' house, and heard laughter and music. The Rabulas were having a party after all. And they were not invited.

A few minutes later, Ahmed walked up. He had a bottle of wine.

"I see you also not invited," he said. Kumar nodded. Ahmed sat down on the front steps.

"Got a glass?"

Kumar brought out two glasses. On the way back to the veranda, he asked Indu to fry some potato chips. "I thought you guys didn't drink?" He said as he gave Ahmed a glass.

"Drinking is against my religion, yes," Ahmed replied, pouring out a glass of wine. "But I am not that religious." He laughed and gave Kumar the bottle. It was the first time Kumar had seen him laugh since the swastika appeared on the sidewalk.

"Everybody is there, huh?"

Ahmed said, gesturing at the Rabulas house. "Even the two lesbians."

"Yes," Kumar said. "Everybody. Even Vivienne and Lauren."

Ahmed pulled out a packet of cigarettes and offered it to Kumar.

Kumar declined. "Against my health," he said, and Ahmed laughed again. He lit a cigarette and started smoking.

"How's Amina, Hala, and Mahmoud?"

"Amina and Hala are good," Ahmed said.

Kumar looked at him quizzically. "And Mahmoud?"

Ahmed was silent for a while. "Not very good," he said.

He looked at Kumar and seeing his concern, explained.

"I dunno. For some time he is very strange now. Talks little. Always on the computer. Don't go anywhere much. Like he is in another world."

"Maybe he has a girlfriend," Kumar said. He quickly realised that might have been the wrong thing to say, considering Mahmoud's rejection by Cynthia. But Ahmed dismissed the suggestion with a wave of his hand.

"Nah!" he said. "If you have girl you happy. But Mahmoud, not happy"

They sat and drank in silence.

"The Bogans are very quiet, hey?"

'Yes they are." Kumar said. "Maybe they can't afford Christmas."

Ahmed said nothing for a while. "Yeah," he said after a couple of minutes. "Christmas is expensive. Ramadan is fucking expensive, I tell you man."

"Maybe you should visit them with some food," Kumar said, and added, with a wink: "You know, as a peace offering."

"Bahh!" Ahmed said. "I will offer them my fist." He balled his fist and shook it at the night air.

Indu now came out with a plate of chips and some chicken wings. She saw Ahmed with the drink and raised her eyebrows.

"He is not that religious," Kumar explained. Ahmed laughed again.

They sat eating the chips and chicken wings and drinking. Ahmed was beginning to get more relaxed.

"It will be great when Abdul comes," he said and looked at Kumar as if to see whether he remembered Abdul. Kumar was confused at first but soon realised to whom Ahmed was alluding.

"Yes," he said. "It would be great. When did you say he was due?"

"June," Ahmed said. "I can't wait."

They drank in silence for a few more minutes.

"You know why I call him Abdul?"

Kumar shook his head.

"I already had one Abdul, long time ago." Seeing Kumar's confusion he smiled and explained. "I had son, Abdul. He two years older than Mahmoud. But he die in 2006." He said.

Kumar saw Ahmed's face gradually assume an expression of great pain. "In 2006 we live in Ghazieh in Lebanon and when Israel attack, me, Amina, Mahmoud and Abdul all get in van and try to get out of city and drive to north." He paused and took a sip from his drink. Seeing that the glass was nearly empty, he refilled it from the bottle.

"When we in the van Israeli plane attack road. I think they think we are Hezbollah. One missile hit car in front and I lose control of van and van run into ditch and van turn over. Me, Amina, Mahmoud hurt. Abdul dead." "He took a very deep breath. "Abdul dead." His voice was beginning to crack.

Kumar sat in silence, stunned by Ahmed's revelation. Ahmed looked at him and saw his surprise and smiled weakly.

"That is why I call new boy Abdul." He took another sip from the glass.

"I never tell you before because I am sad. Amina, Mahmoud and Hala never speak about him. Too sad to speak."

Seeing Rohan approaching, Ahmed stopped talking. Rohan came out and seeing them, sat down with them. Ahmed looked at him.

"No party?"

"Nah," Rohan said. "Not invited."

"I didn't mean that, boy!" Ahmed said, gesturing at the Rabulas' house again. "Don't you have friends to party with?"

"My friend is at the party," Rohan said and smiled sadly. Kumar reached out and ruffled his hair.

"And my other friend is at home."

At the obvious reference to Mahmoud, Ahmed smiled sadly and nodded.

"I am beginning to think, you know, it was not Bogans who throw that brick." He said after a pause.

Kumar glanced at Rohan who was staring at the darkness outside avoiding his eyes.

Nobody said anything for a couple of minutes.

"I am pretty sure it was not them," Ahmed said again, breaking the silence. "And when I find out who do it, I will show them!"

They heard footsteps approaching up the sidewalk. Several shadows emerged, and they heard muffled voices.

"The Bogans!" Rohan whispered.

He was right. The whole Bogan family was approaching. The father, mother, BB1, BB2, BG and the Little Bogan with the Infant Bogan in the stroller. They were chattering excitedly about something. As they approached Kumar's house, their chattering subsided at the sight of Kumar and his companions. Kumar felt his whole body tense with apprehension. Instinctively, he reached out and placed a protective arm around Rohan's shoulder. With his other hand, he gripped Ahmed's hand and squeezed it slightly as a warning for him to stay quiet.

The Bogans trooped past, silent, like ghosts. They did not look at them. They resumed their chattering only after they had got clear of the house.

"Where the fuck are they going?" Ahmed whispered, addressing no one in particular.

"May be going to rob a house," Rohan said.

"The whole family?" Ahmed asked. "Nah, I think they're just goin' out for a little Christmas walk."

They waited in silence as if they were afraid that the Bogans might be lurking around the corner. About twenty minutes later, the Bogans returned. Again they did not look at the little knot of people on Kumar's veranda, but they did not stop their chatter either. At least the Little Bogan didn't.

"Last year we had a tree," he was saying. "Why can't we have one this year?'

His parents did not answer, and the boy asked his question again. Then the Mother Bogan said something, presumably in reply but by then they were almost out of earshot.

A few moments later, a shadowy figure approached them from the street. It was Eric.

"I told Mum I was coming here," he said as he sat down next to Rohan. "So boring there. Nobody to talk to."

Rohan grinned and offered him some chips. Eric took a handful and stuffed his mouth with them.

"Saw the Bogans?" He asked through the chips. Everybody nodded.

"What were they doing?" Rohan asked.

Eric shrugged his shoulders. "No Idea," he said. "They came and stood like ghosts in front of the house and stared at the tree. I thought they were gonna do a run through or something, but they just stood and stared and then walked away."

There was silence for a few seconds. Then Ahmed spoke again.

"Christmas is fucking expensive," he said. "Like Ramadan."

NINETEEN

Things continued as they were for the next few days without any major drama. The only significant development was a falling-out between Vivienne and the Rabulas. Vivienne's attempt to cement the alliance with the Rabulas and Chelliah by inviting them to a New Year's Eve dinner was given short shrift by the Rabulas, who excused themselves by saying they were already booked for that day. Vivienne was convinced that even though the Rabulas didn't mind inviting lesbians to their home, they were not comfortable visiting a lesbian home.

"What they think we going to do? Make them lesbian?" She asked Chelliah, declaring that if not for the Bogans she would have thrown the biggest lesbian street party this side of town just to thumb her nose at the snooty Rabulas. Chelliah promptly carried the news to Kumar and Indu who, like Chelliah, were for once thankful for the presence of the Bogans, even though Rohan expressed grave doubts about Vivienne's ability to organise any party let alone a lesbian street party. And without the Rabulas, Chelliah was feeling awkward about attending the dinner while Vivienne felt equally uncomfortable having Chelliah without the Rabulas.

Determined to have her dinner, Vivienne now made overtures to

Kumar and Indu, denouncing the Rabulas for their attitude to her and Lauren in particular, and to lesbians in general. "They think we dirt," she spat and repeated her threat to kick Mrs. Rabula's big black ass. Kumar and Indu politely declined the invitation saying that they were going to have a quiet family evening. Frustrated, Vivienne returned home, muttering her conviction that now the whole neighbourhood seemed to be against lesbians.

But everybody's plans were laid to rest by the Bogans. Unlike on Christmas, they played the loudest music they had ever played, sending everybody into fits of ill-temper. That night the Bogan men sat around in the park drinking and chatting till the early hours of the morning about what they would do to Ahmed, increasing Vivienne's anxiety and strengthening her conviction that Ahmed should leave the neighbourhood without delay. Following her fall out with the Rabulas, however, she could only fume in private (and occasionally to Kumar) as she had now lost both her allies.

For Ahmed, matters did not improve. He was still shunned by all his neighbours except Kumar and Indu. Mahmoud remained withdrawn. As it was now the summer holidays, Rohan and Eric had no chance of seeing him at school, and he did not return their calls. His Facebook page had also become inactive since the swastika incident. Jimmy had been calling Rohan asking if he could contact Mahmoud as the Ugandan had been hoping to get Mahmoud to help him with mathematics during the holidays. Rohan said there was nothing he could do as Mahmoud was incommunicado.

"I hope he will not turn up at Mahmoud's place," Eric said when he heard about Jimmy's request. "He sounds desperate."

"Yes," said, Rohan. "Very desperate." But he did not think there was any danger of Jimmy turning up again at Park Court. "I think the arrest would have scared him enough to keep him away from here," he said.

Rohan was right. No Jimmy turned up. But Mahmoud still remained withdrawn.

"That boy is like stranger now," Ahmed said to Kumar. "Don't say much, even to us."

That, however, was not enough to dampen Ahmed's spirits. He was looking forward to Abdul. "When Abdul come everything will be better," he said. "Even Mahmoud will change."

But little did Ahmed know that his nightmare was only just beginning.

***

One morning around 3 am, Kumar was woken by a loud noise that sounded like heavy pounding and someone screaming. He stumbled out of bed, opened the window, and looked out.

"What is it?" asked Indu, now also wide awake.

The court seemed to be full of people. It was still dark, but it was not difficult to make out their shadowy forms. There were several vehicles too. Some of the people were carrying torches with very bright beams.

Kumar heard someone yell: "Shut the window and get the fuck inside!"

He shut the window quickly and instinctively and moved away from it. He heard the window in Rohan's room also closing. Then Rohan came into their room.

"Police," he said in a loud whisper.

"Where?" Kumar asked.

"Who?" Indu whispered.

"Ahmed."

Kumar gasped. Ahmed? What on earth had his neighbour got himself into?

They did not sleep after that. They couldn't. Kumar knew well what kind of police came at dawn to arrest people like Ahmed. It was hard to sleep, knowing that. And they didn't open the windows either. They sat on the bed like zombies, motionless, and silent. Rohan also stayed with them in their bedroom. It was as if for once he was lost for words. It was only when daylight had come, and they were sure they had heard the last vehicle depart, that they got up and opened the windows.

The street lay bathed in the morning sunlight. The doors and windows in all the houses in Park Court remained closed. There was no one about, and there was no sign of the commotion last night. Those who had entered Ahmed's house in the night had even taken care to close the gate behind them as they left.

Kumar quickly went to Ahmed's house. Rohan and Indu followed him. They found the front door wide open, and the lock broken. To their surprise, they found Ahmed inside, sitting in the lounge, staring vacantly at them.

"What happened?"

"Mahmoud," Ahmed said. "They took Mahmoud."

Kumar gasped. He felt Indu clutching his arm tightly.

"Where's Amina?" Indu asked.

"Upstairs," Ahmed said. "With Hala. She is not feeling well." Then he began to cry.

Indu quickly went upstairs, and Kumar and Rohan sat with Ahmed.

It took a while for them to put the story together, from the bits and pieces Ahmed was sane enough to explain. The raid was by ASIO, and they had come looking for weapons and explosives. "Where are the guns, you little Arab shit?" They had asked Mahmoud. "Where do you keep your stash of explosives? We know you are planning some shit soon."

"All rubbish! All rubbish!" Ahmed said. "That boy only angry. Very angry. And stupid. Not nasty."

Ahmed told them what the ASIO people had done. "They break door," he said. "Bang! Bang! Crash! Just like that. If they ring bell, I open. Why break door?" He asked Kumar who listened impassively. "And they treat Mahmoud bad. Very bad," Ahmed said. "They call him Arab shit and put him on the floor and stand on him, the bastards!"

Kumar felt sorry for Ahmed, but he was also worried. What had Mahmoud been doing? Kumar asked himself. Was he really 'radicalised' as David had suggested? According to Ahmed, his son had been ranting online against the government and the police for doing nothing about the Bogans, and Ahmed suspected he might also have been saying dangerous things on the Internet.

"But he only stupid," Ahmed kept saying. "Only stupid, not nasty."

Kumar returned home with his family after making sure that Ahmed, Amina, and Hala were alright. Ahmed was going to call a distant cousin to come and stay with Amina and also get in touch with a lawyer and see what he could do. "I am going to fight the bastards all the way," he vowed. "They don't know who they are messing with." Kumar hoped that Ahmed would also not start raving like Mahmoud.

They must have been watching him for a while, Rohan said later when they had returned home. His parents agreed. Kumar realised that there were evidently many people around who thought as David did; people in high places, people who could really get you into trouble. Kumar wondered whether Ayub at work would soon be in trouble too. And who else? He could not help feeling glad that he had remained aloof from the whole affair.

"Maybe this was why the boy was not talking to anybody lately," Indu suggested. "He was talking to some nutters."

"Maybe," Rohan said. He did not reveal that he knew that Mahmoud was chatting to people in Islamic chat groups. It had completely escaped him that this is what Mahmoud would have been doing while he remained withdrawn from everyone else. Now that it has been revealed, he did not wish to share it with his parents. He was not sure how they would have reacted, considering the circumstances. But he was convinced of Mahmoud's innocence, and he agreed with Ahmed that Mahmoud had only been stupid.

"Mahmoud can't plan an essay properly. How can he plan a terrorist attack?" He asked. "In some ways, Mahmoud was just like that Naushad.

A dickhead."

But unlike Naushad, Mahmoud was his friend.

"But why would they arrest someone without any cause?" Indu thought aloud. Kumar thought it was hard to believe Mahmoud was up to anything but then would they arrest someone without a good reason?

Rohan was getting angry now.

"Why do you think they arrested Jimmy?" he asked, his voice becoming shrill. "Did they have a good reason?"

Indu was about to say something when a newsbreak came up on the Television. It was all about the raid, and it revealed more about the arrest. It was not only Mahmoud who had been arrested. A few others, almost all of them teenagers, had been taken in, all across the state, in what the news headlines called 'dawn terror raids.' The arrested were part of a group that had been planning a big attack on Australia Day, the reports said. The names of the suspects were not revealed, but there was enough information in the reports to make it easy for viewers to have a fairly good idea as to who they might be. There were also messages from the Prime Minister, the Premier and the Police Commissioner. "There is no room for terror in this country," they said. "All Australians should unite as one against these heinous criminals who plot to destroy our way of life."

"Oh my God!" Indu placed her palms on her cheeks. "What has this boy been up to?"

Rohan was furious now. In a rare loss of temper, he got up and walked into his room, but not before giving his parents a piece of his mind.

"I know Mahmoud better than any of these fucking idiots who read the news. Anyone who believes their crap is also a fucking idiot!"

He slammed his door shut.

Kumar and Indu looked at each other, startled by the boy's outburst. He was obviously outraged by what had happened. Seeing Indu distressed by their son's behaviour, Kumar signalled her to calm down. This was very unlike Rohan, and he was sure the boy was simply venting his own frustration. He will cool down soon.

At work, Kumar saw that the newspapers too were plastered with reports of the arrests. "Terror Teens Trapped," screamed the *Herald Sun* while *The Age* simply announced "Busted!" Both papers carried multiple reports and stories of the raids and even pictures of some of the homes targeted by the ASIO. The *Herald-Sun* editorial was effusive in its praise of the authorities who, it claimed, had thwarted a massive assault on peaceful Australians which had been deliberately timed to take place on a day that should be special to all Australians. "It was sad to know that there were in our midst misguided youth who did not appreciate the peaceful and tolerant way of life this great country had to offer," it added.

Everybody at work was also talking about the raids. "To think that such people have been living amongst us!" one of the women in Kumar's department said to another, her hand firmly on her cheek in disbelief.

"I don't know why they can't do this in their own countries," Kumar heard a male voice saying as he walked past the kitchenette. Everyone seemed surprised and outraged.

The news reports and the chatter made Kumar feel increasingly uncomfortable. The extent of the raids and the enormity of the alleged plot alarmed him, especially when their details covered so much newsprint and were repeated by so many people around him. What if it were all true? He asked himself again. Were Mahmoud and others really up to something nasty or was he being an idiot to believe what he saw on the news, as Rohan said? But Rohan could be blinded by his loyalty to his friend. If the reports were true, the implications for him could be very bad. Was he on the watch list too, as a friend or associate of Ahmed? What about Rohan? He was a close friend of Mahmoud. Might he get dragged into this mess? Should Kumar himself continue speaking to Ahmed and should he let Rohan go to see Ahmed's family?

As he continued to think of it, his unease grew, his mind niggled by a feeling of increasing uncertainty. It reached panic proportions when he heard Dev, his Indian colleague who was suspected of being gay, telling the Filipina accounts clerk Juanita that he would not be surprised if there were terrorist sympathisers everywhere, even amongst the staff.

At lunch, Kumar approached David again, diffidently. He was not sure what David thought of the whole affair, given the conversation he had had with him earlier about Mahmoud. David was seated in his usual place, sipping a latte for a change, reading the paper, and smoking his pipe. Seeing Kumar approaching, he nodded gravely and showed him the front page of his paper.

"Bad news, huh?" He said, and Kumar nodded slowly, deliberately, to show that he entirely agreed with David.

"I hope they have got all the little rascals in the bag," David said, glancing at a news report and shaking his head as if he still could not believe what he had read. Kumar nodded again. And as he was wondering if he should say that he hoped ASIO had got the right group of little rascals in the bag, David added, as nonchalantly as if he was speaking of yesterday's weather, that Ayub hasn't turned up for work. Realising the futility of saying anything at all, Kumar nodded again.

And as David continued to express his approval of the raids, Kumar realised - to his great relief - that David did not seem as yet to have figured out Mahmoud's connection to the raids. He had either forgotten what Kumar had told him earlier, or Mahmoud's relevance to last night's events had somehow escaped him altogether. Whichever it was, Kumar was not prepared to refresh his memory or help him make the connection, for fear of drawing undue attention to himself. He continued to sit next to David, nodding and shaking his head whenever David made a remark about the dire threats to Australian values and the need for everybody to be vigilant. David seemed pleased with the level of engagement shown by Kumar: he liked his audiences to be silent and agreeable.

When Kumar returned home, he spoke to Indu about David's behaviour and the hysteria at work. Indu too had experienced a similar atmosphere at the bank, and she too had been worried about the implications for them. Will they also be on a watch list because of their friendship with Ahmed and family? Should they continue to see them? But she also felt very sorry for Ahmed and his family, especially for Amina.

"That poor woman is suffering so much because of this silly boy," she said. "And she is expecting another!"

To make matters worse, everyone else believed what the papers and the news said. The raids appeared to have confirmed their suspicions. Vivienne had called soon after the first news break in the morning to say, triumphantly, that what she has been saying all along has been finally proven. "They terrorist, I told you!" She hissed. She warned them not to go to Ahmed's house anymore. "If you go, you next!" she said menacingly, before hanging up.

The Rabulas too called as soon as Kumar returned from work and said that they were disappointed in Ahmed and Mahmoud. They had never thought Mahmoud would go to that extent, but now that the truth has been revealed they were not all that surprised. Chelliah craned his neck over the back fence shortly after that to say that he was glad that the police had acted in time. He was hoping to go to the City on Australia Day, and now he could do so without fear. His only complaint was that although the police had taken Mahmoud, they had not taken the Pakistani flag down. It still fluttered from the rooftop, like a blot on the skyline, he said.

Later in the night Jimmy also called. "Man!" He said to Rohan. "What a bummer, hey? I never thought Mahmoud was into that kind of shit."

"What kind of shit?" Rohan asked, infuriated.

Jimmy said the shit that the TV talked about. Close to exploding, Rohan said that the only shit was what the TV people were talking about.

"And you shouldn't talk shit about my mate either!" He growled and Jimmy, somewhat apologetic, said that he understood Rohan was Mahmoud's good mate. All he wanted was for Mahmoud to get out of this mess without too much trouble.

"He was a good math teacher," he said. "I don't want to be stuck without him next year with exams and shit." Beside himself with anger, Rohan simply hung up.

Eric had made it a point to check Cynthia's Facebook page. "Full of bullshit!" he spat, showing it to Rohan.

"I deplore this insanity!" Cynthia had written. "This terrorising and scaremongering. This has been another attack on the peaceful Islamic community by an Islamophobic government led by racist White men, another attempt to scare us all into submission."

"She's nuts," was Rohan's considered opinion.

"And a hypocrite," Eric chimed. "She is like the government she is condemning, one of them Islamo-people."

Rohan nodded. "A pity we had to find out the hard way," he said.

Only the Bogans seemed quiet.

"There was no way they would have missed the raid in the night," said Rohan. "They don't seem like the type of people who read newspapers, but surely, they've got TV?"

Kumar found the Bogans' strange silence ominous.

"Must be wondering whether they will get raided too," Indu said, but Rohan dismissed the possibility.

"They would have been raided alright if Mahmoud's dad had

complained about the swastika," he said. "But he didn't and look what it has landed him in!" But it was only a matter of time before they did something, he pointed out. "They will strike when they are ready," he said with the air of an expert on Bogans.

But unlike his parents, Rohan had no qualms about visiting Mahmoud. His anger had abated, but he was still convinced that his friend was innocent. "Being an idiot is no reason to be treated like shit," he said. "If that was the case, half the teachers at school should be kicked and dunked in the toilet." Besides, he reiterated that Mahmoud was his mate. He would go and see his family even if his parents didn't.

Shamed by his son's loyalty to his friend, Kumar and Indu decided to go and see Ahmed again that evening. They met Eric near the gate. Like Rohan, he too had decided, in defiance of his parents, to go and support his friend's family. "Mum told me not to go," he said. "But I said Mahmoud is my friend and I have to be with his family. If you lose me like Ahmed lost Mahmoud, how would you feel?" He had asked Vivienne. "Wouldn't you like someone to come and sit with you?" Vivienne had snorted and said if you go I will have no son because then you are not my son anymore. Eric had smiled sweetly and said, don't worry Ma, then I will come and sit with you too.

Ahmed was happy to see them. "You are my only friend," he said, hugging Kumar tightly. Kumar returned the embrace awkwardly; in the circumstances, he felt uneasy at the gesture and tried hard not to show it.

Ahmed continued to pour out his appreciation. "From the day I arrived, you are my friend and now you the only people coming to see me," he said and hugged Kumar again. This time Kumar winced, bringing a smile to Rohan's lips. Ahmed then turned to Indu. "You good woman," he said and then squeezed Rohan's shoulder. "You good boy," he said. "Mahmoud's good friend, even though you swear sometimes." Then he saw Eric and frowned, but greeted him with a nod of cold recognition. Eric bore the chilly reception with a grin.

They had gone to see Mahmoud, Ahmed said when they sat down. He was ok, but now looking very much like the little idiot he really was, he said. "Very quiet, none of that Facebook bullshit now." His lawyer was doing everything he could to get Mahmoud released.

"Where is Amina?" Indu asked. "And Hala?"

"They are upstairs," Ahmed said. Amina had fainted when she was coming out after seeing Mahmoud. "She is better now, but still very upset. Even more upset after going to see Mahmoud. She has her cousin with her. But cousin is not son." He sniffled. "And Hala is missing her brother very much."

Kumar nodded to show he understood. Now more relaxed, he placed a hand on Ahmed's shoulder.

"I am sure things will get better Ahmed," he said. Let's hope for the best."

When Indu came down, Kumar bade Ahmed goodnight and returned home. "Let us know if you need anything," he said. Ahmed nodded absently.

When they returned home, Indu revealed that in the midst of all the misery, Hala had made a touching gesture.

"She offered all the money she had raised for those orphans to pay for Mahmoud's lawyer, you know," she said with admiration. Apparently, she had raised nearly two thousand dollars. Kumar was impressed by the girl's gesture. What he found even more impressive was that Hala had managed to raise that much money. "That is a lot of money for a girl of twelve to raise," he said. Indu nodded.

Eric, who had come with Rohan, shared a look of amusement with his friend. "She is just returning what she took I guess," Rohan said, out of his parent's hearing. Eric nodded. Then he made a revelation of his own.

"She did that to me too, you know?"

Rohan looked at Eric. "What do you mean? Did what?"

Eric explained. The first night he was watching the Bogan girl alone, he had got a bit too excited, he said. He was alone for the first time with the binoculars, it was dark, and the girl was also alone, wearing shorts and a skimpy t-shirt. He got excited, and when Hala suddenly entered the room, she found him in a compromising situation, he said, wincing. As Rohan struggled to suppress his laughter, he went on to say that that was all he was willing to divulge. But Hala had said that if he was willing to pay a small amount weekly, she would not tell her father. Fearful of Ahmed, Eric had agreed.

"How much?" Rohan asked.

"Not much," was all Eric was willing to say. "But a bit more than Mahmoud. She said I got to a private school. I think she must have got money like that from other people too. Two thousand dollars is a lot of money. I don't think it was all voluntary contributions."

Rohan laughed. But he was happy that Hala had not got to him. He tried to console his friend.

"It was all for a good cause. As you can see, she had saved all that, and it is sweet of her to have given all that for her brother's defence, even if some of it was Mahmoud's in the first place."

They both chuckled. "If only that Bogan Girl knows what I had suffered for her!" Eric sighed.

***

But things got worse before they got any better. Especially for Amina who had not been feeling well after Mahmoud's arrest. She had spent the whole morning crying and refused to even answer calls from her family in Sydney for fear of the police listening in. Ahmed and Hala sat with her and for much of the morning Indu, too, stayed with her. But there was little improvement. Ahmed and Hala were not in much better shape either, but Amina was taking it really bad. It was as though Mahmoud was dead. Her condition grew worse after she returned from seeing Mahmoud in custody. She continued to weep softly, refusing to eat anything, and despite the best efforts of her cousin and Indu, and notwithstanding the pleading of Hala and Ahmed, she refused to budge.

By lunchtime the following morning, Amina was experiencing difficulty breathing. She was gasping for air, Indu said later. Terrified, Ahmed called an ambulance and Amina was taken to hospital. There she was stabilised but was kept under observation. Indu, who had gone to the hospital with Ahmed, came home in the afternoon and phoned Kumar at work to tell him that Amina was all right but still not talking to anybody. Ahmed, Hala, and Amina's cousin sister were at the hospital, keeping her company, but there was little improvement in her condition. If she was behaving as though Mahmoud was dead after the boy's arrest, after seeing Mahmoud in custody, she was behaving as though *she* was dying, Indu said.

Then, around six in the evening just after Kumar returned from work, Ahmed came to Kumar's house, crying like a baby, and told him that Abdul was dead. Again, Kumar was perplexed for a moment before he remembered who Abdul was, but he was still confused as to how he could die even before he was born. Then Ahmed explained. "Baby no more," he cried. "Abdul no more." Amina has had a miscarriage. Ahmed believed that it was the shock of the police raid and the trauma of losing Mahmoud that caused it.

He sat in Kumar's lounge and cried for what seemed like an hour. He sobbed and cried, his big shoulders heaving with every violent sob. Kumar sat next to him and patted his shoulder while Indu made some tea and Rohan looked on, utterly subdued. Finally, Ahmed left, saying that he had come to pick up some stuff for Amina who was still in the hospital. Indu wondered why he had spent all that time in their house if he had come to pick up Amina's things, but Rohan said it was probably because he wanted to have a good cry.

Amina returned home the following morning. She seemed to have aged about ten years. Her once jet black hair was now streaked with grey and white, and she appeared to be hobbling rather than walking. Her eyes had also taken on a glazed appearance as if she was looking without seeing.

"The poor woman has died inside," Kumar said. "That's a terrible way to live."

Later that day, they released Mahmoud. No charges were laid. There was nothing to lay charges for. As Ahmed had believed, it was nothing more than silly ranting on the Internet. After the appearance of the swastika and the graffiti he had 'befriended' some foolish people online and had started saying a lot of stupid things, Ahmed revealed. Apparently, he was even threatening to attack Israel.

"How that idiot attack Israel from here?" Ahmed asked, and said again that the police could have easily settled everything by ringing the bell at a decent hour and talking to them in a civilised way. They didn't have to break the door, stand on the boy's back, and kill his wife's unborn child. It was clear he wanted to say more, but after Mahmoud's arrest, Ahmed had become subdued. He probably feared, Kumar thought, that if he said something out of order, and it was reported to the authorities, ASIO will come again, break the door and stand on *his* back.

It was the first time Eric and Rohan were seeing Mahmoud in weeks. He too looked like he had aged. Eric and Rohan were keen to know what the police had done to him.

"Did they beat you?" Rohan asked, and Mahmoud shook his head.

"Did they rape you?" Eric asked, and Mahmoud shook his head even more vigorously.

Kumar looked at Eric, aghast at the boy's temerity and insensitivity.

Even Rohan seemed taken aback. But Eric didn't seem to be concerned by their shock and surprise. He badly wanted to know.

"Then what did they do?" He asked, and Mahmoud began to cry.

But Ahmed's troubles were not over yet. As people gradually began to figure out who the arrested teenagers were, he began to receive calls, mainly from his cleaning clients. They told him that his services were no longer required by them. One or two even said they did not wish to have anything to do with terrorists who have abused Australia's hospitality. Only one woman told Ahmed that she was sorry to hear about what happened, but in the circumstances, she did not feel comfortable employing him.

"They can all get fucked!" Ahmed said. "I will find work again," he vowed, sounding more like a man in despair than hope.

That night Kumar sat with Ahmed in his lounge. Ahmed sat without speaking for a long time, thinking. Mahmoud was upstairs with Eric and Rohan, and Hala and Indu were with Amina. Everybody was quiet, and everything was still. For some reason, even the Bogans did not play their music that night. With the curtains drawn, and only the light over the dining table turned on, the lounge was sunk in a semi-darkness which accentuated the gloomy mood in the house. The atmosphere was sad, depressing, and painful.

Ending his long silence, Ahmed got up abruptly and went upstairs. While Kumar waited, wondering whether to go after him, Ahmed returned carrying what appeared to be a stack of books. They were his photo albums. Kumar had seen many of them previously when Ahmed and his family had moved into Park Court. He showed them to Kumar again now, taking him through every single picture and talking about them. He showed Kumar pictures of him and Amina when they were courting, pictures of their wedding and the pictures of them on their honeymoon. There were pictures of the children when they were young, and pictures of Mahmoud's cousins in Sydney.

"All my life is here," Ahmed said. "All my dreams, my struggles. All that over now." He shook his head in dismay. "All over. All ruined."

Kumar sat in silence, not knowing what to say. Ahmed was right. His whole life was there in those pictures, his life in Lebanon and in Sydney, as a teenager, a young bachelor, a young husband, a father, a professional and finally a cleaner, the long metamorphoses undergone by most immigrants. And Kumar noticed that this time Ahmed was also showing him albums he had not shown him previously. In these hitherto unseen albums, Kumar saw for the first time, pictures of Abdul, Ahmed's first child, tragically killed by a missile. He looked very much like Mahmoud when he was younger, Kumar thought, but with a cheekier smile than Mahmoud whose smile was usually shy, even sheepish. In one picture, both boys were wearing identical t-shirts, arms around each others' shoulders grinning at the camera. They looked almost like twins.

"They look like twins, huh?" Ahmed asked as if reading Kumar's mind.

Kumar nodded. "He looks like a sweet boy," he said.

"Yes," Ahmed said. "The sweetest. And Mahmoud and him very close. Like friends."

He took a deep breath before continuing. "Before I not show you these photos. Because you not know about Abdul. I not know you and I am sad also. But now you know about Abdul and I know you are good man, like brother to me."

He patted Kumar on the arm. "And I not care anymore."

Then he started sobbing.

Kumar felt sad - and awkward. He wanted to put his hand on Ahmed's shoulder and tell him that all was not lost and that he still had his family, and that he could rebuild again as he had done before, but all he managed to do was put his hand on Ahmed's shoulder. He felt it heave with the sorrow inside.

Kumar sat in this manner with Ahmed till Indu came down with Eric and Rohan and told him it was time to go home. He patted Ahmed on the shoulder and got up.

"Take care," he said to Ahmed. "I will see you tomorrow." Ahmed nodded like a man who didn't seem to know what he was nodding at.

Outside Eric lingered behind with Rohan. "I feel bad about what I did," he said. "Shall I tell him I did it?"

Rohan knew his friend was alluding to the brick-throwing incident. He thought for a few seconds and then shook his head.

"Not right now," he said. "But maybe later."

"How much later?" Eric wanted to know.

"Much later," Rohan said. "Maybe when you are married. Or living in another state."

TWENTY

If Ahmed thought his ordeal ended with Amina's miscarriage, he was wrong. The Bogans had been quiet since the police raids. But the day after Amina's miscarriage they struck, just as Rohan had predicted, and in devastating fashion.

In the morning, Ahmed went out to get something from his van and found another swastika and the words 'Muzzy terrorist' scrawled across the side of the van in big ugly letters. He walked around the vehicle, only to find the same sign and words defacing the side of the van that faced the street. The letters were huge, so large they covered the entire side of the van. And they seem to have been scribbled in the same hand that wrote 'fuk off muzzies' beneath the swastika a few weeks ago. And the swastika was once again the same: drawn facing the wrong direction.

Ahmed stood staring at the graffiti for a few moments as if unable to believe it was real. Then he exploded.

"May Allah smite the bastards who did this," he screamed in Arabic. "May Allah break their arms and legs and crush their fingers and leave them limp and worthless for writing this filth on the van of a decent, God-fearing, hard-working man."

Ahmed's outburst was as explosive as it was intense. But it was nothing compared to what it became when he saw the Bogans.

The whole neighbourhood had been sunk deep in its Sunday morning slumber when Ahmed discovered the graffiti. The Bogans, accordingly, were nowhere to be seen when Ahmed let loose his tirade. But, as Ahmed's screams shattered the morning's tranquillity and his neighbours began to come out, wondering what the noise was about, the Bogans too staggered out of their house, bewildered, almost all of them still seemingly half asleep.

They stood on their veranda, staring curiously at Ahmed. But it did not take them long to realise what Ahmed was screaming about. Smiles passed over their lips, and they began to relax. Father Bogan said something to BB1, who laughed raucously and slapped his thighs with merriment while the smiles of the rest of the family turned into broad grins of amusement.

Then Ahmed saw them.

He stood staring at them for a few seconds as if trying to fathom what he was seeing. The Bogans saw him looking at them, and their smiles broadened, BB1 even waving at him mockingly. That was all that Ahmed needed. He erupted again, this time more violently. He began to shake his fists at them like a man possessed. His whole body shook as he poured out his rage at them, shouting even more loudly now so that his words could reach his enemy.

"You bastards!" He screamed, in English, this time. "Not enough for you my family ruined, my business destroyed, my baby killed? Not enough you destroy me and my family? You want to do this also?" He said, pointing to the van. "You want to do this also?" He began banging on the side of the van.

Now others were also coming out of their homes, roused by the screams and the bangs. Kumar was the first to emerge, followed by Indu and Rohan. Vivienne and Lauren too came out soon after, looking as though they were walking in their sleep with Eric not far behind. Chelliah stumbled out too, wearing only a pair of boxer shorts, looking shell shocked, and even more fragile than usual. He stood at the entrance to his drive way, watching cautiously as if expecting to duck behind the little wall should there be any trouble. He even created a minor distraction from the main event as people began casting curious glances in his direction.

Ahmed continued to rant like a madman, alternating between shaking his fists at the Bogans and banging on the van. From time to time he made as if to charge the Bogan's house, but only took a few steps towards it each time, stopping near the driveway and shaking his fists at the Bogans before returning to his van. Sometimes he looked at the sky and raised his arms as if seeking help from the heavens, and sometimes he beat his breasts. And in his words, anger was mixed with tears.

By now everybody realised what the commotion was about as the scrawl on Ahmed's van was clearly visible to them all. But what was surprising was Ahmed's explosive reaction. He had not behaved like this when the swastika had first appeared. He had erupted after the brick was thrown, but that was different. Then he was responding to a specific act of aggression. This time it was significantly different. Now it seemed that Ahmed was hitting out not only at the graffiti, but everything; the graffiti, the swastika, the arrest of Mahmoud, and its devastating consequences. It was as if the graffiti on the van had pressed a button in him, setting off his pent up rage and anguish. It was fascinating to see, as it was frightening.

"I hope he doesn't do anything silly," Indu whispered to Kumar who was watching from the driveway. She was obviously talking about Ahmed charging the Bogans. But Rohan said there was little chance of that happening. If Ahmed wanted to charge the Bogans, he would have done that at the very start. Kumar agreed. Clearly, Ahmed had no such idea. He was simply venting his rage and anguish and being slowly consumed by them. But Rohan could not be so certain in his estimate of the Bogans' possible reactions. If they were provoked by Ahmed's ranting, which at times appeared quite threatening, they might not wait for Ahmed to charge them. They might do the charging themselves. That could be a total disaster, not only for Ahmed but also for everybody else.

Interestingly, however, the Bogans were showing little sign of retaliating. It had seemed at first that they were content to stand back and enjoy the spectacle of Ahmed erupting. After all, was that not exactly what they wanted? They obviously knew about Mahmoud's arrest and had probably seen it too. They evidently knew how to push the right buttons to trigger the explosion they desired and having done that, it would have been just a matter of enjoying the resulting fireworks.

It had appeared initially that this was precisely what they were doing; that they were now savouring the results of their handiwork. They all stood in the veranda watching, sniggering, and pointing. BB1 was even seen giving Ahmed the bird, and the Little Bogan even clapped a few times in dramatic fashion as if he was applauding a command performance at the theatre. They were clearly enjoying the show they had instigated.

But then, as Ahmed continued to rave, they quietened down, the smiles gradually disappearing. They simply stood staring intently at Ahmed, the amusement on their faces gradually replaced by surprise, curiosity, and confusion. Even when Ahmed walked towards their house, a couple of times actually moving a few feet up their driveway to pour out his grief and frustration, they did not move. It was as if they were beginning to sense the extraordinary intensity of Ahmed's outburst; as if they suspected that it was no mere response to their latest act of provocation but something bigger and more powerful than what they could ever have planned. They stood in a huddle, watching, and anyone who cared to look would have seen that they, too, were beginning to appear uneasy. When BB1 tried to whisper something, his mother shushed him. This was not a time for distraction.

On the road, meanwhile, Ahmed continued to pour out his agony, pacing up and down, between the Bogan's driveway and his van, now raising his arms to the sky, now beating his chest with his fists, and now and then turning to the Bogans and standing mutely with his arms stretching out, as if he were lost for words. His voice, Kumar noticed, was beginning to fray, as if sadness was taking over from his anger. Soon he was alternating between ranting and sobbing. And whether ranting or sobbing he was now appearing increasingly like a man in pain rather than rage.

Amina, Hala, and Mahmoud had rushed out of the house when they heard Ahmed's shouting. Amina and Mahmoud tried to calm him down, Mahmoud attempting to pull him in the direction of their house. But Ahmed would not be moved. He shrugged off every attempt and even pushed Mahmoud away forcefully. Finally, they all stood on the sidewalk, helplessly, watching Ahmed having his meltdown. Hala stood clinging to her mother, her little eyes opened wide and filled with tears and fear.

Everybody had gathered in the street now, outside Ahmed's house. Vivienne, Lauren, and Eric stood on one side, in a huddle, Lauren, and Eric slightly behind Vivienne. Chelliah, who had retreated in to his garden to watch the proceedings from behind the safety of his garden wall, went back inside the house only to reappear wearing a shirt. He sidled into the street, and upon seeing Kumar and family already there, stood next to them. Soon, the Rabulas also joined them, Mr. Rabula hobbling after his wife, the faces of both scarred with anxiety.

Everybody seemed to realise they were watching a man coming apart. Under the pressure of months of tension and anxiety, caused by his conflicts with his neighbours and intensified by the arrest of Mahmoud and the loss of Amina's child, Ahmed had been building up to this. The scrawl on the van, so blatantly offensive and insensitive and coming so closely on the heels of Amina's miscarriage, had probably been the last straw, the trigger that had set it all off in one explosive outburst. He was going to pieces in front of their eyes. And nobody could do anything other than look on helplessly.

And the Bogans too continued to watch. They too seem to have fully realised now that they were seeing something more than an ordinary outburst from an angry man. Ahmed's body language and his tone all pointed to a spirit truly distraught, a man steadily disintegrating emotionally. They seemed to be surprised by what they were witnessing and strangely, even shaken by the pitifulness of Ahmed's breakdown. Whether they also heard or understood his lamentation for his dead child, it was hard to say. In stunned silence, they watched, as still as statues on their veranda.

Gradually, Ahmed's pain and anger turned into pure grief. He stopped shaking his fists and beating his breasts and stood in the middle of the road like a man bereft of all hope, looking up at the heavens as if seeking succour there. Then, as the grief overwhelmed him, he shook, shuddered and bowing his head like a man defeated and crushed, began to cry. He wept and cried, sobbing loudly, violently, like a man who had been longing to do it for months but had only now summoned up the courage to do it.

"Why don't you go and talk to him?" Indu asked Kumar.

But Kumar simply stood rooted to the ground. He felt paralysed by the pathetic spectacle before them. This was too big for him, he felt; too big for anybody. This was a serious meltdown, the kind that a pat on the back or a kind word could not check.

Rohan put it into words. "No point talking to him now," he said, gravely, and added with his characteristic practicality: "He can't hear you above the sobs."

At last, slowly but surely, Ahmed settled down, the sobs gradually subsiding, and his crying reduced to mere sniffling. Then, as if weighed down by his grief and the exhaustion of ranting and crying, he sank down in the middle of the road. He sat facing his van, his back to the Bogans. He appeared to be staring at the graffiti on the van, but his gaze was fixed on something faraway, beyond the van, beyond the street and possibly beyond this world.

For a long time, Ahmed sat outside, staring vacantly at the graffiti. Everybody thought that he had spent his anger and grief and was now calming down. After a few minutes, Amina went up to him and said something softly, but Ahmed showed no sign that he had even heard it. Mahmoud went too, and Hala who was crying now, hugged her dad and asked him to come home, but Ahmed did not move. At length, they gave up and returned to where they were standing. Kumar also went and tried to coax Ahmed to get up, but he paid no attention.

"Come and help me," he said to Rohan, and Rohan went and tried to help his father to make Ahmed get up, but soon gave up. "He is too fat," Rohan said. "Too fat to be moved even by the two of us."

Chelliah offered no support. He would have, he said, had his incontinence not been playing up recently. "The slightest strain on the muscle opens up the waterworks," he said. Rohan told him that if it was that bad, perhaps he should stay inside without straining himself too much by standing around. Chelliah simply frowned and reminded Kumar that it was still not too late to thrash the boy.

Mr. Rabula was all for non-intervention. "There is absolutely no point in trying to force him to get up," he said. "The man has been traumatised. He will move of his own accord when he calms down. Better to keep an eye till then though," he advised, and, as if to indicate that he had absolutely no intention of keeping an eye on Ahmed, he promptly left with his wife. Vivienne and Lauren lingered a little longer, but they too drifted back to their house after a few minutes. Eric came and stood beside Rohan.

Kumar glanced at the Bogan house. To his surprise, he saw the Bogans too sitting down on their veranda. It seemed they too had decided to stay and watch, not the way they would enjoy a spectacular display but as they would have watched a disturbing phenomenon. It seemed to Kumar that they did not wish to leave until they ascertained exactly what was going on with Ahmed.

"Wonder what they are up to?" Rohan said, gesturing towards the Bogans with his head. "Yes," Eric replied, glancing at the Bogan house. "They're weirder than usual."

Ahmed continued to sit and stare, seemingly oblivious to everything and everyone around him. It was mid morning now. The weather forecast had predicted a very hot day, and the sun was already blazing above them. If Ahmed planned on having a long sit-in, he was likely to have a very hard time. A cool change was predicted in the afternoon, but by then Ahmed would most certainly have suffered serious dehydration. But he didn't seem to care; at least not yet.

After a few more minutes of waiting, Kumar and Indu turned towards home. Ahmed seemed to have calmed down, even if he was mentally somewhere else, and they concluded there was no danger of anything serious taking place for the moment. In any case, Amina, Mahmoud and Hala were there to watch him, and Eric and Rohan had also chosen to stay with their friend.

Around midday, Rohan came home. Ahmed had finally got up and walked in, he said. Kumar and Indu sighed with relief. "Thank God, he finally came to his senses," Indu said. But Rohan wasn't quite sure if Ahmed had recovered or it was the heat driving him in. "It's like 40 out there already," he said, filling a glass of water from the kitchen tap.

It did feel hot indoors too. Hot and stuffy. And it was still only January, Kumar thought.

"The funny thing is, the Bogans also waited till Mahmoud's dad left, and then only they went inside," Rohan said after taking a long drink. Kumar found it odd too but didn't want to dwell on it too much. The Bogans were too strange for him to try to understand their thinking.

Kumar was about to turn the air-conditioner on when the phone rang. It was Vivienne, and she seemed to be in a panic.

"He is on the move!" She said in a breathless voice.

"Who is on the move?"

"Ahmed!"

Kumar was confused. Rohan had just reported that Ahmed had moved in. Was Vivienne reporting the same thing, in the present tense? One couldn't say for sure when Vivienne was speaking, but her frantic tone was a worry.

"Moving where?"

"To Bogan house!" Vivienne said impatiently. "He is going with package under his arm. Must be bomb!"

Kumar was beside himself. What on earth was Ahmed going to do? Was Vivienne imagining things?

At the other end of the telephone line, Vivienne was getting anxious.

"Shall I call the police or wait for bang first?"

Kumar tried to think. Even in his confused state of mind, he realised that letting Vivienne call the police was not a good idea.

"I'll call the police," he said. "You wait for the bang."

While Indu and Rohan looked on in surprise and confusion, Kumar called the police.

"My neighbours are trying to kill each other," he told the woman who answered the phone.

Then, having given the details of Ahmed's location to the police woman who sounded even more confused than he was, and calling Indu and Rohan to follow him, Kumar hurried out of his house in the direction of Ahmed's.

He found everybody already there. Vivienne certainly knew how to spread the news. But everybody was also keeping themselves at a safe distance from the Bogan house, even Chelliah having crossed the road to be on the other side near Vivienne's house. Amina, Mahmoud, and Hala were also there, their faces contorted with worry.

"What's going on?" Kumar asked Mahmoud.

The boy shrugged his shoulders. "Dad came in, and Mum was getting him a drink and he suddenly went into his room, and came out with a bundle and took off." He said, pointing in the direction of the Bogan house. "He's been there for nearly ten minutes now."

"Oh man, that is not good!" Mr. Rabula said. "What was in the bundle?"

Mahmoud shrugged again.

"I am sure it is bomb," Vivienne said loudly, casting a hostile glance in the direction of Mahmoud. "I think he want to blow up Bogan house." Mahmoud simply gazed impassively at her.

Kumar looked at the Bogan house. It was still standing, and there was no sign he could see of any struggle. In fact, it was eerily quiet.

"It must be a silent bomb. Something that kills without noise and without any damage to property," Rohan said. Kumar looked at him, not certain if the boy was talking tongue in cheek. Realising that he was, he turned again towards the Bogan house. It lay bathed in the midday sunshine, baking in the heat. There was no sign of any movement or life at all.

"Don't tell me they are all dead," Mrs. Rabula said.

Kumar was also getting worried. This did not sound good at all. What worried him most, however, was not what Ahmed might have done to the Bogans but what the Bogans might have done to him. There were six of them, not counting the infant, and at least the two parents and the two older Bogan Boys could easily make mincemeat of Ahmed. That, Kumar thought, might be the reason for the absence of any sound from the Bogan house, not because Ahmed had killed all the Bogans but because the Bogans had killed Ahmed.

He looked up the road. Where the hell were the police?

Suddenly Amina stepped out. "I am going there to see," she announced.

Everybody looked at her as if she had gone mad. Mahmoud grabbed her hand. "Don't, Mum!" he cried, and Hala hung on to her mother, sobbing.

But Amina was unstoppable. "They will not hurt woman, I am sure," she said and began to walk towards the Bogan house.

Mahmoud and Hala looked at her in despair. Then they too followed her.

"This is sheer madness," Chelliah said. "They won't hurt a woman! How can she be so sure?"

They watched in dismay as Amina, Mahmoud and Hala approached the Bogan house, went up to the front door and rang the bell. The door opened, and as they watched wide-eyed and open-mouthed, the three members of Ahmed's family disappeared into the house, as if they had been sucked into a dark hole.

"Oh my god!" Gasped Vivienne. "Amina and kids also gone!"

Then they heard the sirens, and a posse of police cars drove into Park Court, making straight for the front of the Bogan house. There were at least half a dozen of them. Soon, the end of the street was flooded with police officers wearing flak jackets. A few of them took cover behind the short wall, and the rest took cover behind their cars. One large female officer looked at the little knot of people gathered around, and frowned.

"Get away from there!" She ordered. "Move to the top of the road."

They all moved, but only a few paces. Everybody wanted to see what was going on.

An officer produced a megaphone and started calling those in the Bogan house.

"You are surrounded!" He said. "You can't escape. So, don't do anything silly, and come out with your hands in the air."

There was no response from the house. The policeman repeated the words.

"I think they all dead," Vivienne said in a whisper that was loud enough for the police to hear.

"I think I asked you to move away." The policewoman said and started walking towards them as if to move them away by force.

Just then, the front door to the Bogan house opened. Ahmed stood in the doorway, looking dumbfounded.

"Don't move!" The policeman with the megaphone said. "Put your hands in the air and walk towards us, slowly."

"How can he do that if he is not to move?" Rohan asked.

"Quiet!" the policewoman said. "And why are *you* still here?"

"He's my friend's dad," Rohan said.

"I don't care even if he's *your* dad. Move!"

Rohan moved a few feet back, and when the policewoman turned her back, he moved forward again. The rest of the little crowd moved with him.

Ahmed was still standing, stupefied, in the Bogans' doorway. He had raised his hands, but he was not moving. He was probably pondering the same problem that Rohan had pointed out: how to come forward without moving.

Then someone else came out, pushing his way around Ahmed. It was the Father Bogan. Seeing the police, he froze.

"What the fuck's going on?" He asked.

The policeman repeated his previous order, addressing it now to the Bogan.

"How the fuck am I to come forward without moving, you dumbass?" Father Bogan asked.

"Shut up and move forward!"

At this, Ahmed and Father Bogan began simultaneously to move forward. As they did so, leaving the doorway open, the rest of the Bogan family also came out followed by Amina, Mahmoud, and Hala. They all seemed surprised and confused.

"You!" A policeman called out to Ahmed. "On the ground, face down. Now!"

Ahmed began lowering himself to the ground. But Father Bogan was getting angrier now.

"He didn't do anything you cunt!" He cried. "Piss off and leave us alone!" Behind him, the rest of the Bogan family looked equally outraged. Both the Mother Bogan and BB1 started speaking at once but were cut short by the police.

"Shut up!" The cop cried. He pointed his gun at Father Bogan. "You too! On the ground! Now!"

Father Bogan was indignant. "Aww, fuck off!" he said derisively. "You're fuckin' crazy. Why dontcha go and find some real crims to catch," he sneered.

The policeman was unmoved. If anything, he was getting slightly agitated, because, emboldened by Father Bogan's defiance, Ahmed too seemed to be reconsidering his options. He stayed on one knee as if frozen in the process of lying down.

"I am not telling you again!" the policeman shouted. "Down!"

"We are not fuckin' dogs ya pig!" Father Bogan yelled back. "You can't treat us like this!"

On the street, Kumar and the rest of the residents heard the exchange and were beginning to get worried.

"Why don't they lie down?" Mr. Rabula asked. "Why do they have to make it so hard? The police will shoot, you know."

Kumar was thinking on the same line. He didn't like the way things were moving either. He also was intrigued by two things: one, that Ahmed and father Bogan seemed, each of them, unscathed; and two, that Father Bogan was apparently defending Ahmed from the police. But he was really worried that the answers to these questions would never be known given the attitude of the two. If provoked, it was possible that the police would shoot them both. If they did, neither Ahmed nor Father Bogan would be in a position to enlighten them about anything.

But the policeman did not shoot. He put aside the gun and pulling out his can of capsicum spray, began to douse Father Bogan with its contents. Seeing him do this, another policeman joined him, letting Ahmed take the brunt of his canister of pepper spray.

Father Bogan stood his ground for a few seconds before he started reacting as if he was not certain he was being shot or pepper-sprayed. Then when it began to sting, he started screaming, holding his face with both his hands. Soon he was on the ground, rolling, a string of choice expletives pouring out of his mouth. By then Ahmed was already there, having been closer to the ground than the Father Bogan, and equally vociferous but in Arabic. Soon they were both writhing on the ground, together, united in their pain and anger. The furious Bogan children and Mother Bogan and the distraught family of Ahmed were being kept away by the police who seemed as confused as everybody else about what was going on.

But the police never got to find out. They left when they were finally convinced that there had been a misunderstanding between two neighbouring families and that Ahmed had not gone into the Bogan house to kill anybody. They left Ahmed and Father Bogan in their respective homes, still angry but in gradually subsiding pain. For the feuding neighbours, the police had some strong advice: if the police were summoned over trivial matters like this again, they were all to be charged with wasting police time.

"See the number of cars here," one cop said to Chelliah. "These should have been somewhere else going after real criminals."

A policeman looked around at the flags flying from the rooftops. "What's with the flags?" He asked, his eyes narrowed. "A festival or something?"

"A competition, actually," Eric ventured, winking. "I think it's over now, hopefully."

The policeman shook his head in resignation. "Fuckin' weirdos everywhere," he was heard to mutter to a colleague as he got into the car. His colleagues seemed to agree.

The big policewoman had some parting words to Kumar. "You should have thrashed him soundly when he was small," she said, pointing to Rohan. "Then you wouldn't have had to put up with all this cheekl."

"There is a law against that in Australia," Rohan said. "You should know that."

"I meant India," the police woman said. "Where you guys came from."

"And don't expect us to clean that swat sticka `and the graffiti neither," warned a cop who looked like a senior officer, as he got into his car. "We got better things to do. You clean your own shit." Rohan said it shouldn't be a problem as Ahmed was a professional cleaner and he had cleaned it before, but by then the policeman was inside his car and the car was already on the move.

Later they all gathered in Ahmed's house, even Vivienne and Lauren, to find out what had happened. Ahmed was still recovering from his dose of pepper spray, not swearing anymore now, but still in some discomfort. Everybody was waiting impatiently to hear from Ahmed what exactly had occurred.

Ahmed was about to enlighten them when there was a knock on the door. Mahmoud opened it, and they found BB1 on the doorstep. He had something in a bag. When he saw Mahmoud, he smiled diffidently.

"Ya old man left his stuff at our joint," he said.

"Cheers," Mahmoud said, taking the bag from him. "How is your dad?" he asked.

"Oh, he'll be fine," BB1 said. "Still in a bit of pain and pretty pissed off with the cops. Says he'll kill them all. But he'll be fine. He is just pissed off. That's all."

The two boys stood looking at each other awkwardly for a few seconds. Then BB1 spoke. "How's ya dad?"

"Same," Mahmoud said. "In a bit of pain and pissed-off. But I don't reckon he can afford to threaten the cops."

BB1 nodded and again, smiled sheepishly. "Catchya," he said. Then he was gone.

"What was all that about?" Rohan asked, coming into the hallway. "What's in the bag?"

"Dad's albums," Mahmoud said. "From Lebanon."

"Albums?"

"Yeah," Ahmed said, breaking his silence. "From Lebanon."

"This is what you took there?" Chelliah asked.

Ahmed nodded. "We thought it was bomb," Vivienne said and Ahmed looked at her and shook his head in disbelief. Then he looked around and saw that everybody was waiting for him to explain.

"Yeah," he said. "I take photo albums. Of my family, of Amina's family. Of our life in Lebanon."

"What for?"

"I wanted to show them who we are. We are not Muzzies, or terrorists, or savages. We are people. I want them to see that."

Everybody stared at Ahmed, still puzzled.

"And what did the Bogans do?" Mr. Rabula asked after a few moments.

"Wayne," Ahmed said. "His name Wayne."

He saw confusion in the faces of his audience and began to explain.

"The man's name Wayne. His wife is Liz. The oldest boy Richo, the next one Jacko, ..."

"And the girl?" Eric asked, breathless.

"Bridgitte," Hala piped in, winking at Eric, who blushed. Vivienne frowned at Eric, intrigued by his interest in the girl.

"Yeah that's right, Bridg-itt," Ahmed continued. "The little boy Shane and the little one in the pram..."

"Kenny," Mahmoud said. Ahmed nodded. "Kenny," he said, smiling to himself. "That's right. Kenny."

"And they have one other girl child before Kenny," Amina interjected. "She called Anna. But she die in accident."

Everybody kept staring at Ahmed and family as if unable to believe their ears.

"So what did they do when you showed them the photos?"

Rohan asked after a minute or so.

"They show me their photos also," Ahmed said.

There was a slight pause as everybody tried to fathom what had taken place. At last Kumar spoke.

"What was in the photos?"

Ahmed pursed his lips. "Nothing strange. Family photos. Kids playing, young man and woman holding hands, babies laughing. Just like ours."

There was silence again. Everybody seemed speechless. Then, Vivienne spoke.

"Brig-git," she said, struggling with the pronunciation of the name and looking pointedly at Eric. "Funny name!"

"Not really," Rohan retorted. "Perfectly Aussie name. Just like Beer Gut."

"And perfectly Normal," Mahmoud joined in. "Just like Vivi-en."

Vivienne seemed poised to make a feisty comeback when Amina interjected.

"Her grandmother from Belgium," She explained.

"Yes," Mahmoud, said, nodding. "And do you know," He asked his neighbours, "that Wayne is actually part-Aboriginal?"

Everybody looked shocked. Vivienne let out a loud gasp that drowned Indu's less audible "My!"

Ahmed grinned.

"Yeah," he said, nodding. "His father's father Aborigine. He from somewhere up north. He play footy for club there."

"And he got injured in the same accident they lost the girl in," Mahmoud added. "After that, he went into depression and lost his job."

Everybody seemed stunned by the revelations. It all seemed too much to digest.

"*Well!*" Mr. Rabula said after a pause. "Who would have thought any part of him was Aboriginal?"

Chelliah disagreed. He was quick to point out that it was perfectly possible to have two parts without one really showing. "Remember that Andrews fellow?" He asked. "He was Anglo-Indian but could you ever guess any part of him was Anglo at all?" He could totally accept that Wayne had an Aboriginal part to him even though we could not see it.

"Maybe we were looking at the wrong parts," Rohan said. Chelliah frowned.

There was silence for a few moments. It was as if everybody was thinking of something to say. Then Vivienne spoke.

"Maybe I also show you our photos, huh?"

Ahmed said nothing. He simply cast his eyes at the bag with his albums. Behind Vivienne, Chelliah frowned again, and little furrows appeared on Mrs. Rabula's brow.

They heard footsteps coming up the driveway, accompanied by voices. Mahmoud opened the door.

Outside stood Jimmy. Standing next to him was Cynthia. Jimmy was beaming from ear to ear, while Cynthia stood uneasily trying to smile.

"Jimmy!" Mahmoud exclaimed in surprise, grabbing the boy's hand. He fixed Cynthia with a cold stare. The girl pursed her lips but held his gaze, although her eyes were far from defiant.

"I am so sorry about what happened Mahmoud," she said. The customary combativeness was gone from her tone. She sounded doleful.

"I.."

"All good," Mahmoud cut her short. "All good. Not to worry." He turned to Jimmy who was now surrounded by Eric and Rohan.

"What happened to you, man!" Jimmy said, patting Mahmoud on his back. "We thought you were gone forever. Then I heard you got released." He patted him again. "I always knew you were innocent. Wrongfully arrested. Just like us, man!"

They all went inside. Mahmoud's neighbours seemed surprised - even shocked - to see Jimmy. A gasp escaped the mouths of some.

Mahmoud introduced his friend.

"This is Jimmy," he said, indicating the Ugandan. Jimmy introduced Cynthia.

"My fiancée," he said. "Cynthia."

The introduction surprised Mahmoud, Rohan, and Eric. They had first thought that Jimmy had merely arrived with the girl. The revelation was intriguing.

"Which part of Africa are you from?" Mr. Rabula wanted to know. He and his wife had been looking Jimmy up and down as if trying to detect any signs of where he might be from.

As Jimmy seemed hesitant to answer, Mr. Rabula offered his own guess. "You are definitely not from the Sudan," he said. Rohan rolled his eyes at what appeared to be the start of a familiar guessing game.

"He is from Uganda," he said, tiredly.

"Uganda!" Chelliah repeated, then thought for a few seconds.

"Oh. yes! The country of Idi Amin!" He said, remembering. "He was a terrible dictator. Ate human flesh, you know?"

Jimmy smarted from the remark. but hit back with a smile that bared his brilliant white teeth and a glare that suggested that he would be only too happy to eat Chelliah's flesh.

Amina, who had been watching Jimmy, now spoke up.

"I think I see you somewhere before," she said. "That smile looking familiar."

As Hala giggled and Mahmoud turned red, Jimmy's smile disappeared. Rohan intervened.

"Maybe on the street somewhere. His smile is unforgettable."

"He is a sweet guy," Cynthia now lent her voice, still small but gaining in confidence. She reached out and grasped Jimmy's hand.

"So is Mahmoud," Eric said. "You know, he nearly burnt down the ..."

As Cynthia looked quizzically at Mahmoud, the boy winced. "Never mind!" he said. "It's all in the past!"

The mentioning of the kitchen alerted Ahmed. "So this is that.....?"

"Yes," Mahmoud snapped, irritated by the way the conversation was going. "Never mind!"

As Cynthia joined the adults, the boys took Jimmy to a side.

"How the fuck did this happen?" Eric asked, gesturing towards Cynthia.

"When?" Asked Rohan. "Where?" Mahmoud wanted to know.

Jimmy flashed another smile.

"Behind the canteen, man," he said. "Last week of school. She came chasing after some girls who had called her some name and ran into me having a quiet smoko," he smiled at the memory, eyes hooded. "Then, things happened very quickly."

"You understand anything she says?"

"Naaah," Jimmy was positive. "Very little, man. But communication is not just about words, you know," he said winking, then glancing in the direction of Cynthia now busy chattering to Vivienne, Lauren, and Indu about something they evidently didn't seem to understand.

"She is a nice girl. Strong and confident. I have told her, as long as she doesn't try to liberate me, we will be fine!"

People were beginning to drift off now, with promises to return with food for a party they had decided to have at Ahmed's place.

The Rabulas departed first, Mrs. Rabula promising to return with a big pot of goat curry. "All is well that ends well," she said, and Mr. Rabula nodded. "God works in mysterious ways," he said while looking sternly at Vivienne as if expecting a miracle there too. Vivienne waited till their backs were turned and then stuck up her finger before turning to Amina and saying that she will also come later with some beef rendang and rice.

Indu also offered to bring some food, and Eric knew exactly what he wanted her to bring. "Can you bring a big bowl of them wedges with chilli in it?" He asked. "Of course!" said Indu and looked at Mahmoud, and the boy nodded vigorously and said that was exactly what he was going to say before Eric jumped the gun. "I will bring some chicken," Amina said, and Vivienne's eyes lit up. "Can you make it Halal?" she asked, her voice quivering with anticipation. Amina stared at her neighbour as if she thought she was pulling her leg, and when she realised Vivienne was perfectly serious, she simply nodded her head. Yes, she said. She will make it halal.

Chelliah was the only one remaining, and everyone looked at him. Despite publicising his love of cooking, he had never invited anyone to sample his culinary talents. Now he surprised everyone.

"I will bring my signature dish," he said. "Chicken Vindaloo."

As everyone looked at Chelliah in surprise, the boys looked at Cynthia. The girl was gaping at the old man, her jaws wide open.

Chelliah explained that it was the favourite dish of her wife too. They had both loved cooking and had shared all housework equally.

"You mean like 50-50?" Eric asked. Chelliah nodded.

Rohan nudged Cynthia. "Wanna marry him?" He whispered.

Cynthia reddened at the suggestion. The others were too preoccupied with Chelliah's revelations to notice it. They all walked out, chattering excitedly.

After their parents left Eric and Rohan lingered behind with Mahmoud. Rohan was certain Eric was longing to tell Mahmoud about the brick, but he glared at him malevolently and even managed a surreptitious kick to Eric's shin to say that he should keep his mouth shut. Eric got the message and retreated behind a deep sigh and a tight grin. He simply squeezed Mahmoud's hand.

"I am very sorry about everything that has happened," he said.

Mahmoud, unaware that "everything" included the brick thrown through the window, squeezed back and said he was just glad it was all over.

There was a knock on the door again. They opened the door and again found Richo standing outside.

"Hey dude," he said to Mahmoud. "I'll scrub that shit off ya old man's van tomorrow if ya don't mind."

"Yeah, that's fine," Mahmoud said. Richo stood, shifting awkwardly on his feet. Suddenly he was alerted to something behind Mahmoud's shoulder.

"Jimmy!" Richo exclaimed.

As the Park Court boys looked on in surprise, Jimmy brushed past them to grab Richo's hands and embrace him.

"Richo!" He cried. "What you doin' here, man?"

"I live here!' Richo said. He pointed to their house across the road.

Jimmy looked at the house and seemed taken aback. He realised who he was talking to and had the good sense not to push it any further. He simply squeezed Richo's hand and said he was thrilled to see him, which indeed seemed to be the case.

"Obviously you guys know each other," Eric said, still surprised. Jimmy flashed his brilliant smile. "Yeah man," he said, "We working together in the Woolies warehouse. Richo started just last week."

The introductions over, Richo turned to leave. Mahmoud stopped him.

"Whatcha doin' in the evening?" He asked, and Richo shrugged his shoulders.

"Nothing, I guess."

"Come over to our place. With ya family. We got lotsa food."

Richo seemed undecided. Eric decided to help him make up his mind.

"We got chips." He said. "Lotsa chips."

Richo perked up.

"Yeah, that's right!" Said Mahmoud. "Wedges with green chilli on them."

Richo looked as if he had been told something outrageous.

"Who puts green chilli on wedges?" He asked.

"Mum does," said Rohan. "And they taste fuckin' awesome!"

Richo didn't seem to be too sure about that. But he agreed to come with the rest of the family.

"Do we need to bring anything?" he asked.

"Up to you," Mahmoud said. "We got plenty here."

"Mum does a wicked casserole," Richo said. "I'll ask her to make it."

The boys nodded, and Richo walked back to his house.

"Didn't you recognise him when you met him at Woolies, as one of them Bogan Boys?" Mahmoud asked Jimmy as soon as they had closed the door. Jimmy smiled again.

"Nah," he said. "Didn't remember him at all." Then his expression turned quizzical.

"Obviously you guys are all good now?"

"Yeah," Mahmoud said. "All good."

"What was that shit about the van?" Jimmy was keen to know. It was obvious that he had not seen the graffiti on the van.

"Nothing," said Mahmoud testily. "All good!"

That seemed to satisfy Jimmy, and he went into join Cynthia. Eric sidled up to Mahmoud.

"I thought you said they ate only chips?"

Mahmoud shrugged his shoulders. "I seen 'em eat only chips," he said unrepentantly. "How the fuck am I to know they do casseroles? I could only see what's happening outside, not inside."

Suddenly they heard someone yell:

"Woo-hoo!"

They opened the door to find Richo standing in the middle of the road, arms spread, and face turned to the heavens. His brown hair fluttered in the cool breeze that was blowing down the road. He saw them and smiled.

"Woo - hoo!" He said again.

"The fuckin' cool change is here!"

ABOUT THE AUTHOR

Channa Wickremesekera was born in Sri Lanka in 1967 and educated at Royal College, Colombo. In 1990 he came to Australia to pursue his university education, obtaining a bachelor's degree in 1993 and a PhD in 1998, specialising in South Asian military history. He had tried his hand at writing fiction while at school, but it was interrupted by his higher educational commitments. He returned to writing fiction after finishing his PhD., self-publishing his first novel *Walls* in 2001. To date, he has written five novels and novellas and four monographs on military history. His fiction deals mainly with the migrant experience. He currently lives in Melbourne, Australia

FICTION

Tracks, Self-published, 2015.

Asylum, Self-published, 2014, Palaver Books, 2015.

In the Same Boat, Self-Published, 2010.

Distant Warriors, Perera Hussein, Colombo, 2005.

Walls, self-published 2001.

HISTORY

A Tough Apprenticeship: Sri Lanka's Military against Tamil Militants 1979 -1987, Self-published 2016.

The Tamil Separatist War, New York: Routledge 2016.

Kandy at War: Indigenous Military Resistance to European Expansion in Sri Lanka 1594 – 1818, New Delhi: Manohar, 2004.

Best Black Troops in the World: British Perceptions and the Making of the Sepoy 1746 – 1805, New Delhi: Manohar, 2002.

www.ingramcontent.com/pod-product-compliance
Lightning Source LLC
Chambersburg PA
CBHW072351110726
47909CB00003B/675